SWALLOWTAIL BOOKS

Swallowtail Books are republishing classic detective stories. Other titles are:

The Eye of Osiris by R. Austin Freeman
Murder at School by James Hilton

For further details about these books and for future publishing plans please contact:

Swallowtail Books
3 Danesbrook
Claverley
Shropshire
WV5 7BB
England

Telephone number : 01746 710837
E-mail : swallowtail.books@claverley88.freeserve.co.uk

DEATH ON THE OXFORD ROAD

E. C. R. LORAC

Swallowtail Books

SWALLOWTAIL BOOKS

Published by Swallowtail Books
3 Danesbrook, Claverley, Shropshire, WV5 7BB, England

First published by Sampson Low, Marston & Co Ltd 1931

This edition published by Swallowtail Books 2000

A CIP catalogue record for this book is available from the British
Library

ISBN 1 903400 00 7

Printed by Antony Rowe Ltd, Bumper's Farm, Chippenham,
Wiltshire, SN14 6LH, England
Book cover and logo designs by Simon & Erica Minter Design
Services, 96 Cardigan Road, Reading, RG1 5QW, England

All incidents and characters in this book are entirely fictional

DEATH ON THE OXFORD ROAD

CHAPTER I

"The only object of running a car nowadays is that it makes you independent of railway time-tables," asserted Peter Vernon dogmatically, as he refilled his pipe and leant back comfortably in the smooth-running Talbot.

"Motoring for pleasure is a contradiction in terms," he persisted. "Either you stick to the main roads and form one of a procession,—bonnet to tail—reaching from Land's End to John-o'-Groats, or else you take to the by-roads and rattle your car to ruins over ruts and pot-holes until it's not worth anyone's while to salvage the remnants."

"I'm always willing to listen to an honest opinion," replied the driver of the Talbot, accelerating discreetly as he saw the long stretch of open road ahead of him. "Opinions nowadays are derived from two sources; one source is the car-owner class,—hogs to a man; the other is the pedestrian class, the back-bone of England, the fellows who get the work done, and who, by reason of their convictions, (define the word in any sense you like), can't own a car, and are reduced to accepting lifts from the swine who do."

Vernon grinned. "Don't rub it in. I'm enjoying the run at the moment, but it doesn't invalidate my argument. The roads at the present moment are a pleasure to drive on, but as it's past midnight, that fact can hardly be taken as a criterion of their state during the rush hours. I admitted, quite handsomely, that I liked to be relieved of the burden of coping with time-tables. Railway schedules are composed for the purpose of annoying a logical brain."

"Then I take it that your brain is not troubled by them," retorted the driver. "As a matter of fact I agree with you that motoring for pleasure is an over-estimated pastime, but on an occasion like the present, when you have spent a day in Oxford and prolonged the day until after the last train has departed, then a car is not to be despised. . . . Hell's bells! That chap's asking for trouble. . . ."

The last remark was due to the unexpected appearance of a big car from a side turning just ahead. The driver of the Talbot,—by name Robert Macdonald, by nature a cautious Scot—had his car well in control, but he was glad that the road surface was dry and hard as his four-wheel brakes checked the Talbot's progress with a suddenness that made Peter Vernon swing forward in his place.

"Sorry," said Macdonald, "but to try and pass him was to ask for trouble, I should have been driving blind. Now why do drivers swing out of a small side turning on to the main road without sounding a horn, and without bothering to see if the road is clear?"

"A little problem for your deductive brain," responded Peter Vernon. "Probably they've been burgling the local manor, and are hurrying quietly away. More probably they've been to a dance, and counted on the road being empty at this hour. Can't you pass the brute? . . . I hate this procession business."

For a few minutes Macdonald accelerated, and the Talbot crept up towards the leading car; then for a while the distance between the two vehicles remained constant as they climbed steadily up the long hill which leads over the first ridge of the Chilterns. Then, to Vernon's surprise, the pace of the Talbot suddenly diminished, and the speedometer went back to zero, as Macdonald pulled up at the roadside.

"That's a Sunbeam six," he said calmly, as his hand sought for his pipe. "I can't pass him if he doesn't want me to, and I share your views on processions. We'll give him a couple of minutes to get clear away,—I don't want to tail him for miles. Judging by his previous exhibition he doesn't indulge in driving sense."

"Sunbeams are a good breed," said Vernon, "cars after my own heart. You may well snigger,—the grapes are sour, and you damn well know it. If you can't afford a car, the best thing to do is to manufacture reasons for not wanting one."

"I'm with you," said Macdonald, "besides, you don't need a car. I get some perks to help me run mine. Sorry to hear that trade's bad, though."

"Trade's damn' bad," replied Vernon. "Publishing's suffering like everything else these rotten days, and authors are about as plentiful as gooseberries in a bumper season. As for journalism, it's a dog's life. Every specialist in every walk of life is making an extra penny by ramming articles into the Press. The monster's gorged,—and my choicest articles don't even get read."

"It's a hard life," said Macdonald, puffing away at his pipe. "No matter which way you turn, everyone's broke. . . . I should think that blighter's had time to get clear by now. We'll stroll on. As a matter of fact I don't like speeding, it always means asking for trouble in the long run. An average thirty is good enough for ordinary purposes."

Letting in the clutch, Macdonald got going again after a glance at his watch. The time was one-fifteen a.m., just forty-five minutes since they had left Oxford, and they were now mid-way between Tetsworth and Wycombe, having covered the twenty-two miles without a hitch.

"Well, if you're not busy, why not come up to

Scotland with me?" enquired Macdonald, as he drove on. "A holiday's due to me, and I'm thinking of going up to Edinburgh and then north. There's some grand country around St. Andrew's way, and we could carry on right up to Inverness. It's a cheap holiday if you know the way to do it."

"Jolly decent of you, Jock, and I'd give the world to do it, but I've got to keep my nose to the grindstone somehow, and raise a few beans. Writing's a funny job. Just when you need to be at your best you find your brain's gone to pulp, every idea gone west."

"Shows you need a holiday," went on Macdonald. "You'd pick up ideas by the wayside. Think it over."

For the next few minutes they drove on in silence. Once over the ridge the car travelled easily on the downward slope, and they slipped silently downhill under the shadow of the great beech trees which flourish on the chalk. As they rounded a curve they saw the tail lights of a stationary car ahead of them, and Macdonald recognised the Sunbeam which he had pulled up to avoid.

"Now what the deuce is he doing this time, bang in the middle of the road?" he enquired, slowing down as they approached the other car.

"He's got himself into a mess, the damned fool," exclaimed Vernon. "Knocked some poor devil down,— he ought to be hung for the way he was driving."

Macdonald pulled his car in to the side of the road and jumped out without a word; Vernon was right, a man was lying prone across the road, and the Sunbeam, pulled up a few yards ahead, was in a direct line with his body. To the left, the road was bordered by a steep bank of chalk covered with a thick growth of dogwood and wayfaring tree. The body lay well out into the road, and to pass it on the off side would have meant nearly ditching the

Sunbeam.

As he walked into the light of his head lamps, Macdonald was hailed by a young man who had been conferring with someone in the closed car just ahead.

"I say, there's been a ghastly accident. Someone must have run this chap down and left him here. He seems to have been dead for hours. Can you get a doctor, or a bobby, or someone? It's a perfectly horrible business. . . . His face is all—"

Macdonald saw the speaker sway, and he caught him by the arm and pulled him back towards the Talbot, pushing him down till he sat on the running board.

"All right," he said, "sit still and put your head between your knees. I'll see what we can do."

Vernon, who had alighted from the Talbot by the same door as Macdonald, made as though to come forward to examine the still figure which lay face downwards in the road, but Macdonald touched his arm, and motioned him towards the young fellow who was crouched down on the Talbot's running board.

"Keep an eye on him," he said. "It looks a bit odd; also, if you hear another car coming up signal with this" (giving Vernon a flash lamp); "we don't want another crash and there are plenty of fools on the road as well as this one. You'd better leave this to me; it's not a pleasant business."

Just as Macdonald was bending to examine the casualty, another voice called from the Sunbeam, and a girl's head appeared from the window.

"Dick, Dick, can't we get on? I dare not wait any longer."

Macdonald went up to her.

"I'm sorry," he said, "I'm afraid you'll have to wait for the moment. There has been an accident and witnesses will be needed. In our own interests, as well as in the common obligations of humanity, we've got to stand by and do what we can."

Macdonald's quiet voice conveyed a sense of authority, and the girl replied as one who protests against compulsion. She was quite young, and her voice was an educated one, but she spoke breathlessly, as though in a fever of nervousness.

"But we don't know anything about it. It's nothing to do with us and we can't do anything to help. We *must* go on, it's really vital."

"If you go on now, you will still have to give evidence later," replied Macdonald, "and once you move your car you will have destroyed all proof that this accident was nothing to do with you. I can't force you to remain, obviously, but I very strongly advise you to do so."

So saying, Macdonald turned to his task of examining the body in the roadway. It was lying face downwards, and a first glance had shown that nothing could be done to help the poor crushed creature who lay there. Macdonald was not surprised that the young man who had first investigated this accident had felt upset by what he saw; his profession had made Macdonald himself accustomed to the sight of death in strange forms, but the injuries done to the dead man in this case were of a kind likely to cause horror in the most experienced. From the face there was nothing to learn,— it was evident that a solid-wheeled lorry must have been responsible for the damage wrought; Macdonald lifted one of the hands and examined the soiled fingers, noting the rigid joints and considering the temperature of the hands. Glancing up at the chalk bank beside the road, he observed that a footpath ran along the crest of it, some twelve feet higher than the roadway. It occurred to him that the dead man might have fallen headlong on to the road and been stunned by the fall. Next he turned his attention to the position of the car in front of him. Owing to the dryness of the road and the smoothness of the surface, its tyre marks only showed after the brakes had been applied. It appeared that the Sunbeam, travelling on the crown of the road, must have run right over the body, swerved, and been violently braked, so that it had come to a standstill only a few yards further on.

Macdonald turned at this juncture to the young man who had been addressed as Dick. He had got to his feet again and came forward into the radius of the Talbot's head lights.

"I'd better go on into West Wycombe," he said, "there's a telephone box further along the road, and I'll ring up the police station. Can't do anything here, that's plain enough."

Macdonald eyed him shrewdly. It was quite evident that the young man shared his companion's anxiety to get away as quickly as possible, and the Scot had a strong suspicion that the couple wanted to vanish away, and not to be involved in the consequences arising from their midnight drive.

"There's an A.A. box a couple of hundred yards back," countered Macdonald. "I think it would be better if my friend went and telephoned from there. The police can get out here in a very few minutes, and it would be much more satisfactory from their point of view if you waited and gave evidence on the spot. It will probably save you trouble in the long run."

"Their point of view be damned," retorted the other. "You know as much about it as I do, and it doesn't matter to you two chaps if the police ask you questions." Here he hesitated, scrutinizing Macdonald's face. "Be a sport," he urged. "I'm joy riding, you can guess how it is. I don't mind for myself, but I don't want her dragged into it,"— pointing to the girl who had just alighted from the Sunbeam. "I don't want the police asking questions."

In reply, Macdonald turned to Vernon.

"Double back to the A.A. box," he said. "Here's my key. Ask them to put you through to the local station and tell them a police-surgeon's wanted."

Then he turned back to the youth called Dick. He was a big, fair fellow, clad in a tweed coat and flannel trousers, and Macdonald could tell that he was not of the same class as the girl whom he had been driving.

"You say that you don't want the police asking questions," he said. "As a matter of fact, the police are already asking questions. I'm a C.I.D. man. Here is my card. It's a sheer chance that I happened to come across this situation, but it's my business to take control until the local men arrive."

The young man took the card and read it in the light of the head lamps. He learned that the stranger who spoke to him was Chief-Inspector Macdonald, of the Criminal Investigation Department—a name he was likely to remember for a long time to come.

"Now the most sensible thing you can do is to answer the questions I put to you," said Macdonald. "In an accident of this kind it's your business to give evidence to the police, and you won't do yourself any good by shirking the issue. It's no use saying that I know as much about it as you do,—you were first on the scene and it's up to you to give evidence as to what happened. How came it that you drove straight over a man's body which lay right in the middle of the road? Your headlights are good enough."

"Because I didn't see him—it—," returned the other

with a shiver. "I was going fast, and the road was clear, and I suppose I was looking too far ahead; the first thing I knew about it was the bump and the swerve. I stopped at once and got out. I jolly well wish I hadn't."

"It was unfortunate for you that you didn't let me pass you a few miles back,—you'd have saved yourself a lot of trouble," commented Macdonald; "as it is you'll have to face the music. . . . Hullo,—here's one of the county men. He can take over."

His last remark was due to the appearance of a constable who had come round the corner of the road ahead of them. He was on a bicycle, and he jumped off beside Macdonald before he had seen the body behind them.

"Bit of a collision?" he enquired, and then saw the nature of the accident which was detaining the two motorists. With something like a grunt he observed the position of the two cars in relation to the body, and then, having propped his bicycle against the Sunbeam, was about to bend down to examine it when Macdonald said,

"He's quite dead, and been dead for some time. We have telephoned through to the station, and they ought to have a surgeon out very shortly."

"Were you the driver of this car?" enquired the Constable, producing a note-book and turning to Macdonald.

"No," he replied. "That's my car,—the Talbot. I pulled up seeing that there had been an accident. My name is Macdonald, Chief Inspector, C.I.D."

The constable gave vent to a slight whistle, and then turned to the young man called Dick, just as the girl who had alighted from the Sunbeam came to join the group.

"Name and address, please," demanded the constable, determined to do things in their proper order. It was the girl who answered.

"My name's Mary Brown, and this is my brother, Dick. Our address is 520 Banbury Road, Oxford. We don't know anything at all about this. We pulled up when we saw there was a man's body in the road. Since he's dead, and we can't do anything to help, we might as well go on. It's very late and we ought to get home."

The constable scrawled carefully in his notebook and Macdonald turned again to Dick.

"Have you anything to add to that?" he enquired, but the boy shook his head.

"No, sir," he said unhappily, "that's all. Can we get on?"

"I'm afraid it won't do," said Macdonald quietly, turning to the girl. "You see your name isn't Mary Brown, and you don't live at 520 Banbury Road. If you did, you wouldn't talk about driving home when you were intent on getting away from Oxford at the pace of fifty-five miles an hour. I think you'd better show your driving licence."

There was a dead silence, and then Dick broke out into argument.

"What does it matter what our names are?" he urged. "You've said yourself that the poor chap's been dead for hours, and you can see the tracks of the lorry that did him in. You won't do him any good by dragging us into it, and you'll do us a lot of harm. Can't you leave us out of it, or leave *her* out of it, anyway? It's a rotten thing you're doing, making more trouble when there's enough in the world already."

"I'm sorry, but this is one of the occasions when personal convenience can't take precedence," returned Macdonald implacably. "This accident has got to be investigated. All I know about you is this. You came out of a side road near Winchstone and turned on to the main road just ahead of me, taking the corner much too fast; seeing that I couldn't pass you, I pulled up and gave you a few minutes to get away. When I caught you up again a quarter of an hour later, I find you beside the body of a man who was killed some hours ago. Under the circumstances, you'll do yourselves no good by getting away on a false name and address. That makes it look as though you have really got something to conceal."

At this juncture, another car appeared and was pulled up a few yards east of the Sunbeam. Three men alighted and came forward to join the others, and at the sight of them the girl broke into hysterical laughter. Dick caught her by the arm and urged her to be quiet, but her high pitched voice cut across his pleas.

"More and more and more," she cried. "We shall have half the county here soon, asking what Mary Brown's doing in the country."

The tallest of the newcomers, whom Macdonald learnt was the police-surgeon, took the matter in hand. Recognising the note of hysteria in the voice, he caught the girl's arm and led her away from the group of men. In the interval thus afforded, Macdonald gave a terse account of the situation to the Police Superintendent who had arrived in response to the telephone call. A few minutes later, the girl had been seated in the police car with the constable standing by; Dick leant against the Sunbeam, looking a picture of woebegone horror, and the others settled down to their jobs. The police-surgeon examined the dead man, the Superintendent busied himself with the track of the Sunbeam's tyres, and Macdonald did what he had been wanting to do all through the argument,—opened the doors of the closed Sunbeam and began to examine its cushions and carpets.

Peter Vernon came up to him and asked if there were anything he could do. Macdonald answered over his shoulder, preoccupied with his search.

"No. I'm afraid you'll have to wait until I'm through. You're a journalist, aren't you? And this is the sort of occasion that a good journalist often prays for. You've got a scoop,—but you'll have to wait until I give you the word before you can use it."

CHAPTER II

It was daylight before Macdonald and Vernon eventually reached London, but neither of them showed any signs of sleepiness. Vernon was accustomed to being up all night, and Macdonald's mind was too full of the problem which they had stumbled across to be much concerned about the loss of his night's rest. Vernon's only regret anent the night's proceedings was that he and Macdonald were unable to discuss matters as they drove, for they had a passenger in the back of the Talbot. The self-styled "Mary Brown" had proved, on enquiry, to be Diana Hanton, the daughter of Colonel Hanton, of Winchstone Manor, in the county of Buckinghamshire, and Dick Waring, who had been driving her, was her father's chauffeur.

The police authorities had dealt gently enough with the girl, but weariness and shock had combined to upset her to a degree that made her a difficult witness to deal with. Vernon had been full of sympathy for her; she was a beautiful girl, obviously very young, and the journalist had felt indignant that Macdonald had not acceded to Waring's plea, and let her go home without being further involved in the roadside tragedy. Later events, however, had tended to lead him to the conclusion that the Chief Inspector had been justified in his persistence.

As they travelled along the Oxford road in the cold light of early morning, Peter Vernon began to formulate the story to himself. In his capacity of journalist, as well as that of novelist, he knew that Macdonald's terse statement concerning a scoop was true.

The dead man whom they had found lying in the road had been dead for several hours,—on that point both the surgeon and the Chief Inspector were agreed, but they had raised another point, which entirely altered the complexion of the affair. Both were convinced that the man's body had been placed in the road long after he was dead,—that is to say that he had been killed elsewhere, and his body conveyed to the spot where they had found it.

Vernon had not been able to appreciate all the points which led the two experts to this conclusion, but Macdonald had let drop for his benefit one curt sentence which had carried gruesome conviction.

"Not enough mess,—if he had been killed here, the evidence would have been apparent for yards."

The reason for Macdonald's careful examination of the Sunbeam became obvious enough in the light of that statement. It was a horrible thought, but it was clearly possible that the body could have been conveyed to the spot where it lay in the large Sunbeam which Waring had been driving. The car had been driven as though the furies were after it, and the lapse of time between the moment when Macdonald and Vernon had lost sight of it and that when they found Waring standing by his car would have been sufficient to allow the gruesome enterprise to have been carried out.

As Macdonald explained later, he was concerned with

the elimination of useless suspicion as well as the establishing of positive evidence. His first glance at the casualty had told him that the emergency with which he had to deal was more like murder than accident, and his native caution was too strong to allow sentimental reasons to over-ride logic. That Sunbeam had to be examined, and Dick Waring's clothes had to be examined, as much for his own vindication as for any other reason.

There was no apparent mystery about the dead man's identity. A card-case was found in his pocket which gave his name as Bert Rodmell, his address at a village not far from Winchstone, where Diana Hanton had her country home. As soon as his identity was established Macdonald turned to Waring and told him the man's name.

"You know him?" he asked, more in the tone of one who makes a statement than of one who asks a question, and Waring had replied, after a perceptible hesitation, "Yes, I knew him."

The examination of the immediate environment had been quick and thorough; it was soon found that the bushes on the chalk cutting by the roadside were torn and broken, just as they would have been if a man had tripped over the edge and fallen from the path into the road, clutching the bushes as he fell. Vernon had avoided looking at the dead man as he lay, mercifully face downwards, in the road. He had been willing to take Macdonald's word for it that Rodmell had been dead before he was put onto the road, and that a lorry had passed over him since. It was at this juncture that Vernon's common sense had made him say: "Then it's as plain as daylight that those two in the Sunbeam had nothing to do with it," and Macdonald had nodded, but he had not let the unfortunate pair depart. It was not till later that Vernon was allowed to know that Macdonald's search in the big car had brought to light a cigarette case lying in the cushions, and that that case held Mr. Bert Rodmell's card.

These points established, Macdonald and the Superintendent dealt firmly with the man and girl who had been so anxious to depart. Diana had again put up a fight to conceal her identity, but Waring was quicker to recognise the futility of such a course, and he made a clear statement explaining their escapade together.

Colonel Hanton and his family were staying for the season in their London house in Eaton Place, and Diana had taken advantage of the fact that her father was away for twenty-four hours to come down to Winchstone "to see a friend" as Waring expressed it. (Macdonald considered it a safe guess to assume that Colonel Hanton did not approve of the friend in question.) Originally Diana had intended to return home by train, but circumstances had caused her to miss the last train, and she found herself stranded at Winchstone with the prospect of her escapade being discovered. She had then telephoned to Dick Waring who was living in the chauffeur's cottage at her country home, and had asked him to take out the Sunbeam, pick her up just beyond the village, and drive her up to London. The Sunbeam belonged to Colonel Hanton and it was left at Winchstone Manor for the use of the Colonel's invalid sister, Miss Madeleine Hanton.

Now Dick Waring had grown up in the village where Colonel Hanton was squire. He and Diana had known each other as children, when he was a farmer's son, and she, the squire's daughter,—and it was pretty evident that there wasn't much that Waring wouldn't do for her. He admitted to Macdonald that he had been much exercised in his mind when he had received that telephone call. He felt that it would have been much better to tell Miss Madeleine about it, and let her deal with her adventurous niece, but he hadn't the heart to give his idol away. Macdonald, guessing again, could easily conjure up the manner in which Miss Diana exploited the old boy and girl friendship of their youthful days, and persuaded the chauffeur to do her will. Waring had met the girl at the place she mentioned, having taken the car out of the garage at one o'clock in the morning, and was driving her up to town as fast as the Sunbeam would carry them. It was their haste which proved their undoing,—and something else too commented Macdonald to himself,—Waring must have had his attention distracted considerably to have missed seeing that body in the road. He had not seen it till he was on top of it, and could not avoid it. Then, with a feeling of horror, he had pulled up and gone back to see what he had done.

"I thought the poor devil was drunk, and that I had done him in," he admitted to Macdonald. His wits bemused by the catastrophe, he did not know what to do next. He was a decent-minded lad, and it revolted him to leave that body in the road, and drive on as though nothing had happened.

The arrival of the Talbot had occurred just when he had decided to drive on and report the accident by telephone.

"I didn't ought to have started," he said woefully. "I shall lose my job, and Miss Diana's in a worse mess than she would have been if I'd told Miss Madeleine to start with."

This fact was plainly indisputable, and Macdonald had next asked for a few facts about the dead man. Waring told him that Rodmell was an employee in the Hayward

motor factory, and that he lived with his people at
Downfield, a village not far from Winchstone. Beyond
these bare facts he would not commit himself; he said
that he only knew Rodmell slightly, and that Macdonald
had better make enquiries from someone better qualified
to answer than himself.

Asked if he had ever taken Rodmell out in the
Sunbeam, the chauffeur denied it with scorn, and further
stated that be had not seen him that day.

The questions asked of Diana Hanton were very brief,
and her answers told the police nothing at all. Asked, in
her turn, if she knew Rodmell, she said that she had heard
of him, but did not know him personally, and did not
know his people. She had not seen him during the day,
and did not intend to answer any further questions. She
protested vehemently against being detained,—told the
police that they were exceeding their rights in
questioning her at all. From what Vernon could gather
she was an arrogant creature, accustomed to having her
word accepted as law, and the one person of whom she
really stood in awe was her father. When she was told
that the police would not allow the Sunbeam to continue
its journey, she was evidently nonplussed. It was then
that Macdonald had said that he would drive her back to
town in his own car, and leave her at her father's house.
Vernon couldn't help being amused at the way she had
tried to tackle the Chief Inspector when they had once
started on their homeward way.

Leaning forward from the seat at the rear, with her arm
against the back of the driving seat, she had tried to
wheedle Macdonald into promising that the night's
events should be kept secret from her father.

"It will mean an awful row for me," she confided, "and
I had nothing to do with the accident. It doesn't seem fair

to drag me into it when I don't know anything about it. You see Daddy's away, but I've got a latch-key, and if I get in before anyone's awake, they need never know how late I was. Of course I'm sorry that that horrid Rodmell boy got run over, but I don't see how getting me into trouble is going to help him?"

"If you take my advice, Miss Hanton, you'll go to your father immediately he gets back home and tell him the whole story," replied Macdonald; "it's impossible to keep your name out of it, I'm afraid. Waring will have to appear as a witness at the inquest, and one of the first questions he will be asked is what he was doing with his employer's car at that hour of the night. After all, you have got him into a mess, and it's not fair to leave him to bear the brunt. I'm afraid that your father's got to be told."

Diana did not accept the quiet finality of his voice. Evidently her experience of mankind had led her to believe that most men could be coerced into doing her will if she only tried hard enough.

"Dick Waring would never give me away," she asserted, "and if he gets the sack for taking the car out, I can easily get him another job. I simply can't be dragged into a case over accidents to the Rodmell family. People would be horrid over it. Please,—I know you must have a lot of influence with the police,—I could tell that from the way they treated you. People like that always accept a hint from anyone in authority, don't they?"

"Do they?" enquired Macdonald quite unperturbed. "I'm a policeman myself, and I'm not very good at taking hints, but I can't quite see that people need have any reason to be nasty to you about the Rodmell family, because, as you have said, you don't even know them. But if people are likely to be horrid, it will be your father's business to deal with them. You must tell him all about it, and he will be the proper person to see that you are protected from unpleasantness."

"Then you won't do anything to help?" she protested incredulously, and Vernon guessed that tears were not far away.

"Not in the matter of deceiving your father," answered Macdonald quietly, and the girl retorted hotly:

"I see that I was mistaken in my estimate of you. I thought you were a gentleman."

Macdonald only smiled.

"So you see your judgment isn't always infallible," he answered, "you really need your father's counsel in this difficult world."

The girl sank back into her place without another word, and Vernon got out his note-book and began to jot down details of his scoop for the later editions. He had already telephoned to the *Clarion,* and though the facts he was allowed to give had been limited by Macdonald to a curt statement of fact, yet he had been able to establish a priority in a story which promised to provide the Press with a first-class sensation just at the season when news was getting scarce.

"If this affair puts me into a position when I can look my pass-book in the face," he had confided to Macdonald, "I'll take you at your word about that trip to the Highlands."

Macdonald had glowered at him. "Ten to one this banishes the Highlands into the dim and distant future for me," he had grumbled.

There was hardly any traffic as they entered London, and the sun was shining mistily on Hyde Park as they drove along the fine, empty spaciousness of the Bayswater Road. Vernon noticed that it was just five o'clock as they passed Marble Arch, and he wondered what Macdonald would do when they reached Eaton Place, whether he intended to rouse a sleeping household and see to it that Miss Hanton gave a correct account of her night's adventure, or whether he would allow her to creep in unobserved, to make her own explanations if any were demanded of her.

Drawing up the Talbot outside Colonel Hanton's house, Macdonald was on the pavement in a twinkling and he opened the back door of the car before Diana had time to get out and run past him.

"I can only beg of you to take my advice and tell your father exactly what has happened," said the Chief Inspector, as he stood in front of the door. "He has got to hear about it all some time, and it is obviously better for you to tell him yourself than for him to learn about it from the police."

Before the girl had time to reply, the front-door of the house opened, and a tall, grey-haired man came outside and stood on the pavement.

"Diana!" he said, as she got out of the car. "Thank God you're safe! When I came back last night and found that you were not in the house, I was horrified. I have been telephoning half the night to try and find you." Then he turned to Macdonald, his fine lean face drawn and frowning.

"I will ask you for an explanation of this matter later, sir," he said, his voice expressing a cold anger.

"You can have the explanation here and now," retorted Macdonald. "I am an Inspector of the Criminal Investigation Department. Your daughter was involved in the results of an accident on the Oxford road shortly before two o'clock in the morning. As the local police had reason to detain the car in which Miss Hanton was travelling, I offered to drive her home. If you wish to make any further enquiries of me, you can telephone to me at Scotland Yard."

Macdonald took a card from his pocket and tendered it to the grey-haired man. His assumption that the latter was Diana's father had been correct enough, and he stood back from the door of the car, his attitude indicating that he had nothing further to say. Colonel Hanton gave one glance at the card, and another at the Chief Inspector's lean, tanned face, and then said:

"I beg your pardon, Inspector. I am indebted to you for your goodness in bringing Diana home. May I ask you to come in?—you must be in need of breakfast and a rest."

Macdonald smiled at him, his slightly saturnine face altering amazingly.

"No, thank you, sir. I am quite near home, and I shall be glad to get to bed. Your daughter is very tired,—I won't detain you any longer."

As Macdonald drew away from the car, the girl took a step towards him, her face flushed.

"I want to beg your pardon," she said, "I behaved abominably. I'm sorry for what I said, it was—"

"Never mind," said Macdonald quickly. "You were tired and worried and felt that things had been too much for you. Hurry up and get into bed and make up for a lost night;" then with a formal "good morning" to Colonel Hanton, the Chief Inspector got back into the car, and started the engine again, as the girl and her father entered the house.

"Look here, Jock,—you can drop me here and I'll find my way home," said Vernon. "You've had a night of it too; you want to go to bed."

"So do you," replied Macdonald. "I said that I'd drive

you home and I'm going to do it. We didn't reckon on entertainments like the one we met on the road, but it'll be useful to you as material."

"By Jove, it will," answered Vernon fervently. "What did you make of her,—the fair Diana?"

"Bit of a minx," said Macdonald; "she quite mistakenly fancies herself in the role of Sphinx, for which part she's not adapted. She's transparently foolish, but probably well meaning."

"Don't I wish she could hear your opinion of her," chuckled Vernon. "There'd be a natural death from explosion of the spleen. Apropos of Sphinxes, I loved the way she tried the Cleopatra touch on you, hoping you'd oblige as Anthony."

Macdonald laughed. "Not on your life. It's the conceit of these modern products that gets me. That lass thinks the world's a playground for her to play skittles in."

"Feeling elderly, Jock?" enquired Vernon.

"Prehistoric,—in comparison with that," said Macdonald scornfully. "I'm pre-war, and was brought up properly."

Vernon laughed. "Putting aside the girl's conceit and wrongheadedness," he said, "you don't feel inclined to credit her with collusion in to-night's dirty work?"

"No, I don't think I do," answered Macdonald slowly; "though she knows more about Mr. Rodmell than she chose to admit,—more shame for her. The contents of his pockets labelled him as a swine, and he probably asked for what he got, unless— Look here, my brain's fairly addled. I'm not going to start discussing this business now. I'll come and have a yarn after we've both had a sleep. Here's your back door, I'll leave you to it."

They had pulled up on the Embankment, just by the Temple Gardens, and Vernon began to collect his belongings.

"Thanks very much and all that," he said. "So far as you know, will the powers that be down there enlist your co-operation in the hue and cry?"

"G.O.K.," answered Macdonald, "and probably not even G. I'm bound to send in a report and comment on the things which struck me. With due respect to their very pleasant Super., he's a bit satisfied with the extremely obvious, and the case of Mr. Bert Rodmell isn't going to be quite plain-sailing. I'll let you know, and in the meantime don't lose your head and drop bricks in the Press."

"Right oh! Robert. Go to your wee bed and sleep it off. Ring you up later. So long!" And with that Vernon made his way up to the Strand and entered the Temple. To his credit as a journalist be it said, he did not go straight to bed. He did quite a lot of telephoning to this number and that in Fleet Street. Before he went to sleep he had amassed quite a lot of information about the Hanton family and the neighbourhood of Winchstone in Buckinghamshire. He meant to be intelligently equipped when he met Macdonald later in the day,—even the C.I.D. found journalistic information worth having at moments.

CHAPTER III

When he had closed the front-door on Macdonald and Vernon, Colonel Hanton slipped his hand inside his daughter's arm.

"You must be tired out, Diana; I'm not going to ask you any questions until you've had a rest, but you must realise one thing clearly. Later on you have got to tell me exactly what you have been doing since I saw you last. It won't be any use trying to deceive me, you have got to tell me the truth. Now do you want anything to eat? I'll bring you some hot milk up to your room,— coffee will only keep you awake."

The girl shook her head; her face was white and strained, and dark shadows under her eyes told their tale of physical exhaustion.

"No, daddy. I don't want anything. I just feel sick, I'm so tired."

"My child, I can see that without your telling me. Run off to bed and get to sleep. I'll let you have four hours' sleep and then I shall come up and talk to you. If you've been in a smash, the police will be making enquiries, and you had better tell me what happened early enough for me to deal with them when questions are asked."

Still holding her arm he led Diana up the wide stairway to her bedroom and opened the door for her.

"I put a hot-water bottle in your bed in case you were cold, my dear," he said, his voice shaking a little. "I've had a bad night of it, Di. Promise me,—you'll get straight into bed and stay there? No more running about on your own account?"

Diana shook her head.

"I'm too dog-tired to do anything but fall asleep," she said. "I don't want anything, Daddy, only just to go to sleep."

Colonel Hanton bent down and kissed her wan face, and then, closing the door softly, crossed the landing to his own bedroom. Before he reached his door, he heard muffled footsteps on the stairs just above and turned to see a portly figure, wrapped around in a grey dressing-gown.

"Beg pardon, sir. I heard voices and came down to see

if there was anything you wanted."

"Nothing, Bates, nothing," replied Colonel Hanton. "Miss Diana's car was held up by a breakdown, but she is not hurt at all, only tired, of course. I am going to bed now, but see that I am called at nine sharp. You can bring some coffee to my room when you call me. Miss Diana, of course, is not to be disturbed."

"Very good, sir," replied the butler, and turned back to his room, heaving a sigh of relief. He was glad to learn that Diana was safe, but relieved that Colonel Hanton had arrived back unexpectedly to learn about her "goings-on."

"Not but what I wouldn't have tried to help her out of a pickle meself," he soliloquised, "but she's been goin' too far. Goin's on, that's what it is, and it's only right and proper that the Colonel should know. My eye, she'll be for it now, and no mistake. He's a oner once you've roused 'im."

Colonel Hanton went to bed with a heavy heart. He had realised long since that he himself was in good part responsible for his motherless daughter's waywardness. He had adored her and spoilt her; nothing had been too good for Diana, and nothing had been refused her. When she had been at boarding-school, he had missed her bitterly during term-time, and during the holidays he had only asked that she should have a good time. From an expensive boarding school in England, she had gone to a finishing school in Paris, and had returned in time to be presented and to "come-out" for her first season, and now, when she was only eighteen, her father realised that his persistent indulgence had produced a daughter with a character utterly alien to his own.

Diana had always evoked admiration; at school her juniors adored her after the manner of school girls; she was the leader of every fashion, the ideal of the school élite, and when she came out she soon found that her power of dominion was vastly enhanced. Men of all ages "fell for" Diana. Apart from her beauty, and she had been hailed as the loveliest débutante of her season—she had the Charm which is quite distinct from beauty, but which, reinforced by it, is doubly powerful. Peter Vernon had felt it,—if he had had his way Diana would have been allowed to vanish before the police arrived. Even Macdonald was conscious of it, but then he was a hard nut to crack,—Macdonald was more attracted by his own job than by anything else, and he had a singleness of purpose which eliminated other distractions.

Colonel Hanton was continually distressed in his mind by his inability to comprehend the mentality of the young people whom his daughter brought to the house. He was perturbed by their manners—or lack of manners as he expressed it. They were casual—and he was a stickler for etiquette ;—casual in social observances, in their clothes, in their speech, and, it seemed to him, in their morals. He had been horrified over the views which some of them expressed in his hearing, and when he had protested sternly against the licence of their speech, Diana had only said in her most blasé voice, "Oh, Daddy, don't be so stuffy." Later he had enquired if her moral judgment sanctioned the behaviour of some of her friends and she had replied: "Obviously, since they are my friends. It's no use applying a Victorian yard-stick to the nineteen-thirties, Daddy. You had your conventions, we have ours, only we're less furtive about life than you were."

"Furtive." The word rankled. For the first time in her life Diana found herself up against something adamantine in her parent. He who used to be so amenable to coaxing, had decided to turn over a new leaf, and take his daughter's moral welfare in hand while there was yet time. He demanded to know how she spent her time, and with whom. He censored her parties, and would only allow her to visit houses whose repute was, to his mind, unquestionable. He enquired how she spent her allowance, and insisted on checking her pass-book. The consequences, as any more enlightened parent would have warned him, were the opposite of what he intended. Diana, spoiled from her cradle onwards, resented this sudden limitation of her liberty. Knowing that open rebellion would be useless, she played a new game of hood-winking her parent,—and her new motto in life became "Don't let daddy find out." There was pathos in the situation to an outside observer. Diana was far from vicious by nature; she did not understand the complexity of half the problems to which she referred so lightly, and her outlook was that of the young people of her own age who had grown up since the war. It was their convention to be outspoken, to be shocked at nothing, and to despise repressions. If her father had tried to make her understand his ideas of behaviour when she was a child, he might have been successful, but he had taken too much for granted. His interference when it came was disastrous.

Some of these thoughts stirred vaguely in Colonel Hanton's mind when he went upstairs to demand an explanation of Diana's absence. He had ordered her breakfast to be taken in to her, and at ten o'clock he went and tapped on her door. The voice that bade him come in was clear and untroubled, and he entered to find his daughter sitting up in bed, smoking a cigarette. Youth has great recuperative powers, and Diana's clear eyes and fresh skin showed no signs of fatigue. Her bobbed black hair curled demurely round her face, the centre parting giving her oval face a madonna-like aspect. Her wrap of periwinkle blue silk matched to a marvel the blue of her eyes, and she smiled up at her father with the open-faced expression of a child.

"Sit down, Daddy. I'm sorry that you were so worried about me. I telephoned, you know,—you ought to have known that I was all right."

"You telephoned that you were dancing at Lady Bredon's. I am sorry to say it, Diana, but that message did not satisfy me. I telephoned myself to Lady Bredon,—only to be told that you were not at her house."

"That was a pity," replied Diana calmly. She had realised that she was "for it," and intended to take her fences without shirking. "If you insist on treating me as a child, I am driven sometimes into childish evasions for the sake of peace and quietness."

"Childish evasions, Diana! You mean deliberate lies," said her parent.

"Quite," replied Diana. "You don't know anything about children, and I do. All children lie when they're cornered. It's their only form of defence. Don't interrupt, Daddy. You're going to hear the truth this time, and you won't like it. I went down to Winchstone yesterday afternoon to see Philip Hayward. He is,—or was,—a friend of mine—"

"A man with whom I have forbidden you to associate," said Colonel Hanton, his stern face flushed with anger.

"I know," she replied calmly. "That was your mistake, not mine. If you'd let me see a little more of him in a normal way, I might have found out for myself what you disliked in him. As it was, the minute you told me not to see him, I wanted to. He acquired a meretricious value on account of your prohibition."

Colonel Hanton's face was nearly purple by this time to the point of fury; Diana was actually trying to be clever at his expense, rolling out long words which she knew he hated.

"The fellow is a cad," he said, "it's an intolerable humiliation to me that a daughter of mine should be taken in by him."

"Your daughter only possesses the faculties with which you endowed her," retorted Diana. "All this is so silly, Daddy. Why should you and I quarrel over a wretched creature like Philip Hayward? If I admit that I was wrong and that you were right in your estimate of him, won't you admit that you've been hard on me lately? No one takes easily to a tight bearing-rein when they haven't been brought up to it."

Colonel Hanton took a deep breath. To do him justice, he was a fair-minded man, and even in his anger he admitted the truth of his daughter's contention.

"All right, Di, go on,—only for heaven's sake don't try to be clever. It's not the moment for it."

"Sorry, Daddy. Well, I went down after lunch and met him at tea-time for a picnic out in Quarry Woods. Later we had dinner at the hotel there. He was quite amusing, and suggested that we should stop in the woods and hear the nightingales tune up. He had his car there and said that he'd drive me back to Wycombe to catch the ten-fifty train."

Colonel Hanton groaned as though in bitterness of spirit, but Diana went on unmoved.

"Well, he saw to it that I missed the ten-fifty. There's nothing to groan about, Daddy. I'm a bit of a fool, but not nearly such a big one as you're thinking. When I got back to Winchstone, it was nearly one o'clock. I had to walk you see. I didn't want to go to Aunt Madeleine and give her the chance to come it over me with a story like that, so I rang up Waring at the chauffeur's cottage and told him to drive me up. That was where we struck a snag. Someone had run over Bert Rodmell a few miles outside West Wycombe and left him in the road, and of course we had to see what we could do to help. Then the police came up,—that man who drove me home you know,—and they kept us for hours, quite unnecessarily. That's all."

Diana came to the end of her story with a huge sense of relief. She had used all her energies to keep her nerve, and to talk in the sophisticated voice which was habitual to her; but inside she felt queer and wobbly, with her heart pounding away as though it would leap through her ribs. At any rate, she'd got it over; she had realised that Macdonald had been right when he said that her father would have to know about her misadventure on the Oxford road, and that it would be better for her to tell her own story in her own way than for her father to learn it in bits from other people; but she waited in a fever of anxiety for the castigation which she felt was due.

Colonel Hanton was silent for a moment after Diana had told her tale. He sat, with bent head, looking down at the carpet, his hands clenched together between his knees, and when he spoke his voice was very different from what Diana had expected.

"I said just now that I felt humiliated, Diana. It's the best way of expressing what I feel. I am ashamed both for your sake and my own. I spoilt you as a child, and when I saw the results of my behaviour I tried to control you too suddenly. The result was that you rebelled and I lost your confidence. You lied to me because you were afraid to tell the truth and I have myself to blame for that. Perhaps I ought to thank God that we have an opportunity to realise our own mistakes. I only want to make you happy, my child, but happiness and licence are very far from being synonymous. Think it over, my dear. Don't spoil your whole life by sheer bravado."

"I'm sorry, Daddy." Diana had lost her flippant poise, and was trying not to cry by this time.

"I'm so thankful you know all about it. I knew I'd been a fool, but it's better to learn by my own experience, because I shan't make the same mistake twice. Now about those beastly police," and she drew a long breath and wiped her nose, looking more like the child she used to be than the sophisticated young madam she loved to appear.

"Yes, about the police," said Colonel Hanton, as though he, too, found it a relief to turn to practical politics again. "Did you have a collision?"

"No, it wasn't that," said Diana, her smooth forehead wrinkling as she recollected the scene of the night before. "There was a man's body lying across the road and Waring didn't see it in time. It was horrible. We bumped right over him. Waring pulled up and ran back; when he found the man was dead he wasn't sure what we ought to do, and while we were still talking that man called Macdonald came up behind us in his car. He wouldn't let us go on, although he knew we didn't do it,—it was Bert Rodmell, that awful lout who's always tearing round on a motor-bike."

"I remember him,—he lived at Downfield. I have always disliked the family, as you know, Di, but I shall have to write to express my sympathy. Did you hear the cause of the accident? Was he knocked off his bicycle?"

"I don't know, Daddy," replied Diana slowly. "There was no sign of his bike, he was just lying across the road. I tried not to look because it was all too ghastly, but the police were awfully serious about it. They searched our Sunbeam, and then asked Waring and me if we knew

Rodmell, just as though we could have had anything to do with it. I didn't want to tell them my name, but Waring said that wasn't any good. They'd trace the car and find out."

Colonel Hanton looked aghast. His face had lost the violent colour which anger had raised in it and he looked drawn and grey.

"Diana," he said, "have you told me the whole truth? I don't know if you realise the implication of what you say, but remember this. If the police imagine that you know anything about this accident, they will put you in the witness-box and cross-question you in the same way that they will question Waring, or anybody else, from a pauper to a peer. No privilege of class or wealth will help you to avoid that. If you're concealing anything from me, change your mind. Tell me whatever there is to be told. If it's discreditable, it's even more essential that I should know. I am responsible for you, and I can look after you, but you've got to tell me all the facts."

Diana flushed but she looked him full in the face as she answered:

"So far as the accident goes, I don't know anything at all about it,—not one thing. We left Winchstone in the Sunbeam just after one o'clock and we pulled up ten miles further on. After all, the police admitted that Rodmell had been dead for hours, it was obvious that it wasn't our car that killed him,— it's not that that worries me, it's just the thought of being asked to give evidence. You see—"

Here she took a sudden breath, as though her nerve failed her, but Colonel Hanton said steadily: "Go on, Di, get it over."

"I was at Downfield last week," she said; "I went to see Philip Hayward, and walked over to Quarry Woods. I was sitting resting on a stile and Bert Rodmell came along and began to be impertinent. I was furious and got up to go, but he tried to stop me. Just then Waring turned up,—it was in that short cut between Downfield and Quarry End. . . . It ended in Waring knocking Rodmell down,—he simply laid him out, and Waring said he'd break his neck for him next time they met."

For a few seconds there was dead silence in the room, broken only by Colonel Hanton's heavy breathing, and at length Diana broke out, "I'm so horribly afraid they'll dig up that story at the inquest. It was all so beastly."

"Beastly indeed," said Colonel Hanton with a heavy sigh, and then fell silent again. "I shall have to see what I can do," he said. "The only thing to do is to tell the police all they want to know. Wising is the Coroner for the district. I know him well. Once the police are satisfied that you and Waring had no connection with the accident, he'll probably let you off lightly. He's not the type of man to stir up unnecessary trouble. . . ."

Silence fell again, as Colonel Hanton began to plan out what action he ought to take. At length he said:

"Do you remember your mother, Di?" and the girl flushed at the unexpected question.

"Hardly at all," she said. "How she would have despised me!"

"No, not that," he cried out at her. "Not that, Diana. She'd have blamed me. I ought to have looked after you better. I've been blind and negligent. We'll start again, Di, and try to pull together better. I think you should stay at home to-day. I am going to see that man Macdonald. He looked a good type, and he'll probably give me an idea of how things are going. All right, my child. We'll do our best to get things put straight."

CHAPTER IV

When Macdonald had been driving back to London after the delay caused by the discovery of Bert Rodmell's body on the Oxford road, he had been disposed to curse the bad luck which had pitchforked him into another case just when he was looking forward to a holiday. He found, however, that a few hours' sleep and a good breakfast had made a vast difference to the attitude of his mind regarding the matter. The more he thought it over, the more was his mind intrigued by the facts of the case. Here was a problem which called for skilled research, and Macdonald's mind responded to the challenge as a mathematician's mind would respond to the presentation of a knotty problem which came within his scope.

Consequently, by the time he reached Scotland Yard, Macdonald had forgotten all about his holiday, and was hoping that the county authorities would see fit to apply to Scotland Yard for his co-operation in unravelling the mystery which he had happened upon last night. When he learned, on his arrival at the Yard, that the Assistant Commissioner wished to see him immediately, he hastened up the stairs whistling softly to himself, hoping that the summons was concerned with last night's alarums and excursions.

"Good morning, Macdonald," said the Assistant Commissioner, (Colonel Wragley was a fine looking, grey-haired man, with a hawk-like profile and pleasant blue eyes.) "You seem to have been combining business with pleasure last night. The local authorities were so much impressed with your observations that they are anxious to extend this consultation with you. However, I

38

know your leave is due, so I think it's up to you to say what you think of the suggestion."

"Thank you very much, sir," replied Macdonald. "I think my leave won't seem any the worse for keeping a bit, and the more I consider last night's affair, the more anxious I feel to have a finger in the pie. If I'm going to work with the county men, the sooner I go there the better. I want to have a good look at Mr. Bert Rodmell before he's concealed from view."

"So I assumed," replied Colonel Wragley. "In the message which I have received, they tell me that the body has been identified by the relatives. Do you still want to go?"

"Even more than I did before," responded Macdonald. "This is the sort of case which I have been anticipating for a long time. As a general rule, murder's a hazardous business,—there's an element of risk in killing people, however careful you are, but the one fairly safe method of disposing of anybody these days is to kill them in a road accident. Juries are extraordinarily irresponsible bodies,—they'll do anything to avoid bringing in a verdict of manslaughter, even when the facts look like deliberate murder. I've been wondering when somebody would exploit the fact, and it seems they've done it. 'Chap killed on the road,—oh that happens every day, it was probably his own fault, the number of people who try to commit suicide that way is incredible.' You know the attitude of mind, sir?"

"I do," replied Colonel Wragley, with a twinkle, "but I'd no idea you felt so strongly about it. You ought to join the Pedestrian's Association, they'd welcome you with open arms. In the meantime, if there's any point upon which you'd like to consult with me now, carry on. I'm expecting to get away myself in a day or two."

"Do you know anything about a Colonel Hanton, of—Eaton Place?" enquired Macdonald promptly.

"I knew him during the War," replied the other. "He is a man for whom I, in common with everyone else who came in contact with him, had a deep respect and regard. He is a very fine type, sane, conscientious and competent. He is always ready to help any good cause with all his energies. He will be very greatly distressed over the fact that his daughter's name will be involved in this matter."

"Thank you, sir," replied Macdonald. "I'll do my best about it, but Miss Hanton doesn't seem to have very much horse-sense,—discretion if you prefer the word...."

At this moment the telephone on Colonel Wragley's desk cut short Macdonald's sentence, and a moment later the Assistant Commissioner said, "Colonel Hanton has called to see you. He is downstairs now."

"Do you wish to see him yourself, sir?" enquired Macdonald.

"Certainly not," replied the other. "It is for you that he asks, and I have no intention of interfering at this juncture. You talked about horse-sense just now, Macdonald. You've got plenty of that quality yourself. I'll leave you to it. Carry on."

"Very good, sir," replied Macdonald with a twinkle, and hastened downstairs again, his alert mind concentrated on the problem in which chance had involved him.

Colonel Hanton was standing by the window, his hands clasped behind his back, and he swung round quickly to greet Macdonald when the latter entered the room.

"Good morning, Inspector," he said. "It is good of you to allow me this opportunity of thanking you for your kindness to my daughter last night. I owe you an apology for my cavalier greeting when I saw you this morning, but I had been greatly distressed in mind and did not grasp the circumstances."

"Obviously you had no opportunity of grasping them, sir," responded Macdonald, "so an apology is not needed. I am very glad to see you here, because I feel that it is probable that you can assist us in the preliminary enquiries which we have to make in the case which your daughter chanced upon last night."

Hanton studied the younger man's face with his keen, light blue eyes.

"Naturally, any assistance which it is in my power to give, you shall have immediately," he responded. "While I appreciate the fact that it is my business to answer questions and not to ask them, I should be grateful if you could give me any enlightenment in the matter. My daughter told me that Waring stopped the car when he realised that an accident had occurred; she further stated that you searched the car in which she was travelling. Now road accidents are commonly dealt with by police of the county in which they occur, yet I understand you to say that you,—Scotland Yard that is,—are making the enquiries in this case?"

"In co-operation with the county police, of course," replied Macdonald. The Assistant Commissioner's observations about Colonel Hanton and his own judgment of the man, had decided the Chief Inspector that he could afford to be frank on this occasion.

"I will put the facts before you, sir," he said, "knowing that you will realise that my report is absolutely confidential. The county authorities have asked me to join them in this investigation because chance brought me to the spot where I was able to observe the conditions of this seeming accident. Your daughter will have told you that the body of a man was found in the road. So far as his face was concerned, no identification is possible, but the contents of his pockets gave his name as Rodmell. It was evident that the man had been dead for several hours, and I think that further medical examination will prove that the injuries to the face were inflicted after death, rather than being the cause of it. Moreover, the body had been laid in the position in which we found it after death had occurred. The deductions from these facts are patent, and, since I was first on the spot, it is convenient for the county police to have me working with them."

Colonel Hanton had listened with absorbed attention, a furrow between his brows growing more deeply marked as he listened.

"It is clear to me that the facts which you have presented indicate murder rather than accident, and that the murder,—if it be one,—was carried out by people who had little knowledge of criminal research. I also appreciate the reasons which led you to search my Sunbeam."

Macdonald carried on with his previous policy of frankness.

"I myself was returning to London from Oxford with a friend. At the point where the road from Winchstone joins the main Oxford road, your Sunbeam turned on to the main road just in front of me. We were both travelling fast, but after a few minutes I decided to pull up to give the Sunbeam a chance to get clear, as I couldn't pass it. I pulled up at one-fifteen precisely, stopped for about three minutes and then drove on; at one-twenty-five I caught sight of the Sunbeam again, just where Waring had pulled up after running over the dead man. The matter was confused a little further because Miss Hanton made a determined effort to avoid telling us her name and Waring's, and it was evident that both of them were in a fever to get away."

Hanton raised his hand and interposed.

"I should like to explain to you here the reason of my daughter's behaviour," he said, and gave Macdonald an outline of Diana's story concerning her doings on the previous day. Macdonald was very sorry for Colonel Hanton. The repugnance with which he told the story was evident and his efforts to shield his daughter were at war with his obvious truthfulness.

"Thank you, sir," replied the Chief Inspector, when Colonel Hanton brought his narrative to a close. "It is more than probable that Miss Hanton's actions yesterday will not concern the case at all, and you may rest assured that we shall not publish evidence which is not germane to the case. As you can see, I am being entirely frank with you, so you will not take it amiss if I ask you for one explicit piece of information. Did your daughter go to Winchstone yesterday with your sanction, and did you know of her appointment with Mr. Hayward?"

"The answer to both questions is in the negative," replied the Colonel, his stern face flushed. Had Macdonald been less sorry for him, he might have smiled at the stereotyped answer to his query.

"We can leave that side of the matter, then," continued Macdonald, "and get on to more essential enquiries. Can you tell me anything of this man, Bert Rodmell, his circumstances and family?"

"I can tell you quite a lot," replied Hanton, his voice expressing the relief he felt when Macdonald's enquiries were no longer focussed on Diana. "The Rodmells, as a family, seem curiously out of the picture as far as county life and society is concerned. They came to our district just over a year ago, and took the lease of a large house called Beech Grange, mid-way between the villages of Downfield and Winchstone. The family consists of the father and mother, two sons, George and Bert, and a daughter, Vanda. I don't know if you want details of them,—if so, I can provide you with them, but I don't want to waste your time."

"I want all the details I can get," responded Macdonald. "The more fully you can describe them, the more grateful shall I be."

Colonel Hanton leaned back in his chair, his hands stretched along its arms, and looked shrewdly at Macdonald, who had seated himself on the further side of his office table.

"I am not given to gossiping about my neighbours," began the older man, "but the present circumstances call for outspokenness. As I said just now, the Rodmells don't seem to fit. Normally speaking, when a new family comes to our neighbourhood and settles in a place like Beech Grange, other people call on them and endeavour to show them some civility. In this case no one called, for the Rodmells made themselves disliked before they even settled in their new home. The fact of the matter is, that everybody used one of two expressions,—either 'Latin' or 'foreign.' I don't know which, if either, expression is justified, but the family are certainly flamboyant, and nobody can imagine what brought them to a quiet country neighbourhood like ours. The mother, who is neurotic and a confirmed invalid, is definitely foreign. She may be Italian, or she may hail from further East, but English she is not. The father, a stout, dark, greasy-looking merchant, has a villainous American accent. The elder son is the most presentable looking of the lot; he's a tall, dark, well set-up fellow, over-dressed for the country, and always too elaborate. He has interests in the City, I am told, and is only at home for week-ends. The daughter, to add to the family strangeness, is one of the loveliest creatures I have ever set eyes on, white skinned and black haired, as exotic as a camellia. She's the focus point for every scandal in the neighbourhood. The youngest member of the family is Bert. Since he's had the misfortune to get himself killed, it's not decent to say too much about him, but he was as unpleasant a youth as it's ever been my lot to come across. I only hope some decent country lad won't hang for Bert Rodmell's death, for he was the type to go messing around after every petticoat in the place. . . . It's very unpalatable to me to talk about it, but the lout actually had the impertinence to insult my own daughter, and Waring nearly knocked his head off."

Colonel Hanton here took a deep breath and paused in his narrative, as though to give Macdonald the opportunity of commenting on what he had heard, and the latter said:

"Waring struck me as being a very decent fellow. He was a bit out of his depth last night, torn between his natural impulse to be truthful and straightforward, and his equally natural desire to keep Miss Hanton out of complications. People always forget one aspect of the proceedings when they're being questioned by the police, —the fact that the enquiry is quite as much for their own protection as for the discovery of the guilty party. Miss Hanton immediately jumped to the conclusion that the reason of our questions was to incriminate her,—quite the wrong end of the stick. Now to return to the Rodmell family—presumably they are of independent means?"

Macdonald's last sentence had the effect it was intended to have,—it calmed Colonel Hanton's immediate apprehensions, and brought him back to the main point. On the subject of the Rodmell family in general he was quite happy.

"I should say that the father must have a good income; they took a three years' lease of Beech Grange and it's a good-sized property. Rodmell senior doesn't seem to have any regular occupation, unless attendance at race meetings comes under that heading. I can't imagine what brought the fellow to our neighbourhood,—Newmarket or Lincoln or Lewes ought to have been his ticket." Here Colonel Hanton leant towards Macdonald with outstretched hand. "After all, what do you make of it yourself? It's a bit odd to find a family of that type coming to live in a neighbourhood which seems devoid of the attractions natural to them."

Macdonald laughed. "Odd it is," he replied, "but I imagine that you could hazard a guess as to their motive."

Colonel Hanton waved a deprecating hand.

"I don't like gossiping; unpleasant thing to spread tittle-tattle, but I have an invalid sister who lives down at Winchstone. She seldom goes beyond the grounds, but what she doesn't know about her neighbours isn't worth knowing. This Rodmell family has given her more entertainment than a movie story. A very fair analogy that," exclaimed the Colonel. "They look as though they might have come straight off a film. Well, Madeleine,— that's my sister,—says that the reason the Rodmells came to Winchstone was to be near the Haywards. Old Vincent Hayward, as you probably know, is the owner of the Forward Car Works. He's made a pot of money, and he's an old man now. He has a son Richard, a fellow of thirty or so; according to Madeleine, Vanda Rodmell's setting her cap at Richard Hayward, and Hayward's under her thumb. He'll be a very wealthy man when his father dies, and I believe that is likely to happen at any time, for

Vincent Hayward is over seventy and is said to be in a bad way. . . . Now you know all the village gossip."

"Apart from the fact that it's my business to acquire all the information I can when I'm working on a case," said Macdonald, in his quiet, pleasant voice, "I find that I get enormously interested in the ramifications of small events which concern the personalities with whom I'm brought into contact. There's hardly a village in the country which couldn't supply material for a story by Trollope. Stories about people are much more absorbing than stories about events. Now you've given me an idea about Rodmell's *père* and *mère*,—the one a race-goer, the other a nervous invalid. Then there's their son George, who has interests in the City, an over-picturesque exterior and an over-extensive wardrobe of the wrong clothes; item, Miss Vanda Rodmell, beautiful, film-starish, said to be intrigued by Richard Hayward and his prospects. What about Bert? I'm told that he was in the Hayward works."

"Quite right," replied Colonel Hanton. "Talking about novels, I should think you could write one yourself. . . . Bert Rodmell had a faculty for engineering. He was said to be either too lazy or too stupid to be trained into the pukka engineer, but a very clever fellow mechanically. He worked at the Forward factory as a mechanic, and I think they used him as a driver to test their cars. I know Waring said that what Bert Rodmell didn't know about motor-car engines wasn't worth knowing. I believe he intended to buy a big garage sometime; give the devil his due, he liked his job and really enjoyed working, otherwise he could just have stayed at home and sponged."

"So he had that to his credit," commented Macdonald. "I'm interested to learn that Waring thought well of Rodmell's mechanical ability, because it may explain another point which rather puzzled me. You learnt from Miss Hanton that we searched your Sunbeam. The only item of interest to us which we found in it was Bert Rodmell's cigarette case."

"Good God!" exclaimed the Colonel, his face suddenly horrified, his exclamation more like an appeal to the deity than any form of profanity, and Macdonald hastened to reassure him.

"I shouldn't worry about it too much, sir," he said. "I am anxious to be quite frank with you, because I know that you are deeply distressed over this affair on account of your daughter's having stumbled across it, but if I let you see the trend of our enquiries, you won't need to worry so much. Now about the business of the cigarette case;—if Waring has been in the habit of having Bert Rodmell into your garage to discuss mechanics with him, it's quite obvious that Rodmell could have dropped the cigarette case himself."

"I'm very much indebted to you for your sympathetic attitude towards us," said Colonel Hanton; "you have behaved to both Diana and myself with the most marked consideration, and I am exceedingly grateful, but this last factor seems the most unpleasant part of the whole thing. I told you myself that Waring recently gave Rodmell a thrashing, I have also told you that Waring had the fellow at our garage on occasions. I'm not a detective, but the implication is too obvious to ignore."

"It's also a bit too obvious to consider," replied Macdonald. "Say that Waring cracked Rodmell's skull in a rage, and then decided to put him on the Oxford road, so that he looked like a casualty,— in that case he'd have taken good care not to pull up and be found by the body a few hours later."

Colonel Hanton sat with a worried face.

"You're exceedingly good in trying to spare me worry, Chief Inspector," he said, "but I can't help seeing that the business looks a nasty one—a very nasty one indeed. You will be interrogating Waring?"

"Obviously," answered Macdonald. "We shall interrogate Waring very closely, and also examine your garage and the chauffeur's cottage. After what I have said to you to-day you will not have to suffer under any misapprehensions as to the causes of my enquiry. As you know, you and I, and your daughter, and Waring are all equal in the eyes of the law, and we all have to answer for our actions when we become involved in a case of this kind, but it will be of immense assistance to me if I can count upon your friendly co-operation. A hostile attitude on the part of those living in a locality is a great hindrance to us in our work."

"I am a law-abiding man, and I should count it as my duty to assist the police in any way within my power," said Hanton. "In this case I shall be even more glad to help you in any way that I can. I feel that I am under an obligation to you. You brought my daughter safely home, and you have treated me with a consideration which I shall never forget."

Macdonald laughed. "I'm a policeman, sir; the popular adage—'ask a policeman'—speaks well for the force. You'll find we're not a bad lot taking us all round. Now I must be off to the focus point of proceedings. If I need any local information I shall apply to you."

When Macdonald saw the much reassured Colonel to the door, he was told that another gentleman was waiting to see him.

Going to the waiting-room to collect his fresh visitor, Macdonald led Vernon along the passage, a friendly hand hooked in his arm.

"What's up, Peter? Looking for the lost property office?"

"No, I'm not. I'm looking for Mr. Bert Rodmell," was the journalist's unexpected answer.

"Well, you won't find him here, and that's all that I can tell you about him for the moment," answered Macdonald.

"Right oh, Jock. Be a clam if you like, but if you try the official manner on me, I go berserk. It's my story, you know."

"Keep calm, laddie. We don't need to fight over it. What do you want to do?"

"Are you on in this act?"

"I am that."

"Then take me with you."

Macdonald paused for a moment.

"No. I'm thinking that would be foolish. You're no fool, Peter, and you might be useful. I'll tak' the high road and you'll tak' the low road. You can go down to Winchstone on your own bat (your paper ought to pay your railway fares), and you can ingratiate yourself into local society in any capacity that suits you, and you can tell me anything you notice. You're a noticing wee fellow in your own way."

"Just one question first, Jock?"

"Oh, come along upstairs then. You can't ask questions in the corridors. It's against regulation 251."

Once behind closed doors Vernon said:

"Was that corpse, which I avoided looking at, what it pretended to be? I mean was it wearing its own clothes?"

Macdonald laughed.

"I take you. Well the relatives have identified said corpse as Mr. Bert Rodmell."

"I see. And you didn't care for the fit of his boots,"

answered Vernon.

"He wore boots which were two sizes too big for him," replied Macdonald, "but tell it not in Gath. Publish it not in the streets of Askelon."

"You know quite well that I'm not likely to, so don't waste your wind," retorted Vernon. "I'll take your tip and go study local colour in the capacity of a gentleman, a part for which by nature I am eminently well equipped. You shall hear from me later. Going down in the train I shall write an essay exposing the fallacy which attributes the virtue of taciturnity to the most garrulous nation under the sun."

"It all comes from your being paid by the line," answered Macdonald equably. "You have to spin words out. I shall be at home this evening, probably, if that suits you. Say nine-thirty?"

"Right!" replied Vernon.

CHAPTER V

Leaving London soon after eleven o'clock, Macdonald drove back along the Oxford road. Once clear of the traffic in the Uxbridge district, he made good speed and drove on through Denham and Gerrard's Cross and Beaconsfield, past High Wycombe with its busy factories (he would have to return here later to visit the Forward Motor Works where Rodmell had been employed). A few miles further on he stopped at a roadside inn and lunched off bread and cheese and cider. As he expected, the folk at the inn were full of last night's accident and the maid who brought him his meal was only too willing to chat about it.

"This road's a fair death-trap at nights, you take my

word for it," she asserted. "It's something shameful the way some of them drive. Not but what there's drivers and drivers," she admitted, remembering that Macdonald had himself arrived in a car. "It do seem a funny thing that Mr. Rodmell should have got himself run over. He was a fair terror on that bike of his, and when he took his father's car out, he used to just swank through the village at umpteen miles an hour. He took me out once, and once was quite enough. I was glad to get home alive. Besides my young gentleman didn't half go on about it. Mr. Rodmell was always after the girls, and that sort's never no good."

"You're quite right," said Macdonald sagely, "but unfortunately all girls aren't so sensible. I expect that you saw a good deal of this young fellow since you tell me he worked at the Forward place. His road would lie past here on his way to work?"

"That's right, sir," rejoined the girl. "Past here he was at eight-fifteen every morning. He always tooted, just to make me look out."

"He liked a cheerful greeting on his way to work," answered Macdonald. "Did you see him in the evenings as well?"

"Not half," replied the other. "Always came in just after six o'clock for a gin-and-bitters, though I told him it wouldn't do him no good. If a chap wants to drive in motor races he'd better keep off spirits. Beer's much better for him and I told him so."

"And jolly good advice too," applauded Macdonald. "Then I suppose you saw him on his way home yesterday evening?"

"No, I didn't," replied the girl. "Funnily enough he wasn't here yesterday at all. Now you come to think of it, that might explain a lot. I bet he went out on the ran-dan and came home mixed. He must have got pretty merry, or he'd never have been walking about on his two feet. Just hated walking, he did. I wonder where he left his bike,— lost it in a ditch, I expect."

"It's a pity he didn't stay in the ditch with it," answered Macdonald. "Nice safe places, ditches. Well, I must buzz off. P'raps next time I look in you'll be able to tell me if they found his motor bike. Thanks very much."

"Thank *you,* sir," replied the girl with a grin. "Always glad of a chat."

Macdonald's next port of call was Police Headquarters, where he met Superintendent Hastings, the County man in charge of the case.

The Superintendent welcomed Macdonald cordially, and showed his appreciation of the work which the latter had done in the early hours that morning.

"It's a fine old puzzle, and that's what it is," said Hastings cheerfully. "When we 'phoned through to the Rodmells, they were all at sixes and sevens. The father and elder brother were away, and the mother's an invalid. Seemed she was having a bad turn and Miss Rodmell wouldn't leave her. However, she gave me her elder brother's 'phone number in town,—Mr. George Rodmell, that is,—and we got through to him. He set out early this morning and got here by eight o'clock. He identified the body as his brother's without any hesitation."

"Very kind of him," said Macdonald thoughtfully. "What else had he to say?"

"As a matter of fact I didn't ask him a lot of questions," replied Hastings. "I thought it better to leave things as they were, because we don't want to ask the same questions twice over, and I thought if you, and I, and Dr. Renford had a chat, we should know a bit better how to carry on. Anyway, Mr. Rodmell told me that his

brother had been away for the week-end. He,—George,
—had been at Beech Grange on Saturday and Sunday,
but he'd gone back to town on Sunday afternoon, and
Bert was still away then. I told him I'd call to see him at
the Grange some time to-day,—seemed the best thing to
do under the circumstances."

"Good work," said Macdonald. "You've done exactly
what I should have done, left all avenues open without
committing yourself at all. Now what about Dr. Renford?
He's the chap I want to see."

"Just so," replied Hastings; "I made an appointment
with him to meet us at the mortuary, at one-fifteen, after I
got your 'phone message saying you'd be down soon
after midday, so if we go along there now we shall be in
good time."

"Excellent," replied Macdonald, and the two men
entered the Chief Inspector's Talbot and drove to the
mortuary, a short distance away.

Macdonald had met Dr. Renford on the Oxford road
the previous night, and had summed him up as a
competent, cool-headed individual. A few minutes after
Macdonald had started his examination of the body,
Renford came and joined him, and the two settled down
to their business of measuring and observing.

The body was that of a well-built, muscular fellow, the
neck and arms considerably sunburned, the whole
physique telling of good condition. The hair was black
and curly, the skin dark in tone and there was no
deformity or deviation from the normal to be noted. The
only identification mark which distinguished the remains
was an old scar on the thigh, whose nature Macdonald
recognised immediately.

"That was made by a bullet," he observed, and the
doctor nodded in agreement. Over this point the

Superintendent had something to say.

"That's the odd part," he said. "George Rodmell, when he identified the body, said that that scar settled the matter. Young Rodmell got a shot through his leg in South America, the family all lived out there until a few years ago."

"Quite," said Macdonald. "Anyone else able to give confirmatory evidence about that scar?"

"Well, Mr. Rodmell said the rest of the family could; they all remembered the circumstances, but apart from them, I don't see how you're going to get any evidence along those lines. The same point occurred to me, but I don't see how to get any further. This isn't a bathing resort!"

Under other circumstances Macdonald might have laughed over the disgust in the Superintendent's voice, but he was deep in thought as the doctor remarked:

"If we could get hold of a doctor who'd vetted him, we could soon get that point decided, but we're not going to have any such luck. I'm told that Bert Rodmell was the world's healthiest! They'll probably tell you he's never seen a doctor since he was born. Anyway, here's the gist of my report on this corpse as far as I can go, until after the autopsy. Deceased is a man in the prime of life; my own estimate of his age is thirty-five to forty, though there's no exact criterion to give a ruling. At any rate I feel safe in saying that he couldn't have been under thirty. He is five foot, seven inches in height and solidly built. You'll find he weighs between eleven and twelve stone. The body shows no evidence of disease, and there is no deformity of any kind. Owing to the damage done to his head I can't give you an exact description of his teeth, though judging by what I can see at present they were unusually good ones. The only definite identity mark is the scar on the right thigh."

"Well, that gives us something to work on," replied Macdonald. "The next step is to get an accurate description of Bert Rodmell. Judging by his clothes, I should say that he is a taller fellow than this one, and not so broadly built; also his feet are a good half an inch longer and thinner at the heels. . . . Have you taken finger-prints,—of the corpse, I mean?"

The concluding question was shot at the Superintendent, who shook his head.

"No, you've caught me napping there," he answered.

"Well, just see to it, and then we'll examine the prints on the card-case, and the pleasant photographs in Mr. Bert Rodmell's pockets. Doubtless the latter exhibits will give good definitions of his not over-nice fingers, but the two sets won't coincide."

"You sound pretty certain," replied the Superintendent, and Macdonald turned away from the mortuary table.

"I am. Dead certain. That chap there wasn't a lad of twenty. Reliable criteria, or none, common observation tells me that. In the meantime you'd better collect your finger-print man and his apparatus, so I'll run you back to the Station."

As they drove to the Police Station again Macdonald enquired:

"What do you make of it, accepting the fact that that body is not Bert Rodmell's?"

The Superintendent did not hesitate in replying; he had evidently thought out the answer to this question already.

"I'd say it was a pretty safe guess to assume that young Rodmell killed this chap and cleared out himself. He's not been at his job since he left midday Saturday, and no one at the works knows where he is."

"Then if that's the case," said Macdonald, "we must

also assume that Mr. George Rodmell's an accessory, since he's identified another man's body as his brother's."

"Not of necessity," argued the Superintendent. "Say if that bullet mark was a coincidence,—that Bert Rodmell *had* got a scar of that kind, then it's probable that the brother's identification might be honest, but mistaken. After all, people aren't as used to corpses as you are, and nobody's going to look at that one longer than's necessary."

"Oh, I see what you mean all right," responded Macdonald readily, "but experience hasn't taught me to trust coincidences of that kind. To me it looks far more as though George Rodmell knew that the dead man had that scar, and used his knowledge to carry conviction in identifying the body as his brother's. However, that's a point which can't be settled until we have further data to argue from. Say if we try to make a reconstruction of what might really have occurred in this case, basing your argument on the facts we have gathered so far. I expect you've worked out some sort of idea?"

The Superintendent pondered for a moment or two before he answered, and then he spoke cautiously as a man feeling his way.

"Let's take the facts we're certain of. Deceased has been run over by a lorry, and he's wearing Bert Rodmell's clothes and he's not Bert Rodmell. Then I should say that deceased was a lorry-driver, and that Bert Rodmell killed him, drove off afterwards in the lorry, and then made himself scarce."

"Now that's a good logical effort at honest reconstruction," applauded Macdonald. "It takes most circumstances into account and gives us something to work on. Point one, find the lorry and the man who drove it. If your theory's right, we shall get reports of a missing lorry and a missing driver. Bert Rodmell wouldn't have taken another man's lorry back to the works, or garage, or wherever it came from. Then there's another point,— does it look to you as though this job could have been carried through single-handed? That chap in the mortuary is a good weight, and unless Rodmell was unusually muscular he'd have had the deuce of a job to lift him. Say if brother George lent a hand? Between them they'd have no difficulty with the weight-lifting. The more I think about it, the more certain I feel that I'd better go straight to see George, and find out what he's got to say for himself. About the lorry—I think you're more likely to think out means of running it down than I am. It's a game of hide-and-seek in the dark, but we might try to eliminate a bit. Personally I think that lorry is likely to be a local product, because the whole affair is definitely local. If the murder was committed a considerable distance away, I don't see the point of bringing the body back to where we found it. They'd labelled the remains Bert Rodmell, and the label was clear enough wherever the body was found. Now assuming that death occurred about six o'clock yesterday—Monday—evening, the body must have been concealed somewhere for at least six hours. At present we don't know what traffic passed along the main road last night between midnight and one-thirty, but I've advertised for that information, and we ought to be able to narrow down the time. In your experience, do you think it's probable that an hour might elapse without any traffic passing that particular spot?"

"Sheer guess-work," replied the Superintendent, "but I should say that it's very unlikely an hour could elapse at that time without something passing. Well, let's say at a guess that the body was brought in a lorry somewhere about one o'clock, and that the lorry was driven on in the direction of Wycombe soon after one. Now it's up to me to think out where that lorry came from, assuming, as you say, that it's a local product. I reckon I can kill two birds with one stone to start with. I'll go up to the Forward Works and put in all the enquiries I can about young Rodmell and lorries as well, and I'll put another man on to speed up the enquiries we're making hereabouts. Also I'll get photographs of those finger-prints."

"Good," said Macdonald, "you're the sort of chap I like working with. Well, I'll drop you here and carry on to Beech Grange and see George."

"Right oh, and when you come back you might put a few of your ideas on the table," replied the Superintendent, and Macdonald laughed.

"If you go on anticipating me with the right sort of ideas, I might as well keep quiet. You haven't needed much help so far."

Hastings grinned broadly. "You're a cunning one, Chief Inspector. You noticed his boots didn't fit, and then put me wise about finger-prints. No help at all."

"Well, good hunting!" answered Macdonald. "Perhaps I shall be able to subscribe a few ideas after I've had a chat with brother George."

So saying, he let in his clutch and drove on over the ground which he had crossed in the early hours of the morning. In less than a quarter of an hour he pulled up again and came to a halt on the same spot that Colonel Hanton's Sunbeam had stood some twelve hours earlier; here he found a constable on duty, patrolling up and down the road beside the chalk cutting. Macdonald, having introduced himself in his official capacity, asked the man if he had been one of those who had helped in the search of the spot directed by Superintendent

Hastings earlier that morning, and the man nodded his head.

"That's right, sir. The Super had three of us on the job as well as himself, but we didn't find a thing. I've been peerin' round a bit meself, and I've found this article,—sheer luck it was. I lay on me back in the road and looked upward so to speak, and the light 'appened to catch it."

As he spoke the constable produced his handkerchief from his pocket, and unrolling it carefully he displayed to Macdonald the stub of a short yellow pencil, about two inches long.

"Good for you, constable," exclaimed the Chief Inspector. "It's all very well to talk about luck, but dogged does it. It was a good idea to look from beneath so to speak,—that's what I call intelligence. Where did you find it?"

For answer the constable, putting down the pencil wrapped again in his handkerchief, solemnly laid himself on his back at the base of the chalk bank and pointed upwards, Macdonald crouching beside him.

"Just by the base of them roots, sir, where the bushes is broken. You couldn't see that pencil no other how; it was just under a branch."

"A jolly useful find," said Macdonald, lifting the pencil gingerly, a finger at either end. "This isn't everybody's pencil by any manner of means. In fact the number of people who would use it is distinctly limited, so it may be a very useful clue. Now I'm just going to have a look at the path at the top of this bank."

So saying, he walked back along the road some fifty yards, and made his way up the little footpath which climbed steeply over the chalk bank parallel with the road. At the summit of the path he stopped, and his lips formed a noiseless whistle; it had been dark when he was at the same spot during the night, but he had made a guess at its strategic value, putting himself into the position of those who had left their victim below in the roadway. The crest of the little path commanded a view of the road both eastwards and westwards. Towards Wycombe the road sloped downhill, curving southwards, thus forming a bend which hid the road in front as you drove along it, but from the path where Macdonald now stood, he could see bits of the main road more than a quarter of a mile away in each direction. In fact he guessed that at night you could see the oncoming lights of a car for a considerable distance either way.

"Say if they brought a lorry up to the bend in the road, close against the bank," he mused. "One chap keeps cave up on the path, to signal if anything's coming. The other gets the passenger out of the lorry, backs a few yards and then drives on. . . . The watcher slides down through the bushes to save time, jumps aboard and the two make off. . . . Well, I can't track the lorry and George simultaneously, so I'll leave the lorry to Hastings."

Back in the car again, Macdonald drove on until he reached the turning from which the Sunbeam had appeared the previous night, and then turned southwards up the side road whose signpost announced, "Downfield 2, Winchstone 1½' The road to Winchstone appeared a little further on as another side turning on the right; the ground rose steadily as Macdonald approached Downfield, and the road was shaded by magnificent beech-trees. The surface, though less good than that of the main road, was not of the kind to show any tyre marks, and Macdonald knew that he wouldn't get any help that way.

He found the entrance to Beech Grange on the left-hand side of the road, about a mile away from the main road. A short drive led up to the house, which was a big, modern, red-brick building, gabled and half beamed.

"Edwardian-suburban," said Macdonald, who took a dislike to the building at sight. "Opulent and convenient but an outsider of a house all the same. Porch late-perpendicular, and ye bell all in keeping."

The manservant who answered Macdonald's summons on the offending bell seemed a suitable retainer for the Rodmell family, judging by Colonel Hanton's description of them. The man was "dark, stout, and greasy," and his American accent was pronounced, so that Macdonald found himself wondering if he ever got mistaken for his master. However, after a glance at Macdonald's card, he led him into a small room at the back of the house, and asked him to be seated. While he waited, Macdonald looked around him with his usual lively interest in other people's houses, but found nothing to indicate the character of anybody who owned it. The furniture was modern and new, everything was neat and well kept, and the only comment that came into the Chief Inspector's mind was:

"Why, it's a dentist's waiting-room, all complete, down to the copies of the *Illustrated* and the *Tatler,* laid out to console the intended victims. No smoking by suggestion."

But Macdonald had not long to wait. A very short time after he had been shown in, the door was opened again and a tall, dark man came into the room.

"Good afternoon, Inspector. You wish to speak to me?"

"Mr. George Rodmell?" enquired Macdonald, and the other gave an affirmatory nod. "I am in charge of the enquiry into your brother's accident," continued Macdonald, "and we need your help in elucidating certain points."

"I shouldn't think much elucidating was needed," responded the other. "It looks plain enough to me. I drove past the spot where you found him and I thought it self-evident. Bert lost his footing on the path and tumbled on to the road under a lorry. A ghastly accident, but you've got to take care of yourself on main roads these days. . . . Sit down, won't you? Hot to-day, isn't it?"

Here George Rodmell pulled a handkerchief out of his pocket and mopped his forehead. He was a tall, heavily built man, disposed to stoutness although he was still young. His hair and eyes were black and his complexion olive-toned; he wore exceedingly correct dark clothes and a wide black tie, and would have been good looking save for his tendency to obesity, but his good looks were of an un-English variety, and even his dark tie and careful tailoring could not prevent him from looking a trifle flamboyant.

"Fact is, I've had a most distressing day, and I'm feeling the strain a bit," continued George. "I went up to town on Sunday because I'd got an important bit of business on hand. Worked like a dog in the city all yesterday, and was woken up in the middle of the night and told that young Bert had got killed by a lorry. . . . Shocking business. My father's away and my mother's ill. . . . hopeless invalid, by the way. . . . nerves. . . . We're keeping this from her at present. She's in no state to stand the shock. Well, then I had to go to the mortuary. . . . Fairly bowled me over, I can tell you. I only hope the poor chap was killed instantaneously. Can't bear to think of it. Care for a drink, Inspector?"

"No, thank you," replied Macdonald promptly, glad of a chance to stem the tide of staccato sentences. "As you say, it is a shocking business, and I can quite understand that the mortuary upset you, but I should like you to give me an answer to this question. Are you satisfied beyond all doubt that the remains you saw this morning are those of your brother?"

"Satisfied?" echoed George, his jaw first dropping in amazement, and then closing with a snap. "What the devil do you mean? That's an odd question to come asking a man who's just identified his brother's body. Of course I'm satisfied,—if you like the word. Damned ill-chosen to my mind."

"Then may I put it in another way?" answered Macdonald. "Are you absolutely certain that the remains are your brother's,—certain beyond the possibility of a doubt?"

George mopped his brow again.

"Look here, Inspector; I went to the mortuary this morning and I identified the—er—remains. I told the man in charge there my reasons for being able to identify. D'you think I'm likely to have changed my mind since I came home? If that's the sort of question you want to ask, you might as well pack up and not disturb me any longer. You may not seem to realise it, but I've had a trying day, and I'm not in the mood to be worried by foolish questions."

"I'm sorry that my questions should seem either offensive or foolish," said Macdonald quietly, "but it's our business to go very carefully. You have assumed that your brother met his death by accident as you described. I regret to state that we consider that assumption untenable. There is every indication of foul play, and the possibility I am investigating is that of murder."

George Rodmell sat very still. If Macdonald's last words came as a shock to him, he showed it by sitting very still, his black eyes fixed on the other's face as though to read his thoughts. Finally he answered in a monosyllable.

"Why?"

"I found your brother's body lying in the road in the early hours of this morning," replied Macdonald. "According to medical evidence, death must have occurred fairly early on Monday evening. It is obvious that the body could not have lain in the road all that time without being reported. As a matter of fact we know that it did not. Therefore the body was placed in the road several hours after death had occurred."

"My God!" said George Rodmell, and it was evident enough that he was perturbed this time.

"What do you want me to do?" he demanded miserably.

"I want you to answer my questions as fully as you can," replied Macdonald, "We have to find out exactly what your brother was doing during this past week-end and where he has been staying. I should like a good photograph of him, if you have one, also his passport,— and it will be desirable for me to examine any letters and papers of his which are available. First, can you tell me where your brother was staying? I understand that he was away from home during the week-end?"

"That's right," answered George. He heaved a large sigh, straightened his tie and sat up with the air of a man making an effort. "This is a blow to me," he added as an afterthought. "Accidents are bad enough, but murder,—I only hope you're mistaken, Inspector, awful thought that, murder. . . . About poor Bert. I'm afraid that I can't tell you where he was this last week-end. You see I didn't come down here till Saturday evening, and he'd gone away then. I didn't ask where he'd gone to at the time. He was always one for playing his own little games, was

Bert. Quite likely he went to town to see some of his pals. He'd a lot of friends, had Bert, though I don't know much about them. He was a lot younger than me, and we didn't go about together much. Then he may have taken a trip over to France,—I've known him to do that in a week-end before now. I'm afraid you'll have to wait until my father comes home. He ought to be back this evening. I've wired to his clubs and done my best to get in touch with him. He was in town yesterday, but I think he took the night train up to Liverpool to see an old friend of his off to America."

Macdonald was relieved when George stopped to take breath, and promptly asked:

"Could I see your sister, then? As you are not able to give me any information, and time is an important factor, perhaps she could help."

"Right oh, I'll go and find her. I expect she's with mother. I told you, didn't I, that my mother is an invalid? She's not fit to hear this shocking story. We must keep it from her. I'll go and fetch Vanda."

So saying George walked out of the room, shutting the door behind him. Macdonald heard his retreating footsteps and then he himself went to the door of the room and opened it. He heard George mount the stairs and open and close a door on the first floor. For a few moments there was silence, then came the sounds of a door opening again, and a high-pitched querulous voice, speaking with a foreign accent.

"There is a mystery in this house. You always deceive me, you try and hide things from me, but I will not allow it. No, I will not stop in my room, I will not be a prisoner. I want to know who is in the house. I will be mistress here."

Macdonald heard two other women's voices, one soft

and gentle, evidently Vanda Rodmell's, trying to persuade the first speaker to go back to her room and rest, and another shriller voice speaking in tones of protest. As he heard footsteps on the stairs, Macdonald set the room door wide and stood waiting to see what would happen next.

A few seconds later he saw a tall, grey-haired woman, wrapped in a violet silk kimono, standing in the hall. Catching sight of Macdonald she came straight towards him, supporting herself with a hand on chair and table as she passed.

"What are you doing here and what do you want?" she demanded. Macdonald was filled with pity at the sight of the worn, ravaged face. Her great black eyes seemed to gaze sightlessly at him, the pupils expanded right over the iris. Her skin was yellow and creased, but the face retained traces of great beauty. At her side, putting out a restraining hand stood a girl whom Macdonald promptly recognised as Vanda, the white-skinned beauty whom Colonel Hanton had likened to a camellia.

"Mother, why must you worry like this? I do beg of you to come back to your room and rest. This gentleman came to see George on business, and we mustn't interfere with their talk."

Mrs. Rodmell gave a great sigh.

"It's always the same. You say I mustn't interfere. I tell you there is trouble in the air. I know I am ill," this time she addressed Macdonald, "but they won't give me my medicine. They want me to die. I'll go and look for it upstairs. It must be somewhere there."

She allowed herself to be led away by a woman in nurse's uniform, and George and Vanda came into the room with Macdonald and closed the door. The girl looked Macdonald straight in the face with her magnificent dark eyes.

"I'm sorry," she said, "but it's difficult to control her. She ought perhaps to be in a home, but quite often she's normal for weeks together, and only has these bad times occasionally. George says you want to see me about Bert?"

"Yes, Miss Rodmell. I am sorry that your mother is ill, to add to your other anxieties, and I'm afraid that my questions must seem an additional burden, but can you tell me where your brother spent the week-end and when you last saw him?"

Vanda Rodmell seated herself in a chair at the table, and answered promptly and quite simply.

"I last saw Bert at breakfast time on Saturday. Shortly before one o'clock he rang me up and said that he was going to spend the week-end in town and wouldn't come home to lunch. Father went up to town immediately after lunch the same day, and he hasn't been back since. I don't know where Bert went, but he often stayed at the Strand Palace when he was week-ending. My father rang up from town yesterday morning, about eleven o'clock, to tell us not to expect him before to-night. . . . If that's all you want to know I'll go back to my mother now. I'm worried about her."

"Just a moment, Miss Rodmell. Has your brother told you that the inquiry into Mr. Bert Rodmell's death has led us to dispense with the assumption of accident? I think you ought to know, for we are afraid that he was murdered."

Macdonald's plain speaking was deliberate; he wanted to see how Vanda Rodmell reacted to that portentous word. He saw her shiver and her hand went to her throat, but her voice was quiet enough when she spoke.

"How horrible. . . . Oh, why should these appalling

things happen to us? I do so long for just an ordinary happy existence like other women have. . . . I suppose you want to ask me if I can tell you who murdered him. Well, I can't. Some plough-boy, I expect, because Bert was an atrociously behaved creature. I suppose I ought to be sorry but I'm not. I just resent it."

And with that Vanda Rodmell got up from her chair and walked out of the room, leaving the embarrassed George to face the situation.

"I say, Inspector, that's a bit thick, but she's a selfish little wretch, is Vanda. Too damned good-looking,—turns a woman's head. You must have got a devilish queer impression of us, but we're not at our best just now. . . . You said you wanted to look through poor Bert's things. If you'll come upstairs I'll show you his room, and that photograph you mentioned."

Still talking, George led Macdonald out of the room and up the stairs. On the second floor he opened a door and ushered him into a bedroom; closing the door he stood with his shoulder against it and gave Macdonald the oddest look.

"No chance you're mistaken, is there, old boy? What I mean is, do you think the verdict may be accidental death? Just a chance so to speak?"

"No chance at all, in my opinion," retorted Macdonald curtly, and George answered:

"Well, it's a shocking business, that's what it is. If you don't mind, I'll just get a drink. I need it. See you later."

CHAPTER VI

If Miss Madeleine had heard her brother describing her to Macdonald as "an invalid," she would have been very angry, and would have resented the description as another of those inaccuracies of the masculine mind which a logical woman takes pleasure in refuting. Certainly the word "invalid," with its suggestion of feebleness, was not a good description of Miss Hanton. Although she was crippled by muscular rheumatism, and unable to walk without aid, she was a woman of great ability and energy of character. The Hantons' friends were wont to say that if Madeleine had been a man, she would have had a much more distinguished military career than had her brother, for she had an exceedingly active brain, in addition to a vivid imagination and powers of understanding.

When Miss Hanton heard vague reports from her maid that Waring the chauffeur had been "getting into trouble with the police," she lost no time in sending for him, and demanding an explanation of the trouble. Dick Waring was as wax in the hands of the capable lady who cross-examined him, and the whole of the night's misadventure was laid before Miss Madeleine after breakfast on Tuesday.

"Waring, you ought to have had more sense," she pronounced. "If you had come to me and told me of Miss Diana's message, we could have avoided all this fuss and to-do. Surely you know me well enough by now to realise that I'm not lacking in common sense. However, it's no use crying over spilt milk. What I want to know is this. If the man was dead before you arrived, why are the police bothering about you?"

Waring was only too glad to lay his troubles before Miss Hanton, and he described Diana's efforts to conceal her identity and to get away, and finally the finding of Bert Rodmell's cigarette case in the Sunbeam. Asked for an explanation of its presence there, he was quite unable to give one, but he produced another disquieting fact. The Sunbeam had been taken out of the garage without his knowledge; there was a dent or a scratch on the off mudguard which had not been there when he washed the car on Monday morning. Miss Hanton was intensely interested to hear this. Instead of bursting forth into weak lamentations as an invalid might have been expected to do, she sat up very straight in her wheeled chair, her eyes bright and alert.

"Now let's get all this into proper order, Waring. You washed the Sunbeam yesterday morning and ran me into Tetsworth before lunch. You locked the car into the garage at one o'clock, and at two o'clock you went into Oxford to your cousin's wedding. What time did you get back to your cottage last night?"

"Just after eleven, Miss," replied Waring. "We all went to the theatre, same as I told you. . . ."

"Yes, yes, I know all about that," answered Miss Hanton. "The point to be remembered is this. Your cottage was empty, and anybody could have got into the garage while you were away. I always told the Colonel that the lock of the garage door was an idiotic affair,—I believe I could have opened it myself with a hair-pin. . . . Where do you keep the key by the way?"

"Hanging up in the kitchen, Miss," replied Waring.

Miss Hanton was off on another tack.

"You tell me that Bert Rodmell had never been in the Sunbeam, but he'd helped you overhaul your motor-bike some weeks ago. Did you have him in the kitchen at the cottage?"

"Yes, Miss. He came in to clean himself up," answered Waring.

"And doubtless noticed where you kept the key," retorted Miss Hanton and grew thoughtful for a moment or two.

"How long did they say he'd been dead?" she asked.

"Hours," replied Waring tersely. "I think I heard the police doctor say six or seven."

"Good gracious me!" replied Miss Hanton, her mind busy with the impossibility of a body lying undiscovered in the main road for that length of time.

"I don't wonder they searched the Sunbeam, Waring; and it's a good thing for you that you were with a party all the afternoon and evening, or it might have been awkward."

"Well, they say it was a lorry finished him," said Waring, "though that's not much to go by. Some of these lorry drivers aren't any too particular. If one of them ran over him before I did, it's more than likely he'd have driven on and said nothing about it."

"Hm . . . how far could you trace the lorry wheels?" demanded Miss Hanton.

"About twenty yards," answered Waring. "The road had been gravelled not long since and . . . but it's not the best sort of story to tell a lady, Miss," he finished inconclusively.

"Rubbish, Waring!" snapped Miss Hanton. "How old are you? Twenty-three? Well, when you were seven years old, I was Commandant of a hospital in France. I've been bombed, and I've been torpedoed, and I've bandaged men who were half blown to bits. If you think your corpse on the road is going to upset me, you're making the mistake of your life. I only wish I'd been there,—I'm much more observant than most people, and corpses were commonplaces to me at one time."

"Well, Miss, it was a nasty business, and it fairly turned my stomach," he persisted. (Afterwards when he retailed the story to Miss Hanton's maid he told her that Miss Madeleine was a fair corker,— no flies on her).

"Well, it seems to me that the police were satisfied that young Rodmell was dead before the lorry went over him, and they thought it possible you'd put him where he was," said Miss Hanton calmly. "I'm not one to waste time on useless sentiment, and it strikes me as an amazingly interesting problem. If this man Macdonald comes to see you, Waring, I shall be interested to have a few words with him. If he's any *nous* at all, he'll want to get *au fait* with the neighbourhood, and there's not much I can't tell him about local atmosphere. If he turns up, you'd better 'phone through. I'll come down and see him."

Miss Hanton's next activity, after she had dismissed the chauffeur, was to ring up her brother. She learnt from him that he was just off to Scotland Yard, but that he thought he had better run down to see her if he could get away.

"You'd better bring Diana with you," said Madeleine. "She'll be just as well down here for a bit, and if she has to appear at the inquest, she'll be on the spot and perhaps I can put some sense into her head. Don't lecture her, John. You'll only make more trouble if you play the heavy parent. . . . I know you've been worried, poor old chap, but you must keep a sense of proportion."

Colonel Hanton duly arrived, shortly after midday, bringing a rather subdued Diana with him.

"My dear, you look charming but a bit washed out," said Miss Madeleine to her niece. "I don't wonder, your first season's a wearing business. I liked your presentation dress, and thank God for long skirts. The gels a few years ago looked as though they were in their shifts. If you're not above making yourself useful, you might try to think out a new scheme of decoration for my bedroom. Not too far-fetched, but it looks a bit Edwardian at present."

Having hustled Diana upstairs, Miss Hanton set to work to cross-examine her brother, and soon learnt all that he could tell her, both concerning Diana's luckless expedition and Colonel Hanton's own interview with Macdonald.

"He seems a sensible creature, that's one comfort," she commented. "You'd better leave Diana to me. I'm very sorry for you, John. You've had a difficult time bringing up a motherless girl. You men all make a hash of managing daughters, particularly when you've an only child. It was of no use for me to interfere, though I've told you dozens of times that you were laying up trouble. I do beg of you not to brood over this till you get it out of all proportion. Diana's a fool, but there's no vice in her, and I hope she's learnt her lesson. She'll know better than to flirt with the wrong type again."

"The fellow's a damned cad," began the Colonel, but Miss Hanton cut him short.

"There are plenty of that type of cad about, married and unmarried," she retorted calmly, "and a girl's got to know the difference nowadays. I'm sorry that it was Philip Hayward though. His cousin Richard is a very decent sort and quite neighbourly. Now, don't get heated over it," she continued, anticipating her brother's next speech. "I'm quite capable of realising for myself that it's no longer desirable for me to receive Richard Hayward. We all have to be responsible for our family shortcomings, and Philip was staying in Richard's house."

Colonel Hanton went back to town after lunch, and Diana went up to her room to make up for last night's arrears of sleep. Not that the loss of a night's sleep troubled her, but she was in no hurry to have a tête-à-tête with her aunt,—she knew that Miss Madeleine was capable of making her feel very small indeed.

Her brother and niece disposed of, Miss Madeleine got herself settled into her electrically propelled motor-chair. It was a neat vehicle and assured her of "independent mobility" when she wanted to be on the move. This afternoon she decided to inspect the garden, particularly the shrubbery near the chauffeur's cottage; if the Scotland Yard man were to arrive, Miss Madeleine intended to have a word with him.

She drove herself out on to the big lawn in front of the house, and inspected the rose trees with the eye of a connoisseur, being accustomed to superintend gardening operations from her chair. The main drive curved round on the south of the lawn and she had a view of any visitors arriving. Shortly before three o'clock a car appeared in the drive; seeing the driver, Miss Madeleine waved a friendly hand, so that when he alighted, he came across the lawn to meet her.

"Talk of the devil," she said to herself. "Here's Richard Hayward, and I'm wondering what *he* wants."

Her visitor was a tall, well-built man, pleasantly dressed in well-cut tweeds, as though he were going golfing; he had a square, sunburnt face with a resolute jaw and fine grey eyes, and carried himself well, walking with a long stride.

"Good afternoon, Miss Hanton. I hoped that I might be fortunate enough to catch you in the garden this fine afternoon, so as I was passing I thought that I'd drop in, and save you the trouble of answering a letter. We are hoping that you will be kind enough to give the prizes again at our Ambulance Competition at the Works. The men said that the speech you made last year was far and away the best they'd ever had made to them."

"Very nice of them," said Miss Madeleine. "At least I knew what I was talking about, tho' I'm no good at frills. There's a seat over there under the trees. Shall we go across?"

So saying she led the way in her chair, and Richard Hayward followed her; when he was seated Madeleine said:

"I'm very sorry, but I'm afraid I can't accept your invitation to give away the prizes, Mr. Hayward, much as I enjoyed it last year. It's no good beating about the bush, for I'm afraid I've got an unpleasant statement to make. My brother has been much put out by a friendship which has sprung up between your cousin Philip and my niece Diana. My brother totally disapproves of this friendship, and is very incensed with your cousin. Now I have no intention of going into the rights and wrongs of the matter, but my niece is staying here in my charge, and this is my brother's house. Without being unfriendly to you, I can only say that I respect my brother's point of view. Under the circumstances I can't give away the prizes."

Richard Hayward flushed, and his face showed that he felt the rebuff he had received.

"I'm exceedingly sorry, Miss Hanton. I know Philip is a fool and that he can be an unpleasant fool, but I'd no idea that he had offended your brother. I quite see your point of view, but I feel very sick about it, for I was proud of being friends with you. . . ."

"Life is very difficult at times," said Madeleine, "and we can't always do as we wish. How is your father? I was sorry to hear such bad reports of him."

"A hopeless case, I'm afraid," rejoined Hayward. "It's just a matter of time. His heart can't last out much longer, but he likes us to carry on as usual and tries to pretend that nothing's the matter. I'm hoping he won't get on to the news about young Rodmell, that's bound to upset him further."

Madeleine had made no bones about showing Richard Hayward that her acquaintance with him was about to cease, though she hadn't put it into such plain words; but she had no objection to prolonging the present conversation, if her visitor showed no resentment at her cavalier dealing.

"I'm so sorry," she said. "It must be very sad and worrying for you to have your father so ill. Did he then know young Rodmell?"

"Oh no, it's not that," replied Hayward. "As a matter of fact this is quite confidential, Miss Hanton, but it's a positive relief to talk to you about it. It appears that Bert Rodmell robbed Mellon's safe before he left on Saturday, and of course the police are fairly buzzing about it."

"But however have you proved that?" demanded Madeleine, all other thoughts out of her head, save the one engrossing mystery.

"It's all a bit vague, but it boils down to this," answered Richard Hayward. "On Saturday morning about noon, Mellon (he's our works manager, you know), had Rodmell into the office to haul him over the coals for some negligence. While he was talking to Rodmell, Mellon was called away from his room to speak to me. He left Rodmell alone in his office for five minutes, and apparently the key of the safe was left in the lock. Inside the safe were the drawings and full description of a new type of shock absorber that was being worked out. Unfortunately it was only just completed and we hadn't covered it with a patent. Well, that has disappeared, and a bundle of £1 notes which were Mellon's private property. Mellon wasn't at the works yesterday, he was ill, and consequently he didn't discover his loss until this morning, but he's certain that Rodmell's the culprit. The safe was locked after he'd gone, and he was the only person to be left alone in the room while the safe was open."

"What an extraordinary affair!" exclaimed Miss Hanton. "It looks as though young Rodmell had every intention of absconding with the loot, and yet he's found down here, murdered apparently, two days after the theft. Can you make any sense of it, Mr. Hayward? It seems a most extraordinary sort of story."

"I don't know what to think," replied Hayward, "I can only imagine that Rodmell came back late at night to fetch something from his home, and that he got into some sort of row and got knocked over the head. Anyway it's all very disturbing, and what with being worried about my father and this story of Mellon's as well, I've had a rotten day of it. . . . I'm sorry you won't give our prizes away, Miss Hanton. Would it be of any good if I called on your brother and apologised for my cousin's behaviour, whatever it was?"

"No, I'm afraid it wouldn't," said Miss Hanton decidedly. "This is one of the occasions when least said is soonest mended. I'm sorry you're so worried, Mr. Hayward. . . . Good-bye."

For some time after her visitor had gone, Miss Hanton sat still in her chair, her hands idle in her lap, but her mind exceedingly busy, turning over one idea after another concerning the "Rodmell business," as she styled it to herself. At length she got her chair moving again and went down the drive to the chauffeur's cottage. The garage at Downfield Court was situated well away from the house and close to the road. Colonel Hanton had refused to spoil the beauty of his house by adding a garage on to the main building, and he had not considered the old stables a suitable place for a car. Consequently he had built his garage close to the road and had put up a small cottage for the chauffeur close by. (His sister said that the arrangement was dictated by her brother's dread of fire. He never really trusted motor cars and declined to have one actually "under his roof".) The drive branched before it reached the road, giving access to the garage.

Just as she came within view of the main gates, Miss Hanton saw the bonnet of a car turned into the drive. She rang the bell on her chair vigorously and the car pulled up, while the driver leaned out and called to her:

"I'm so sorry, I'll back out."

"Don't," called Miss Hanton promptly, "I'm not coming out, I'm just turning off to the garage," and off she went down the side turning. Rather as she had expected, the stranger in the car followed slowly behind her and pulled up in the clearing outside the garage. As he alighted, Miss Hanton studied the driver with thoughtful eyes, watching him carefully as he walked towards her. She saw a tall spare man, lithe and well proportioned. He had a well shaped dark head, and lean, sunburned face, and very keen grey eyes. Standing with his hat in his hand, he bowed to the lady in the chair without a scrap of self-consciousness or gaucherie.

"Miss Hanton?"

"Chief Inspector Macdonald?" shot out Miss Hanton in her deep voice, and the tall man smiled back at her, his grey eyes lit up as though in pleasure.

"My brother, Colonel Hanton, spoke of you to me, Inspector, and told me that you would be coming to see Waring. I know you're busy and I don't want to waste your time, but if you will come up to the house to speak to me for a few minutes when you're through here, I think you might find it worth while."

"Thank you very much," rejoined Macdonald. "I will come as soon as I have finished with Waring."

"Then I won't stay where I'm not wanted," volunteered Miss Hanton crisply, "you'll find me in the garden," and her chair moved off up the drive.

Macdonald spent about twenty minutes talking to the chauffeur, and then made his way towards the house, wondering what Miss Hanton had in store for him. He found her seated by a tea-table under the big beech tree on the lawn, her hands busy among the tea-things.

"Sit down," she said. "A cup of tea won't come amiss, and you can drink while I talk. Sugar? Cream?"

"Neither, thank you very much," said Macdonald, and was rewarded for his discrimination by a cup of China tea such as he was seldom offered.

"I have been told the outlines of this Rodmell story," said Miss Hanton without wasting time over preliminaries. "I know all that Waring and my brother can tell me, and I have just seen Richard Hayward. In case you should feel apprehensive, I can assure you that I know how to hold my tongue. I've been an active woman in my day and no one has suffered through giving me their confidence so far. . . . Now your enquiries at the Works have brought to light this story about Rodmell robbing Mellon's safe?"

"They have," assented Macdonald.

"The idea that occurred to me has probably occurred to

you too," went on Madeleine. "You've only Mellon's word for it that Rodmell stole those papers,—apparently there's no confirmatory evidence. Now Mellon's house is only a couple of miles from here. He's a wealthy man, and one of his hobbies is gardening. He's levelling out some land to the north of his garden to give him more room for experimental bedding, and he's had a lorry up there to help clear the stuff. That lorry has been in the open for a fortnight. All this came into my head after Richard Hayward told me about the safe being robbed. I don't know if it's of any use to you, but it seemed worth mentioning. . . . More tea?"

"Thank you," said Macdonald meditatively, and handed back his cup. "Very few people have tea like that, it's perfect. Before we get back to Rodmell & Co., weren't you Commandant of the Noyons hospital?"

"I was that," returned Madeleine, "I sometimes wish I were still. . . . And you?"

Macdonald tumbled to the query pretty promptly. "First battalion, London Scottish," he said. "I went out with them in December, 1914. . . . I think you and I will understand one another very well, Commandant. . . . Getting back to that story again, the lorry is the part that intrigues me most. If Mellon borrowed it from the Forward works, he didn't report it to us. But it's not so simple as it looks though. . . . You're getting your news twenty-four hours ahead of the inquest, so you understand it's not for publication. That corpse on the road wasn't the body of a boy of twenty, as you would have guessed as quickly as I did, if you'd examined it."

"You surprise me," said Miss Hanton calmly, and sat deep in thought for a moment. "Still, I think it was worth while telling you about that lorry."

"It certainly was," replied Macdonald, "and I expect

you can tell me a good many things which I should like to know, but I'm so intrigued about the lorry that I'm going to ask if I may use your telephone."

"First door on the right as you go into the hall," answered Miss Hanton. "The front door's on the latch, you needn't ring."

When Macdonald returned, he found his hostess smoking a cigarette, and she pushed the box towards him.

"Smoke a pipe if you've got one, and would rather," she said, and Macdonald promptly produced his pouch. "What else can I tell you?" she went on, "I haven't thought of anything myself."

"Tell me all you can about the Rodmell family. Your brother quoted you to me as the local authority."

"If he told you I was the scandal-monger, I'm not," retorted Miss Hanton. "Somehow, I get told all the news, but I never let it out of the family. I chatter to my brother, but he's safe enough. You know from him a little about the family. They made their money through winning a Spanish state lottery. The father is a British subject, born in the West Indies, so were the children. The wife is a Portuguese poor soul. I've never seen her, but I can guess the nature of her malady."

"So can I," replied Macdonald, "I saw her to-day. She's a drug addict."

Miss Hanton nodded. "George likes to describe himself as a city man," she continued. "He's sent me prospectuses of some of the companies he's interested in, and I should imagine he's likely to lose all he possesses and more. I've met him and Vanda at fêtes and other charitable functions. I don't want to be cattish, but they try to buy their way in. Vanda and George both yearn to be 'county,' as they'd put it. They do all the right things in the wrong way. The father is even less desirable than

George, he's frankly intolerable. Vanda's out to marry Richard Hayward, bad luck to her,—I hope she doesn't net him, though she won't while old Hayward's alive. Have you seen Vanda?" Macdonald nodded.

"No need to enlarge on her then," continued Miss Hanton. "I don't know how you reacted, but the young men round here dote on her, poor fish; but Richard Hayward's going to be an exceedingly wealthy man quite soon."

"Give me a line about them too," said Macdonald.

Miss Hanton lifted her eyebrows.

"As you like," she assented. "The father, Vincent Hayward, is a self-made man. He's been twice married. I believe he had a son by the first wife, but he was killed in the war. Old Vincent married again in 1900. The second wife was one of the Gloucestershire Wynns; you see he had made money by that time, and aspired to Debrett, but his second wife didn't live long either, and there's only the one son, Richard, quite a pleasant fellow and generally accepted. Old Vincent's ambitious, he wants his son to marry a title. He's actually talked to me about it, and got the lady cut and dried, but Richard doesn't see eye to eye with the old man about it. Now you've heard enough local gossip to make you a highly dangerous person."

Here Miss Hanton lighted another cigarette.

"A *quid pro quo,* Inspector, I've trusted you with my reputation as a woman who knows how to hold her tongue. Who is your wayside corpse?"

"I don't know," replied Macdonald. "Honest to God I don't," he added, as he saw Miss Hanton's expression. "In the first place Waring identified him by his clothes. Then we found a card case in his pocket; then brother George kindly identified him. What I want to do is to get to grips with the father." He pulled a card out of his pocket. 'H. H. Rodmell, Potboilers Club, Swallow Street, W.' "Can you beat it?" he asked.

Miss Hanton gave a gasp. "What was the name on the cigarette case you found in our Sunbeam?" she demanded.

"Bertie," replied Macdonald, "and the card of Bert Rodmell's was inside it."

Miss Hanton leaned forward. "Last year Rodmell senior came to the Agricultural Show down here, and with him was a fat woman whom he called his cousin. She kept on shouting out, 'Now then, Bertie.'"

"Losh keep's!" cried Macdonald, "have you hit it? How old is he,—the father?"

"Fiftyish, but well preserved," replied Miss Hanton.

Macdonald rose to his feet.

"I know it seems churlish, but I must tread on the gas,—George's expression, not mine. *Au revoir,* and a thousand thanks."

"Don't forget your pipe," replied Miss Hanton.

CHAPTER VII

Macdonald returned to London on Tuesday evening in a rather exasperated state of mind. He had done a lot of satisfactory investigation to clear the ground, but each time he seemed to be making headway something else had cropped up, and every theory which had entered his head had to be abandoned before it was even clearly formulated.

Miss Hanton's information that Henry Hubert Rodmell, Esq., was called Bertie by his intimates was one of the most valuable items that he had learnt that day.

George, of course, had identified the cigarette case as his brother's, and Rodmell *père*, when he had arrived home (which he did about six in the evening, rather to Macdonald's surprise), had upheld George stoutly. The corpse was undoubtedly that of poor Bert; when Macdonald had sprung upon the sorrowful parent the fact that a cigarette case, with his own or his son's name upon it, had been found in the Hantons' car, Mr. Rodmell had at first been at a loss to account for its presence, and then had indulged in a tirade against Waring.

"If the police were looking for trouble, why damn it, they'd got a clear enough pointer."

As for alibis, both Rodmells, father and son, were impeccable in their description of how they had spent the previous evening. George had been at his city office until five o'clock. From there he had gone to his club in Cork Street, where he had played bridge until seven. From his club he went to his chambers in Mount Street, dined, and went to the theatre with his friends the da Costas, ("very well known society people, if you wish to know, Inspector,") and later they had had a spot of supper at "the Troc." George had finally got to his virtuous bed at twelve-forty-five.

All of which Macdonald filed for future reference, and then turned to the father for an account of his doings on the previous evening. Mr. Rodmell had travelled with a friend on the five-fifty train from Euston and had arrived at Liverpool at nine-thirty-five. He had stayed the night at the flat of his friend, Mr. Rosario, who had sailed for Buenos Ayres in the *Melitic* at ten o'clock on Tuesday morning.

Under the circumstances Macdonald did not press the matter further; he had enough information to set his enquiries on hand, but he mused over the two Rodmells as he drove home in the beautiful evening light. Neither of them had challenged his right to enquire into their doings, on the contrary, it seemed to him, they had welcomed the opportunity to describe their doings.

"Greasy beggars," muttered Macdonald to himself.

From neither father nor son had Macdonald been able to elicit anything that was helpful concerning Bert's doings during the week-end. Mr. Rodmell told him with a wealth of detail that his younger son had come to meet him at his club on Saturday afternoon, and told him that he intended to stay with some friends "down Streatham way" during the week-end. The name of his friends Mr. Rodmell was, alas, unable to supply.

"It's like this, Inspector. Bert wasn't a kid. He'd turned twenty and he was a bright young fellow. Now I've always held that a bit of liberty's good for young 'uns. No use for apron strings. No, sir. Let 'em find their own way about. I trusted my boy, no need for me to ask where he went to, every darned minute. . . . 'Down Streatham way,' that was what he said."

And no one, apparently, had bothered to make any enquiries when Bert had not reappeared by Monday morning. Mrs. Rodmell was obviously too fuddled to observe much, and Vanda's reply to the question was characteristic.

"It's not my business to play nursemaid to Bert. I didn't approve of the way he behaved in any sense. He was a disgrace to us all, and if he chose to prolong his week-ends, that was nothing to do with me."

"Nice sister, that's what you are," growled Mr. Rodmell. "Bert dead and stiff, and all you can think of is your own affairs."

"Well, if I didn't consider myself, no one else would," she retorted calmly, and George, perspiring more than ever, rebuked her with:

"Don't talk like that, Vanda. It's rank bad form."

Macdonald returned to London convinced that the whole family was cognisant of the crime, and that Vanda's attitude was a pose to conceal the fact that she, like her father and brother, was endeavouring to protect the younger brother.

Meanwhile Macdonald had many activities to set on hand. The Rodmell family needed watching, and he got Superintendent Hastings to agree to having a Scotland Yard man put on to watch them. Advertisements must be published to get news of Bert Rodmell's week-end activities. Apparently Bert had gone up to London on his motor-bike, dressed in the same conspicuous tweeds which Macdonald had first seen in the Oxford road. But the most pressing question of all remained to be answered. "Who was the dead man?" Someone must have disappeared on Monday evening, and no disappearances had been reported or observed in the locality of Winchstone and Wycombe.

Having been into Scotland Yard to put matters in train, Macdonald returned to his flat and there he found Peter Vernon waiting for him. Macdonald had forgotten all about the invitation he had issued that morning, and the sight of Peter's long boyish figure, tied up into knots in one of his usual odd attitudes, had caused the older man genuine surprise.

"What,—are you still living?" he enquired. "I'd completely forgotten your existence."

"W.A.F.," retorted Vernon, "which is, being interpreted, What a friend, oh Damon cum Achates. I, to the contrary, have had you in mind all day, while I worked on your behalf."

"How did the gentlemanly touch work?" enquired

Macdonald. "I don't know if you've eaten, but I have not, and I'm going to eat now. You can tell me all the horrors while I get outside this. Losh! What a day!"

"Echo answers what," replied Vernon. "Is that beer? I talk better when I'm damped, tho' I talk well at all times. Before I start,—who's the corpse?"

"G.O.K.," retorted Macdonald.

"I know that one," said Vernon. "Still nameless and yet in Bert's clothes. Well, here's my doings. After having gone to the *Clarion* offices and wangled a free hand, I went down to Wycombe by train, you having cast me off, and as I went I considered the gentlemanly touch, and voted it no go for the moment. You were so obviously bound for the seats of the mighty that I felt I didn't like to compete, so when I arrived I made for the pub. that was nearest to the Forward Works. It was lunch time,—hooter gone and all that, and the place was bung full of Forward blokes. I stood beers all round and talked about the morning's tragedy. You ought to have made for that pub., you'd have learned more about Bert Rodmell there than you did in high life. Now there was one old boy, a Sussex man I discovered,—who was full of the Rodmells, and I managed to get him to myself for a few minutes, and he told me some queer things. First he said that Pa Rodmell had made his pile in the Spanish Lottery, and there'd been a picture of him in one of the Sunday papers long before he came to Downfield. Now I began to get a bit suspicious, and asked my old boy how he knew that and why he'd noticed it."

"I've guessed," interrupted Macdonald. "You said the old boy came from Sussex. There's a place near Lewes called Rodmell. Your old boy hailed from there and noticed the name."

"Yes, confound you, he did," replied Vernon.

"Southease and Rodmell, that's the place, but I haven't done yet. He'd read more than that in the Sunday papers. A few months before winning the lottery, a Henry Hubert Rodmell was charged in company with four other men under the Prohibited Drugs Act,—cocaine my old boy thought—, but Henry Hubert was discharged—no evidence against him, Well, that was that. The pub. as a whole thought it not unnatural that Bert should have been found with his face bashed in, but my old boy thought it'd be even more apposite for Pa Rodmell to have been found ditto."

"Have some more beer," urged Macdonald. "I've never known you to be so interesting before. Incidentally Pa hasn't had his face bashed in, I've been talking to him."

Vernon twisted his thin legs round one another in a fresh attitude, his keen face alight with joy as he swallowed his beer.

"Jock, I've hardly begun, I've got a story which will take hours. . . . There was a game-keeper in the pub. who came from a place called Warlington, about a couple of miles from Downfield, and he said he'd seen Pa Rodmell at Warlington just after six yesterday evening."

"Got his address?" cried Macdonald.

"Trust me!" replied Peter. "Well, what did I do?"

"Rang me up and reported information to hand," said Macdonald, a shade bitterly, and Vernon's face fell.

"Sorry, but it didn't seem worth making a fuss about, and I didn't know where you were. Anyway, I was so full of it that I thought I'd do a bit of tracking on my own. I went back to town first, and got hold of old Angus McLean. He's a journalist who drinks too much, but I knew he could do what I wanted. He's a boozer, and he's been fired from every job he had, but he's competent when he's not canned. I told him to search the files of the Sunday Press, and pester all his acquaintances in Fleet Street until he'd got me those Press cuttings about Henry Hubert Rodmell. I wanted the photograph you see. . . . Then I rang up the Rodmells at Downfield and got H.H.'s address at the Potboilers' Club and went there. Some hole, Jock; it's worse than its name. Riff-raff with a bit of money and no hope of getting into any club you'd call a club. H.H. wasn't there. I didn't think he would be, but I talked like a mother to the porter of that hole. Every club gets the porter it deserves, and if it'd been a decent club—"

"Don't stress the obvious, you juggins," interrupted Macdonald. "Have some more Bass and get on with the story."

"Ha! said he, scenting the battle from afar. . . . It's a pathetic story. I soon found out that Henry Hubert didn't always spend the night at his club when he was in town. For instance, he was in town on Saturday and Sunday, but he didn't sleep at the P.B.'s on Saturday night. If you'll believe me it took a five pound note and all my noted charm and address to get any further. No one ever offers me a fiver for saying where anyone didn't sleep. Now the porter was a cautious bloke, he wanted to know what I'd got on H.H., and suggested a move round the corner for a cup of tea. Said it was a pity about them licensing acts and eyed me up and down. I told him—all so candid and sweet—that I was a journalist, and that I'd got a tip for H.H. which was the real thing. Porter bloke looked me up and down. 'That's as may be,' he said, 'but you're not a cop, and you're not a dun, I can see that. I'll risk it if you'll swear you'll not let on to the management.' I swore,—trust me, and he breathed out in my inmost ear, 'You try 345 Charlotte Street. That's it,' and off he went with my fiver."

"The *Clarion*'s fiver I hope," said Macdonald, "and cheap at the price. Go on. You went to 345. . . ."

"I did, as the arrow and all that," continued Vernon, "and I thought I'd been sold a pup, but I was just in time. Just in time, Jock, as the duchess said. . . ."

"Can it, do, and get on with the doings," groaned Macdonald.

"Well, you'd have been too late, that's my one consolation," said Vernon, emerging from his very adequate glass. "Now the landlady at that abode was a very repulsive female. Nasty, she was, not to say contumacious, as someone's butler once said. I was discretion personified, wished for rooms and began to ask terms. She showed me in and exhibited one of her rooms,—may the Lord in his infinite mercy preserve me from ever sleeping in such,—and then I told her that I'd been recommended by Mr. Rodmell, and she got all heated.

" 'Don't know 'im, never 'eard of 'im,' she said, and got nasty all of a sudden. 'Don't want none of your sort in my 'ouse,' she said. 'Trying to get honest lodgings under false pretences. I'll trouble you to get off my premises.' Well I was annoyed, I can tell you, I tried to argue."

"No use," cut in Macdonald, "not with that sort: I seem to remember something about a predestinate scratched face. . . ."

"Well, I only just avoided it by inches," said Vernon, "I told her it wasn't she I was scared of, but blood poisoning. 'Git,' she says,—so I got. . . . No, I haven't finished yet, laddie, I've hardly begun."

Macdonald got up from the table and walked to his big chair by the window, facing the river. Producing his pipe, he tossed his pouch over to Vernon.

"Somebody mentioned the word garrulous once, a very, very long time ago. It's an unmannerly sort of word, not one I'd use of a pal. Now, above all, don't hurry, Peter. I hate to have a good story spoiled, and we've got another night before us."

"If you imagine I'm going to cramp my style on your account after the sort of day I've had, you've guessed wrong," said Vernon. "Each morning sees some task begun, each evening sees its close—"

"Pray the Lord the good beer's not gone to his head," said Macdonald, when he had got his pipe going. "What time was it then, Peter? You've got me all addled."

"Left the Forward pub., 'Goat and Compasses' it was,—at two o'clock. Left High Wycombe two-thirty. Paddington three-fifteen. Interval for Angus McLean. Potboiling at four-fifteen. Charlotte Street five o'clock. Evicted five-five," said Vernon, all in a breath. "I walked along to the next corner a sadder and a wiser man. Then I recovered my breath and decided to root out McLean again. Heaven it was that made me turn round, Jock. . . . I saw an aged and seemingly indigent female emerge laboriously from the area of 345, and decided to have a shot at retrieving bits of my fiver. I met the old girl and walked along aside her. 'Madam,' I said, 'I am in need of information for which I am willing to pay, and I believe that you can do both yourself and me a good turn if you are willing to consider the matter.' Well, I found myself pretty soon in a tea shop for the second time that afternoon. A.B.C. it was, quite classy. My poor old girl ordered a 'coupl-a poached eggs on toast and beans with it, miss' and I reckon she needed 'em. She was the occasional char at 345 and she'd just been sacked for breaking an egg. Poor old misery, she was about 105 in the shade. . . . Yes, you're getting to it, old patience on a monument. Henry Hubert retains a suite in that classy establishment."

"He would," said Macdonald dryly, "he looks it. Any more, Peter?"

"Loads more. I've hardly begun." Here Vernon pulled out his note-book.

"Henry Hubert didn't sleep at 345 on Saturday night, but he turned up there on Sunday and stayed the night. He had a pal to see him in the evening, name of Rosary or something like that."

"Rosario," corrected Macdonald, "carry on."

"My old char, Mrs. Rummidge—happened to hear the name because she was sent up with drinks. Well, H.H. went out on Monday morning and blew in again just after lunch. Mrs. Rummidge was giving his room a good doing, seeing he wasn't expected just then. Anyway he spent a few minutes hunting up a railway time-table, told Mrs. Rummidge that he was off to Liverpool, picked up a suitcase and slung his hook. Well, I left the old girl to finish her poached eggs, and telephoned to McLean. Found him at home, and he said he'd got my pretty picture for me. I told him to meet me at Marylebone Station."

"Peter," cried Macdonald, "you're a P.B.W. Have some more beer. You then took the train to Warlington?"

"You've got it, Jock. I reached Marylebone at six-fifteen and found there was a train to Princes Risborough at six-thirty-five. I wanted to see old Angus before I went, and I was all in a sweat in case he didn't get there before my train went. I spent the time studying time-tables, I'll tell you about that later. Angus arrived just after six-thirty with my picture and all. Here it is . . . no, don't interrupt. I got to Princes Risborough at seven-thirty-five and hired a car, and was at Warlington at eight o'clock. It's only a wee station, and the man who took the tickets had been there the previous evening. He recognised my little picture. H.H. got out there at six-eleven yesterday evening."

"Well done, Peter," said Macdonald softly. "Now here's to you! You've been doing my work for me with a vengeance. *Moitié fait quand bien commencé,* and thanks to you, we've jolly well got going."

"One more word and then I'm done," pleaded Peter. "Ever since I heard old Velveteens mention Warlington in the 'Goat and Compasses', I've been wondering *why Warlington*? And the great idea I got was this. If Henry Hubert was doing dirty work down Winchstone way, he wouldn't have travelled by train to Wycombe where he was known by everybody, and he didn't go there by car, because Velveteens saw him on foot, and he wasn't in the neighbourhood during the day, because Ma Rummidge saw him at 345 in the afternoon."

"That's why she was sacked," said Macdonald. "Sorry, go on."

"Well, I worked it out this way. He took a train from Marylebone to Aylesbury where he wasn't known at all, and changed there on to the Warlington line. It's a wee one-horse line, but he'd have been away from his usual haunts, so to speak. He could have done it, Jock. He left 345 just before three o'clock. Marylebone three-twenty-five. Aylesbury four-forty-eight. Left Aylesbury five-thirty. Warlington six-eleven. Q.E.D."

"And jolly well proved too," applauded Macdonald. "H.H. has produced an alibi of course,—that I expected. He says that he went up to Liverpool to wave good-bye to your Rosary merchant,—I expect it's the same bloke, one Juan Rosario."

"There once was a man named Rosario," chanted Peter,
  In behaviour a perfect Lothario,
  As I said at the time,
  He was expert at crime—"

"You can't find another rhyme," said Macdonald, "but it doesn't matter. Well, Rosario's name is on the passenger list of the *Melitic,* and he sailed all right. Details of the alibi are being gone into by Jenkins. I got a photo of Henry Hubert out of Bert's room."

"Now say if you tell me all your doings, categorically and in order," suggested Vernon. "'Sno use telling me to keep my fingers out of the pie and mind my own business, because I've stuck 'em in already, all ten of 'em."

"And likewise pulled out a plum and said what a good boy am I," answered Macdonald. "You've earned your right to the day's news, Peter, but tell me one thing first. What made you freeze on to Henry Hubert like that? Why not brother George?"

"Journalistic instinct," replied Peter promptly. "What I want is copy. Now I learned two things about H.H. in the first round. He'd won the Spanish Lottery, and he'd been concerned in a Prohibited Drugs case. There's promising copy in that. 'H.H., you're the lad for me,' quoth I, and backed him forthwith."

Macdonald nodded thoughtfully. "Reason, not instinct," he said, "but we don't want to argue over that. Here's my tale."

Macdonald was briefer and less exuberant over describing his doings than Vernon had been but at the end of his recital Peter exclaimed:

"Cripes! it's a corker! What do you make of it, Jock?"

"Make of it?—why nothing for the moment," replied Macdonald. "It's a tale told by an idiot. Now let's cut all the redundancies and see if we can reduce it to sense. The corpse is that of a well-nourished, muscular bloke, used to the open air. His body's in fine condition and he has well shaped, powerful hands, with well kept nails. Also I should guess he had his shoes made for him, because his feet are in such good trim. No corns or calluses. I can't make any guess at his identity except this. The skin of his arms and neck are tanned more deeply than seems consistent with his residence in England. It's not the sort of sun-burn you'd acquire from a holiday at the seaside, it's much more like the result of exposure to a southern climate, as though he had lived in Australia or South Africa."

"Or South America," interpolated Vernon.

"Quite. Well, that being so, he may have landed only recently in this country, but we're bound to get some report of him. He'd have had luggage and it's been left somewhere. . . . Now let's do a little wild imagining. This man comes to England to give H.H. beans, and H.H. asks him down to the country, all friendly like, and does him in, somewhere between six and seven o'clock yesterday evening. Leave it at that for a minute or two. Corpse in a chalk pit somewhere. . . . Now H.H. had seen Bert in the afternoon and heard the story of his depredations. 'You're a bad lad but I'm a good father,' says H.H. 'I'll get you out of the country. You'd better change those fetching tweeds for something milder. I'll hide the tweeds in my suite at 345'. . . . Leave Bert for the moment . . . as you were between six and seven o'clock, Monday evening. Corpse in a hidey hole. Run up to town and get Bert's clothes. Back again to hidey hole. He must have had a car,—losh! that might fit. . . . Dress corpse in fetching tweeds. He did it jolly well, too; I bet it's not easy. Borrow Mellon's lorry and trundle corpse on to the Oxford road and hope for the best. How's that?"

"Cunning, Jock, cunning,—but I bet Bert helped. It took two men to do all that, unless H.H. is in better condition than seems consistent with his manner of living. Do you reckon H.H. borrowed the Hantons' Sunbeam?"

"Seems likely. Now how did H.H. know that Waring was going to be away? . . . I bet there's a maid at Beech Grange who went to that wedding and H.H. would be smug and confidential with maids. I'm getting smug too, Peter. It's all too easy. Do me another reconstruction to blow me sky high."

Peter Vernon puffed away furiously at his pipe for a minute or two, his hands behind his head, his legs over the arm of his chair.

"H.H. has a brother who resembles him considerably," he said at length, "and for some reason it is desirable to bump said brother off. Possibly, since H.H. is aping the gentry, he wants to conceal his unpromising beginnings, and brother is a nuisance. Anyway, the whole crime has been arranged beforehand, including shipping Bert off to sunnier climes, so his little affair with Mellon's safe is a final *jeu d'esprit.* Anyway, someone 'phones to brother that H.H. wants to see him on the q.t. Will he kindly come down, via Warlington, and a car will be sent to meet him at a certain spot. Here he sees Bert complete with bike. Loving nephew says, 'Hullo, Uncle. Sorry the car's gone blotto for the moment, we didn't want to hire another. Jump on the pillion seat, it's not far.' Nephew drives off with uncle behind, and turns up a side road into the woods. Short cut and all that. Suddenly bike coughs like a horse and jibs. Nephew swears. 'Sorry, Uncle, hold the old bus a minute. I'll get her right in a brace of shakes.' Spanner out from somewhere, and one on the boko for uncle. Corpse and bike concealed quickly in undergrowth. Then a nasty period of waiting. An empty house or bungalow or something, quite near. Change clothes. Alter uncle's face. Go and get lorry. Must be after dark. Can't convey uncle in lorry because there's no tarpaulin. Go and get the Sunbeam. Drive uncle to strategic point. Leave him on the road and hope for the best. Best comes off, very little traffic at that time of night. Change from Sunbeam into lorry. Drive back with lorry and finish the job."

Here Peter looked at Macdonald with one eyebrow raised high, but Macdonald shook his head.

"Lots of ifs and holes, Peter. You're assuming a brother, we don't know of one."

"We do!" cried Peter. "We! the British Press. This is my last rabbit, Jock, up the sleeve and out of the hat. McLean got hold of the reporter who wrote up the Prohibited Drugs case. H.H. was accused of taking a packet from a certain gentleman at a certain place. He proved that he couldn't have done so because he was at another place at that time. Faced with the cop who saw him, he said pleasantly, 'I'm afraid you mistook me for my younger brother. He's said to be very much like me.' Of course he couldn't produce the brother—a very unsatisfactory member of the family. Sad case and all that. Yoicks, likewise Tally Ho! Either he's got a brother or he hasn't. You see to it, Jock."

"I will that," responded Macdonald. "If it's as you say, Peter, Bert had to have help. He couldn't have done it alone."

"What price George?" demanded Vernon.

"No go. His alibi includes too many people."

"Well, then, H.H.—though I'm dead keen for him to have been with old Rosary. . . . 'The hours I spent with thee dear heart'—swipe in the eye for you and all that."

"Peter, you're enough to give any man a sick headache. Any more ideas?"

"Just one before I toddle. I'm sleepy. Up all last night. Corpse is old Rosary and Bert changed clothes and got away on his ticket and thoughtfully produced alibi for father. Ideas?—our telegraphic address is Notions. I've got to write up some unoffending lines to tickle the palate of the public on pedestrians and post mortems. Coming events by one who knows. . . . So long, Jock. See you to-morrow. The Inquest's the place for me. Password, Reconstructions. . . ."

CHAPTER VIII

"You seem to have landed yourself into a lively story at a very apropos moment, Macdonald," said the Assistant Commissioner, after he had greeted the Chief Inspector on Wednesday morning. "Got it all cut and dried for me?"

"Far from it, sir," replied Macdonald. "We have a mass of probabilities and surmises, but nothing proved. The only things I can prove definitely are that the corpse is not Bert Rodmell's,—and even that wasn't too easy to prove,—that the injury done by the lorry was post mortem injury, and that the corpse was put where we found it between twelve-forty-five and one-twenty-five. Taking these points in order; my suspicions about the identity of the body were based on the fact that the clothes did not fit. Now I expected to prove that point beyond a shadow of doubt by comparing the finger-prints of the corpse with those of Bert Rodmell, assuming that the contents of the pockets being Rodmell's, they would show his finger-prints. Not a bit of it, we found a letter case, a purse, loose coins, some keys, a packet of cigarettes, a petrol lighter and some photographs. There were remarkably few finger-prints on anything; but one of the photographs, the petrol lighter, and the packet of cigarettes gave us good prints which coincided with those of the corpse."

Colonel Wragley raised his eyebrows.

"Sure you're right about the corpse, Macdonald? Not a case of wish being father to the thought?"

"No, sir," answered Macdonald. "The corpse is two inches shorter than Rodmell and much broader in build. I've got Rodmell's measurements from his tailor,—there's no probability of error on that point. I examined Rodmell's bedroom and tried to get finger-prints there. That room has been swept and garnished with a vengeance. It's reasonable, in a well kept house, to find the wash-stand and dressing-table well rubbed and polished, but everything, glasses, mirrors, brushes and boxes, had been well rubbed, likewise door handles and finger-plates, bed-posts, drawers, chairs, and everything else you're likely to finger. No books, no letters. . . . His boots and shoes were all freshly cleaned, his trouser-press polished. . . . I've never seen such a thorough job in my life."

"Hm. Fishy's the word for it," murmured Colonel Wragley.

"Fishy! It's just one vast herring!" exclaimed Macdonald. "I have absolutely failed to get any finger-prints out of that room which can't be accounted for by the household, save one, and that's a lovely clear one on a pocket mirror,—the corpse's, of course."

"By gad, this is really interesting," said Colonel Wragley. "Looks as though the household is being obliging."

"Obliging really described them rather well," said Macdonald. "Both George Rodmell and his father ended up by being amiability itself. Only too anxious to help. Now analysing the foregoing facts, these points occur to me. Whoever was responsible for the crime was acquainted with criminal procedure as far as fingerprints were concerned, but apparently ignorant of post mortem examination. They assumed that the corpse would be taken for granted, despite the evident fact that it had been dead a greater number of hours than it could have lain where it was found."

Colonel Wragley put out a protesting hand.

"You may have got that point the wrong way round, Macdonald. Perhaps your murderer was one of the modern thinkers who knows how dangerous it is to dogmatise about the time of death from rigor and temperature. You know more about that than I do."

"I quite see your point, sir," answered Macdonald. "The onset of rigor varies enormously, of course. It has been known to set in less than two hours after death, but a case of completely developed rigor forty-five minutes after death is unbelievable. That body wasn't on the road at twelve-forty-five. Also, the murderer forgot that post mortem injuries can be detected from the other kind. I still think our corpse manipulator was ignorant about medical details."

"Any theory concerning said manipulator?" enquired Wragley.

"Lots of them, sir. The most obvious being Bert Rodmell himself, but if he is the culprit he must have had someone to help him. From various enquiries I've made it's evident that he was of poor physique and in no sort of condition. In order to lift that body, one of two qualities is required, muscular strength or training at the job of lifting. Apparently he had neither. When we look for an accomplice, the most likely suggestions are the father or the brother. George is right out of it. He was where he said he was,—first at the Gaiety, then at the Trocadero, then at his own flat. The only interesting thing I've learnt about him is that he had a 'phone call at three o'clock in the morning. He was connected with a public call-box near Charing Cross. The conversation was a long one, the operator remembers it all right, because there were very few calls going thro' just then. The conversation was in a foreign language,—Spanish, I expect. The operator heard that much through butting in because the conversation was prolonged and more pennies were needed."

Colonel Wragley smiled. "When all telephones are automatic we shall lose the human touch which is so often helpful."

Macdonald laughed. "That's true enough. Well, I should imagine that that call was to instruct George about identifying the remains. I might bluff it out of him later when I've found out if the family habitually use Spanish or Portuguese as their private medium. Before we leave George, I might add that he's in a mess financially. After his father won his lottery, George interested himself in Brazilian coffee, and lost a lot of money. Since then he's tried his hand as a director on the board of an Argentine company and some Export Board in Chile, both on the rocks at present. I only mention that point because, in spite of their lottery,—the family are heading for Queer Street,—often a useful point to remember."

"Your department must have had a busy day of it Macdonald," commented Colonel Wragley. "You seem to have covered a lot of ground."

Macdonald laughed. "A bit in the nature of a circular tour, so far, sir. Nor much headway on the main problem. Now as to the father, Henry Hubert Rodmell. He has undoubtedly been mixed up in some queer doings in his time, notably the drug traffic, but we have never succeeded in proving anything against him. On Monday night he states that he went up to Liverpool by the five-thirty train with a friend named Rosario, and that he saw his friend off by the *Melitic* next morning. Of course we wirelessed the *Melitic* and got her commander to interrogate Rosario on our account, without letting the cat out of the bag. Rosario,—also of course,— testified to H. H. Rodmell's accompanying him to Liverpool and seeing him off. That's not very impressive, one obviously expected it, but Jenkins managed to get hold of the Dining-Car attendant on the Liverpool train who recognised Rodmell's photograph as that of a fare the previous evening. In fact Rodmell was very chatty with him and the fellow remembers him perfectly. Against this is some information Peter Vernon raked out on his own account. Vernon is a journalist, and he was with me on Monday night when we first came across the business."

Here Macdonald retailed the gist of Peter's doings including the information concerning the brother of H. H. Rodmell. Colonel Wragley nodded his head.

"Then it looks as though the brother worked the alibi with Rosario, while the Downfield Rodmell was busy in his own neighbourhood,—or vice-versa."

"Yes, sir, but we shall have to get the thing much clearer than that before it's any good to us, though. At present it's just one man's word against another's. To conclude the story about the Rodmells, Vanda, the daughter, took it into her head to go to the mortuary, saying that she also wished to identify the body. Hastings took her in, after warning her that she was likely to be considerably upset by what she saw. Apparently she was calm enough and never turned a hair until she examined the hands of the dead man. Then she staggered back and fainted. When Hastings got her outside and she'd recovered, she wouldn't say anything for a minute or two, as though she were making an effort to pull herself together Then, when she spoke, she affirmed what George Rodmell had said,—that the body was Bert's. Hastings is convinced, and I think he's probably right, that she recognised the dead man, but decided to stand in with the family."

"All of them in it, apparently," said Colonel Wragley, "and you've no news of Bert since Saturday?"

"Nothing, sir. We're advertising and broadcasting, so perhaps we shall get some help. Now just a word about other people in the neighbourhood. I'm satisfied about Waring, the chauffeur. He was in Oxford when the man was killed, but I'm a bit puzzled about Mellon, the manager of the Forward Works. He told Hastings about the theft from his safe, and seemed convinced that Rodmell was the thief. At Hastings's request, he made enquiries about the lorries belonging to the works, and was able to assure him that none of them could have been taken out on Monday evening, but he omitted to say that he had had a lorry up in the grounds of his own house which could have been misappropriated with very little trouble. He had been having some ground levelled, and the lorry was used for carting the loose stuff away and pitching it into a chalk pit close by. Here's a sketch map of the neighbourhood. Downfield and Winchstone both lie to the south of the main road and are just over a mile apart. Mellon's house, Ridgeways, lies about one and a half miles to the north of the main road; Ridgeways is rather isolated, there is no other house close to it and it stands in big grounds,—some six acres. The ground which was being cleared, and the chalk pit also, lie to the south of the house, between it and the road, and the lorry was left standing by the chalk pit, about fifty yards away from the road leading to the house. The ground in which the lorry stood is enclosed of course, and the gate in the fence locked with a padlock, though anybody could have lifted the gate off its hinges. When Hastings asked Mellon about this lorry, he said in a pained way that the only lorries he'd been asked about were the ones at the Forward Works. The one in his grounds had been hired from a local contractor's and had been returned yesterday—Tuesday—morning. To cut a long story short, Hastings saw the lorry at the contractor's. It was undoubtedly the one which had been over the dead man, and its on-side wheels had had a bucket of water thrown over them. You could see the marks of the water on the grimy surface."

"The point which strikes me most forcibly in that story is that Mellon seems to be an almighty fool," said Colonel Wragley.

"Exactly, sir," replied Macdonald. "Assuming that he'd got nothing to do with the case at all, it seems feeble-minded not to have reported that lorry to us immediately. When people say 'you know it never occurred to me' over such a point as that, I immediately ask myself 'Why didn't it occur to you? Either you're a fool, or else you're trying to cover something up.' Now Mellon isn't a fool; he's a first-rate business man who has got an important position."

"Exactly," replied Wragley. "Has he an alibi?"

"None whatever, that's one of the points in his

favour," replied Macdonald. "If there's one thing that makes me more suspicious than another, it's an elaborate, convincing alibi. All the best rogues have one. Now Mellon had been away from the works on Monday. He'd had a feverish cold, quite genuine, apparently. He stayed in bed all Sunday, felt weak in the knees on Monday, but got up and pottered around a bit in the garden. It was a lovely evening, and after tea he went and sat out in the garden, out of sight of the house, and no one saw him between five-thirty and seven-thirty. He went to bed early, at nine o'clock to be precise, and no one saw him again till the next morning."

"Hm,—gives him plenty of time for everything," answered Wragley.

"It does that, sir," said Macdonald, "and there's another little point. The constable on duty at the spot where the body was found picked up a pencil, or the fag end of a pencil. It was a Koh-i-Noor HH, very carefully sharpened by someone who knew how to make a decent point. Now an HH isn't everybody's pencil. It's more useful for tracing or fine draughtsmanship than for writing in the usual way. Mellon keeps HH Koh-i-Noor pencils on his desk at the Forward Works. It's not very important, because obviously Rodmell or anyone else could have helped himself to a pencil from a tray, but I do think that this particular pencil was sharpened by Mellon. I examined the ones he has in use, and his method of cutting the wood away with a long slope has quite a character of its own."

"Finger-prints?" interpolated Colonel Wragley, but Macdonald shook his head.

"None at all, sir,—only smears. Koh-i-Noor pencils are hexagonal in shape and you'd hardly expect to get a print."

"What was Mellon's attitude to the Rodmells? Did he know them?"

"Only Bert," replied Macdonald, "and Mellon seems to have had a down on him,—distrusted and disliked him. . . . I can't make him fit, anyhow. Assume that he was an accessory, or assume that he was the murderer, it's equally improbable either way. How did he get Bert Rodmell's clothes?—and why do the entire Rodmell family back him up by identifying his unknown victim as Bert Rodmell? On the other hand, if he knows nothing about the case at all, why did he omit to mention his lorry, and the fact that he ordered the contractors to come and fetch it away before his levelling was complete? It's a point I can't ignore."

"Is he shielding someone else? Say if he knew that the lorry was used, and knew who used it," suggested Colonel Wragley.

"Exactly, sir," replied Macdonald. "In which case one is led to believe that it was not the Rodmell family, because I see no point in his shielding them."

Colonel Wragley smoothed his chin with a thoughtful finger.

"Is Mellon a bachelor?" he enquired, and Macdonald laughed aloud.

"I see your bent, sir. That Mellon is another of Vanda Rodmell's conquests? He's a bachelor certainly, but he's a man of fifty, and if he's acquainted with Vanda, no one seems to know of it. Also if Mellon were trying to ingratiate himself with Vanda, why did he inform us that Bert was the only person who could have robbed his safe and made off with his Treasury notes?"

"What did he keep a supply of pound notes for at his office?" demanded Colonel Wragley.

"He told me that he intended going abroad quite

shortly, and that he finds English pound notes a convenient way of taking his money. Anyone on the continent will change them. That's quite true, of course, though in these days of travellers' cheques it seems a bit feeble. However, since he told us himself about the notes, I don't suppose it's relevant. He hadn't got their numbers of course."

Both men were silent for a moment or two, thinking hard; eventually Colonel Wragley enquired:

"What are you going to produce at the inquest?"

"I've thought about it a lot, sir. First, we shall call Waring, who need only give evidence as being the first to find the body. There's no need to call Miss Hanton. She didn't get out of the Sunbeam until after I arrived. Then we shall call George Rodmell and his father on the question of identification. Then the police surgeon, Dr. Renford. He can spring a mine on them with his evidence about post mortem injuries, the age of the dead man and his measurements. Then I shall also give evidence concerning measurements. Finger-prints we shan't mention at this juncture, hoping that the jury won't ask awkward questions."

"What verdict do you expect?"

"You never know which way a jury will jump. I expect it will be wilful murder, possibly by Bert Rodmell. That ought to be useful, whether it's right or wrong. We want news of Bert and his doings since last Saturday, and the greater publicity the better. We're up against a dead wall as far as he is concerned. He left the Potboilers' Club by himself, with a raincoat over his tweeds, and vanished. He must have left his motor-bike somewhere, but we haven't traced it. He must have parked it on some friends because Hastings got its number and advertised for it yesterday—broadcast and evening papers. If it had been in a garage we ought to have heard of it. On the other hand, if Bert Rodmell is still in this country, concealed with some of his friends, we shall hear about him somehow. You can keep a man hidden for a short while, but not indefinitely. Someone always talks eventually. That's why I'm willing to give the reporters something to say at the inquest. In some cases, publicity at an inquest is a great mistake,—but on this occasion, the more publicity the better, to my way of thinking, that is."

Colonel Wragley nodded his head. "I agree with you," he replied. "There are a lot of points on which the public may help you. As you've said before, somebody always notices something. You want to get any information you can about Rodmell and about the family in general, and you want to get reports about anybody who may be missing either from a hotel or anywhere else. You've got enquiries going about the Rodmells out in South America of course?"

"Yes, sir. We've cabled at length and ought to get answers from Buenos Ayres any time now. Also I have fixed up a consultation with the men who were on the job when Rodmell père was charged with handling Prohibited Drugs. We have plenty to do, the case isn't what you'd call at a dead end by any manner of means."

"So I observe," replied Wragley. "You certainly haven't wasted any time so far. I have decided to put off my own holiday for the time being. This case is an unusually interesting one and I want to keep in touch with it. Carry on then, Macdonald. I won't detain you. any longer."

Thus dismissed, the Chief Inspector returned to his own room, where he found Inspector Jenkins awaiting him.

"Morning, Jenkins. Been studying the facts of the

case? What do you make of it so far?"

"Too much Rodmell about it for my liking," returned Jenkins. He was an older man than Macdonald, and had not the same class of mind, but he was exceedingly competent, and Macdonald preferred Jenkins to any of his other colleagues. There was about him a certain common sense, and power of dogged persistence which were the qualities which Macdonald most needed in the men who worked under him. However unpromising the clue, and no matter what drudgery was implied in following it up, Jenkins stuck to his job with a thoroughness which few men can command.

"It's like this," he went on, "this case just reeks of the Rodmell family,—you can't get any other scent at all, so to speak. If I'm smoking a cigar, I can't smell another fellow's cigarette."

"Go on, Jenkins," encouraged Macdonald, "I seem to smell an idea."

"Well, here it is for what it is worth," said the other. "If a pal of mine wanted to commit a crime, how'd it be if he got my finger-prints on his jemmy and dropped the jemmy and a handkerchief of mine before he left? Nice definite little clue, easy to pick up. Now he'd arranged with me beforehand to look after myself. All the clues prove I did it, but I was busy at a party with about fifty witnesses to say I didn't. Now hauling me in as a red-herring lets the real scent cool off a bit."

"Good enough," said Macdonald. "Moreover, your pal could have borrowed your handkerchief and finger-prints without your knowledge, but I don't suppose anyone borrowed Bert Rodmell's kit without anyone noticing it."

"Now we're getting to it," replied Jenkins. "You've got a body identified as a man when it's not him at all. How do you know you haven't got a suit of clothes that are identified as Rodmell's without being his?"

"You're a man after my own heart, Jenkins, wherefore you shall take those dreadful plus fours to Miller Bros., who retailed them,—guaranteed to fit, in quarter sizes with suitable variations for unusual figures,—and see what you can do about it. All we know is that Bert Rodmell did have a suit like that one. I see your reasoning. Any of the objects found in the pockets of those clothes could have been bought by the dozen anywhere,—except the keys. I'll make it my business to see to them. Still you know, the father and brother did the identifying. You can't leave them out."

"I'm not leaving them out," said Jenkins sturdily, "but there's more than one way of looking at it. Bert Rodmell would have found himself in prison pretty quickly after his little affair with Mellon's safe. Say if his people, knowing that, decided that the accident business was a god-send? If Bert's officially dead, he can't be arrested."

"You're confusing two lines of thought, Jenkins, and your original one was the better. Some pal of the Rodmells' had planned out a little game of his own. Bert is only too willing to be shipped to sunnier climes for a suitable consideration. Father and brother arrange alibis and tell the other chap to get on with it. That's assuming that at least four people are in the know. A bit dangerous, isn't it?"

"Well, there's another point to be considered," said Jenkins. "Doesn't it strike you as a bit funny that Miss Diana Hanton had her night out at the same time that all these other doings were on the tapis? And what about her father? He lives in the Rodmell neighbourhood. What was he doing on that evening? It's a funny thing. He was expected to be away all night and came back late in the evening instead. Do you happen to know what he was doing that evening?"

"No, Jenkins, I don't. Quite honestly I'd consider it waste of time even to ask, unless we can find something to connect him with the case, quite apart from his daughter's presence at the scene of activities. You might as well ask Vernon and me what we were doing."

Jenkins grunted. "I know what you were doing sufficiently well to know that you couldn't have been driving Colonel Hanton's Sunbeam during the evening. Come to think of it, it'd be easier for him to have taken that car out of its garage than for anybody else."

"Quite true," said Macdonald, "but in that case he worked in collusion with the Rodmells, and it won't wash. I have always said that the way a criminal gets caught is when he fakes evidence. It's the most difficult thing in the world to get away with it. Now somebody left a mirror with the dead man's finger-prints on it in Bert Rodmell's room. That was the act of a fool, thinking he was being cunning. It told us that the individual we're looking for is to be found in the Rodmell household. Now I do agree with you that this is a job needing an accomplice, and, as you say, the Rodmell trail is so obvious that we must be careful not to lose sight of the other angle of affairs. I also agree with you that we haven't any unassailable evidence that the clothes we found were actually Rodmell's clothes. Anybody can buy a suit and wear it till it's old and put another man's name on it. It's important, because one of the points I've been arguing on is that the murderer must have had access to Rodmell's clothes. You might collect evidence on that point from his friends at the Works, as well as trying the makers here in London. There may be alterations or some way of identifying them. Now I want to see Wilkins about the charge against H. H. Rodmell, under the

Prohibited Drugs Act, to see what we can make of that. In my opinion there are two readings of this case. One is that Bert Rodmell had prepared to vanish and took the opportunity of committing a murder before he went; the other is that circumstances made him decide to bolt suddenly, and that someone else thought it a heaven-sent opportunity to get rid of an enemy, and so faked the accident. In either case the family is in it up to the hilt, but it's probable that someone outside the family is accessory. I'm willing to suspect the whole of England in the latter capacity but the last man I'd put my money on is Colonel Hanton."

"Very good," said Jenkins quite unruffled. "I'll go and see if Wilkins has come in yet."

CHAPTER IX

"I'm sorry that I can t give you a better report about your father, Mr. Hayward, but it's useless to indulge false hopes. After this last attack, I don't think his heart will keep going for more than another twenty-four hours. Both the nurses are very able women, and they know exactly what course to follow. Of course I'll come immediately if you send for me, but there's no object in my staying here at the moment. It's improbable that there will be any change during the next twelve hours."

Richard Hayward looked at Dr. Forrester with eyes that were both tired and sad.

"Thanks very much. I quite understand," he said quietly. "Of course we have been prepared for this for months, but it's a shock all the same when the end draws so near."

"You look as though you're in need of sleep yourself,"

said the doctor. "You've been having a worrying time lately, and that inquest was a bit disturbing on top of other things. I believe the Rodmells are friends of yours?"

"Acquaintances expresses it better perhaps," replied Hayward. "I went to the inquest assuming that the enquiry would only concern Bert Rodmell,—as one of my father's employees I was naturally interested in the finding of the jury, but I didn't imagine we were going to get such a bombshell in the way of evidence. What's your own opinion on the matter, doctor?"

Forrester paused in the act of pulling on his gloves, and gave a slight shrug of his shoulders.

"My only knowledge of the matter is second-hand, since I didn't attend the inquest," he replied. "If Renford and the C.I.D. people say that the body could not be that of Rodmell, I think that you may be satisfied that they're right. They wouldn't have risked making an error of that kind. As for the family identifying the body as they did, it's quite conceivable that they were honestly mistaken, especially with that curious coincidence about the old bullet wound."

Here the doctor paused and studied Hayward's face.

"What's about your reading of the facts, Mr Hayward? You know the people in question and I don't."

"I can't make head or tail of it," replied the other. "It all sounds too absurdly fantastic, this supposition of faked corpses,—a revolting thought. I only wish that Scotland Yard might have made a howler. An inquest on an accident is by way of being a decent straightforward proceeding, but this tarradiddle was a bit too much to swallow."

Forrester shook his head. "Scotland Yard don't make howlers of that kind. They may not always catch the murderer, but when they produce facts at an inquest, you may accept those facts as being well grounded. I must be off. Ring me up if you want me again between now and after dinner. I'll call in about eight-thirty in any case."

Having seen the doctor to the front door, Richard Hayward returned to his desk and picked up some letters which he had been answering, but he was interrupted again within ten minutes as the butler came in with a card on a salver. Hayward looked up irritably.

"I told you I would not see anybody, Winter. Whoever it is, explain that my father is dying. I can't be bothered with anyone at present."

"I'm sorry, sir. I told the Inspector that you would not receive any callers, but he insisted that I should at least bring in his card."

Hayward picked up the card from the salver and read the name on it. "The Scotland Yard man," he said. "Oh, confound him! Send him in."

Pushing back his letters, Hayward swung round in his chair and frowned up at the newcomer as Winter stood at the door and announced sonorously:

"Chief Inspector Macdonald."

"What is it, Inspector?" said Hayward. "I hope you'll be as brief as possible."

He spoke in the tone of a sorely tired man, and Macdonald's tone was very apologetic as he answered:

"I am exceedingly sorry to bother you at such a time, sir. My excuse is that the matter is urgent, and I couldn't undertake the responsibility of postponing it. After the inquest this afternoon a woman named Harrison came to me. She said that her nephew, Charles, had disappeared since Monday, and that she had reason to believe that the body on which the inquest was held was that of her nephew. Since Harrison was your chauffeur, and, until very recently, in your employment, I would be glad if you would answer a few questions about him."

"Harrison!" exclaimed Hayward. "The idea is ridiculous."

"Then you know that Harrison is living?" enquired Macdonald.

"I? No,—I don't know anything about him," retorted Hayward.

"Then you can't be absolutely certain that the idea is ridiculous, I take it?" enquired Macdonald mildly.

Hayward swore beneath his breath.

"Sit down," he said wearily, pointing to a chair beside the desk. "As you say, I can't be exactly certain,—that was a mere figure of speech. Sorry if I seemed a bit impatient, but I'm a bit edgy just at present. Was the aunt able to identify her nephew?"

"She was like you, sir. She couldn't be quite certain."

"Do you expect me to be able to identify him then?" enquired Hayward, a tinge of sarcasm in his voice.

"No, sir," replied Macdonald, "I don't. As you must have realised, since you were at the inquest, identification in this case is not an easy matter. I want you to answer a few questions about Harrison if you will."

"Go ahead," replied Hayward.

"When did he leave you, and under what circumstances?"

Hayward stretched out his hand for a cigarette and lighted it; then with a glance at Macdonald, he pushed the box towards him.

"I sacked Harrison on Saturday morning, paid him an extra week's wages, and told him to pack up and go. On the previous evening I caught sight of him driving one of our cars, with a young woman sitting beside him. He had no business whatever to have the car out. On Saturday morning I sent for him and told him that he could leave at the end of the week. He was impertinent. Consequently I told him to clear out at once. I have no use for a chauffeur I can't trust. There are plenty of good men out of a job, so there was no object in keeping a man who's proved himself irresponsible."

"Thank you, sir," replied Macdonald. "Have you seen him since Saturday?"

"No, I haven't. Why do you ask me that?"

"We have heard that he was seen in this vicinity on Monday evening," replied Macdonald in his even, courteous voice. "As you can guess, there is always a fine crop of rumours in any neighbourhood when a case of this kind occurs, and people are busy fitting Harrison into the story."

Hayward glanced at the clock on the mantelpiece and Macdonald made a little movement as though he were about to get up, but the man at the desk said:

"No, don't go. When I saw your card I was exasperated, because my mind was full of other things, but I can't help being interested. Perhaps if you will tell me a bit about the rumours, I can help you to weed them out. Harrison has been with us for a couple of years; he's a very good chauffeur, an excellent mechanic, and he has a large knowledge of roads and distances. I never liked him much, but he's a clever driver, lots of road sense. What are they saying about him?"

"It appears that at one time he was friendly with young Rodmell," said Macdonald. "The latter appears to have been acquainted with most of the chauffeurs in the district. Anyway, rumour has it that Harrison and Rodmell fell out over some girl in Winchstone. Harrison was making the running, and Rodmell butted in and sought to ingratiate himself in the same quarter. The theory advanced by the villagers is that Rodmell and Harrison came to blows on Monday, and that Harrison was killed. If that happened the rest can be surmised easily enough. Perhaps you would give me your own opinion of Bert Rodmell, sir? I understand that he applied to you personally for his job at the Forward Works."

"Yes, that is so," replied Hayward. "I happen to have met his people,—I know the brother, George Rodmell, very slightly, so I gave Bert a trial at the Works. It appeared that he was clever; he had the makings of a first-class mechanic, and I'm told he had some inventive faculty, but apparently not the brains for paper work. I can't tell you much about him, I never came into contact with him. He seemed to have been an unpleasant type from what I hear, though the social failings of our employees don't concern me. At any rate, he was very much inferior to his elder brother in every way. George is not everything that could be desired, but he's presentable and well behaved in comparison with the younger fellow. The latter was a lout,—that's all."

"So I gathered," replied Macdonald. "He was also, apparently, a dishonest lout."

"You're referring to Mellon's story?" enquired Hayward. "All that I can say about that is that I consider his charge is not proven. His evidence against Rodmell is very circumstantial. Personally I blame Mellon. The man had no business to leave his keys in the door of the safe. It's putting temptation in some poor devil's way. That sort of carelessness breeds theft."

"I quite agree with you, sir," responded Macdonald. He was beginning to like Hayward; the latter's straightforward speech and lack of mannerisms made him likeable. Also he appeared to speak of people without any bias, judging them fairly.

"Did Mellon have any reason for disliking or distrusting Rodmell previously, to your knowledge?" Macdonald continued.

Hayward reflected for a little.

"Well, since you ask me, I admit that Mellon did dislike him," he answered. "I've heard him complain of Rodmell on the grounds that he was familiar,—disrespectful was Mellon's expression. There's nothing in that. Mellon's old-fashioned. He came to the works before the war, when cap-touching was more conspicuous than it is now. *Autre temps, autre moeurs,*—the men are less inclined to be respectful, so far as lip service is concerned, nowadays, but if they do their jobs I can't see that it matters. I have already said that Rodmell was a lout; he was inclined to have a swelled head. His people were well off—are well off, I should say. I'm getting muddled with all this mess up at the inquest. Also he knew that his brother and I met on equal terms. Hence he didn't touch the cap for Mellon sufficiently."

During this conversation with Macdonald, Richard Hayward's tone had changed from a rather irritable condescension to that of a man speaking to an equal. Macdonald noticed it, but retained his own manner of official courtesy. He had succeeded in making Hayward talkative under circumstances when he had not hoped for that success, and he continued in the hope of getting further information out of him.

"Speaking in the strictest confidence, sir, we were not very satisfied with Mr. Mellon's evidence in the first case. It is of the utmost importance to us that all questions should be answered as fully as possible, and as early as possible. We asked Mr. Mellon for information concerning the lorries at the works. He furnished that information very promptly, but he omitted to tell us that he had had a lorry in his own grounds which could have been available for the purpose we were considering."

"Good God man, you'll drive me demented!" burst out Hayward, his jaw literally dropping at Macdonald's last statement. "What are you driving at? At the inquest all your evidence goes to incriminate the Rodmells, because they made a mistake in their identification. Next you involve my ex-chauffeur in the affair, and now you're as good as telling me that Mellon—the most God fearing, law-abiding, old Puritan under the sun, has had a finger in the pie. You're pretty catholic in your suspicions, but I'll tell you this. Mellon may be a conservative old stick, what's described as one of the old school, but he's the soundest, most honest and most humane man who ever lived. Mellon! I tell you he's a monument of integrity."

"I'm glad to hear you give him such a wholehearted testimonial, sir," replied Macdonald smiling a little. "We have to be catholic in our enquiries. It's no use confining our enquiries to suspicious characters, we have to envisage everybody. I myself was present when Colonel Hanton's chauffeur had just stopped his car, and Superintendent Hastings was perfectly correct in asking me and my companion to account for ourselves."

"Well, after all these disquieting rumours you've sprung on me, I think it would be only fair if you were to give me an idea of how the matter looks to you, Inspector," said Hayward. "I take it that you're not going to oblige me with a confession that you and your companion were responsible?"

Macdonald's eyes twinkled. "No, sir. I'm afraid not. You rather hit the nail on the head when you accused me of talking vague rumours. The fact is, we're up against it for the moment, and the only thing to do is to sift the rumours as they crop up. That's where it is helpful to get the opinions of men like yourself. You know the parties concerned and I don't, and it's very easy to lose one's sense of proportion about people when one has no background to envisage them against. Take the Rodmells for example,—I come across them at every turn, and they simply monopolise the landscape." Hayward studied the Chief Inspector with shrewd, observant eyes.

"So you want me to spread myself on the Rodmells?" he enquired.

"I should value your opinion, sir," answered Macdonald. "Nearly all the accounts I have had so far are obviously biased. The Rodmells, being comparatively new comers to the district, and differing in type from the country man's criterion of gentry, seemed to be regarded with general suspicion and dislike. You have a dispassionate mind, so your account will probably be nearer the truth."

Hayward's mouth twitched a little.

"You flatter me, for purposes of your own," he answered, "but you offer me an opening and I take it. The Rodmells are not so black as they're painted. Take the father;—he's flamboyant and expansive, a good bit of a fool and an even larger bit of a bounder, but that doesn't prevent him having good qualities. He's devoted to his family, and generous to a fault. He can be taken in by anybody, but he's always anxious to do anyone a good turn, and I've never observed any real vice in him. George resembles his father considerably, but is more pretentious, and consequently less generous minded. Bert I have already mentioned. He's an absolute puppy and none too nice minded, but he's not the stuff to make a murderer. Not got the guts for it."

"And Miss Rodmell?" enquired Macdonald.

Hayward frowned.

"Leave her out of it, Inspector. You're not imagining that this was a woman's job?"

"No, I'm not," replied the other, "but when you get a young woman who is as beautiful as that one, and according to rumour, none too scrupulous, it behoves one to be observant. If you take the majority of murders in this country during the last few years, you can put them under three headings. Murder for sheer robbery, murder of a woman by a man who has tired of her, and murder of a man by a woman who wants to get rid of him. Examples, one, the Oxford murder, two, the Crumbles one, three, the Thompson and Bywaters case."

As Macdonald spoke, his quiet placid voice never altered in tone, but he watched the expression on Richard Hayward's face with great intentness. It was evident that the latter did not think of Vanda Rodmell with the dispassionate aloofness which Macdonald had mentioned. Pushing back his chair, Hayward ground out the stub of his cigarette and lighted another before he answered, and when he spoke it was in tones of sheer weariness.

"Yes, yes, you needn't labour the point. It's all so intolerably beastly when it comes to bandying a woman's name in connection with a crime like this, especially when it's a woman one knows. You say according to rumour. Well, isn't it fairer to speak your rumours aloud, and give a woman a chance to protect herself, than to insinuate God knows what against her? Hang it all, you're not an uneducated constable, Inspector. Your outlook and mine were found under similar conditions, or I'm a bad judge of men. Say something definite, or else withdraw your suppositions altogether."

Macdonald's eyes lightened; he gave Hayward credit for his speech and didn't respect him less for having scored a point.

"You're perfectly right from your point of view," he said, "and I apologise whole-heartedly. I didn't mean to be offensive, but you're wrong in saying that our outlooks must be similar. I am a policeman, and it's my business to regard everybody, men and women alike, simply from the angle of the police. I try to correct the possible errors of that angle by taking counsel with men like yourself and Colonel Hanton, for instance. Your outlook puts women in a privileged class, mine does not,—that's all. Now say if we leave that point altogether, and get back to the original object of my call. You told me that Harrison left you on Saturday morning. He then went to his aunt's at Winchstone, and stayed with her over the week-end. On Monday he went out after tea and he hasn't been home since. The only news I have of him is that he was seen near this house late in the evening. He has, as might have been expected, been uttering threats against you, and I wondered if some such impulse brought him in this direction. I wondered if you, or any of your household, might have caught sight of him?"

"I can only answer for myself," replied Hayward. "I didn't see anything of him. I came in,—oh about six o'clock or a trifle earlier, and I didn't go out again. I was working in this room after dinner, say from eight until bed-time, and as the window looks out only on to the garden, I shouldn't have seen Harrison unless he actually came prowling up to the window. What time was he seen hereabouts?"

"After nine o'clock," answered Macdonald. "If I may I'll ask your servants the same question. You see, the whole case is so obscure. You can't look round for motive or reason when you don't know who the dead man is. If there's any way of identifying the body as Harrison's, we ought to go ahead."

"What would your argument be in that case?" said Hayward.

"It seems definitely established that Bert Rodmell and Harrison had been quarrelling over a woman. It's conceivable that Rodmell, if his affections were seriously engaged, came down here after dark on Monday, either to say goodbye to the girl, or to try to persuade her to go away with him. You will see that I am assuming Mr. Mellon's suspicions to be well grounded. In other words, Rodmell helps himself to papers which he may be able to realise for a considerable sum in another country, and then prepares to clear out. That theory accounts for his non-appearance at the works on Monday. Now if Rodmell and Harrison came to blows, it's conceivable that Harrison got a knock on the head and was killed,—possibly unintentionally. That being so, Rodmell (you said he had an inventive faculty) decides to change places. It's an obviously ingenious idea, given time to carry it out, and there was plenty of time, because several hours elapsed between the probable time of death and the time when the body was placed on the road. Then Rodmell would have known of the existence of Mellon's lorry so that he could have got at that without any difficulty. It seems a possible theory."

"More than possible," assented Hayward. "So you are of the opinion that the jury was right, and that Bert Rodmell was the murderer?"

"The jury certainly showed a reasoning faculty in coming to that conclusion," answered Macdonald. "Whether or not they were right, time will show."

"I wonder," said Hayward thoughtfully. "It depends on whether you catch Rodmell,—poor wretch! It must be an awful feeling to be hounded down. What are the chances that he'll get clean away?"

"Very slight, in my opinion," answered Macdonald. "He couldn't have got out of the country before Tuesday morning, and we've been pretty well on the *qui vive.* He must have taken his passport with him before he left home apparently. At any rate it can't be found. . . . The most amazing part of the whole business is the way the whole Rodmell family identified that corpse. Do you consider that Harrison and Rodmell were sufficiently alike in physique to make such an error possible, bearing in mind that one's mental attitude would be biased by the fact that the clothes and other belongings weighed heavily on the side of the balance indicating Rodmell?"

Hayward paused to consider.

"Why, yes, now you come to think of it. It's quite feasible. Harrison was about the same height and lanky in build. Dark haired and fairly dark skinned. . . . He's older, of course, but a layman wouldn't appreciate that as you and Dr. Renford did. Also, Harrison fought in the war, and had been wounded, which would account for the bullet scar. Odd, isn't it, to think how I scorned the idea, when you first mentioned it. It shows you're right in talking about the strength of the preconceived notions. In spite of the evidence at the inquest, I came away with a fixed idea that you and Renford were both wrong. It seemed so insane, and the interpretation of an accident to Bert Rodmell,—he drank incidentally,—seemed so probable, and more in line with the facts of everyday existence."

As he ceased speaking Hayward glanced at Macdonald. The latter was sitting by the desk, fiddling with a carving on the cigarette box, his long thin fingers tracing round the shape of William of Wykeham's roses.

Hayward drew a bow at a venture.

"That box is a relic of days when I was up. Were you there too?"

Macdonald looked up with a start.

"New College? Not I. I was a poor man. I was at Pembroke, if you want to know."

Hayward laughed aloud.

"It's good of you to cheer me up, because I'm honestly amused," he said. "You come and sit in that chair, trying to look like a good, solid, unimaginative bobby—only you haven't the physique for it. You're an Oxford man, as I am, and you called me 'sir'—only you haven't the voice for it. Finally you elicit very neatly, just what I was doing on Monday evening, under guise of enquiries about my prowling chauffeur. You get my opinions on all my friends, and you are scrupulously careful not to divulge your own. Chief Inspector, if ever you get retired from the Force, and want a job, come to me. You're a man after my own heart."

Macdonald smiled. "I was born north of the Tweed. That accounts for all your observations. It only remains for me to thank you for your courtesy in answering all my questions. It was good of you to see me at all at such a time."

Hayward sighed—a long-drawn, heavy sigh, which seemed to escape involuntarily.

"It's a sad time for us all in this house. My father has been a great man, and I know of nobody who won't regret him."

"That's a good thought," said Macdonald quietly, "we must all die some day, but to have earned the respect of one's fellow men is worth having lived. . . . Good day and thank you for your help."

CHAPTER X

Macdonald's visit to Richard Hayward had been prompted mainly by two fresh pieces of evidence which had come in, the first being the confused story told him by Mrs. Harrison, the chauffeur's aunt, the second being produced by Diana Hanton.

On the Tuesday preceding the inquest, Macdonald had been too busy absorbing the principal features of the case to give any time to Diana, but she had remained at the back of his mind as a person who must be interrogated when an opportunity arose, and the circumstances of his visit came about in the following manner.

The inquest had been held at noon, and Miss Madeleine Hanton had just finished her lunch when Waring came in to see her with the news of the verdict. Having succeeded in extracting from him a good idea of the evidence which had been produced Miss Hanton went into her own sitting-room and sat pondering over the matter. Colonel Hanton, who had intended to go to the inquest, had been summoned suddenly to the bedside of an old friend. He was faced with the choice of failing his friend,—a dying man—who had sent an urgent message for him or not attending the inquest. While he had not hesitated in making his decision, he had announced that he would instruct his lawyer to go to the inquest to represent him, for he had a worried feeling that Diana's name would surely be mentioned during the giving of evidence, and he wanted some responsible person to be there if this occurred.

Waring, however, assured Miss Hanton that Diana had not been mentioned. Waring's own actions were enquired into, and he had stated that he had been driving the car back to Colonel Hanton's house in town, and the statement had passed unquestioned. While Miss Hanton was telling herself that Diana had had more luck than she deserved, the telephone bell rang at her elbow. Answering the call, she heard Macdonald's voice enquiring for her, and learnt that he wished to speak to Miss Diana Hanton. Miss Madeleine promptly acquiesced, and Macdonald said that he would call about four o'clock. Miss Madeleine rang the bell and sent for Diana. When her niece appeared, the older woman told her that the Chief Inspector was coming to see her, adding:

"Now I haven't asked you anything about your doings on Monday, Diana. If no other enquiries were going to be made, it was nothing to do with me, but since it appears that enquiries are on foot, you'd better tell me the whole story. I know quite enough about giving evidence to realise what you must say and what you need not, but I can't help you if you keep anything back from me. The Inspector's coming at four o'clock, so you'd better get your ideas arranged beforehand. He's not the sort of man you can fool."

"Hell, said the duchess!" replied Diana. "Don't I know it! He's the man of all others whom I hoped never to see again. I made the world's fool of myself so far as he was concerned, and he thinks I'm a cheap half-wit, no blame to him. You'd better hear about my début with Scotland Yard, and then you can tell how pleased and happy I am at the thought of meeting him again."

Here Diana lighted a cigarette and blew the fragrant smoke in vigorous clouds up to the ceiling.

"I'd had a pretty poor evening, Auntie,—I'll tell you about that in a minute,—but once I'd got into the

Sunbeam I thought I'd pulled it off, and should get back home with no one but myself any the wiser. When that Macdonald man wouldn't let us go, it was simply the last straw,—I could have killed him! Then I thought that there was no reason why I should give him my name,—I hadn't done anything—nor Waring either, so I told him that my name was Mary Brown and I lived at 520, Banbury Road, Oxford. It was pretty feeble, but I was dead beat and my brain wouldn't function. Of course Macdonald saw through it at once,—I'd got on that diamond brooch Daddie gave me for one thing, with "Diana" an inch long on it,—I saw his eyes read it,—also I don't believe there is a 520, Banbury Road, and he knew it. However, he was quite polite, he always is,—a sort of placid politeness that makes me hate him."

"Well, Diana, considering that he got his first impression of the family from you, I think his subsequent behaviour is vastly to his credit."

Diana had begun to laugh. "I can't help it, Auntie, I must either laugh or cry. I feel so awful over having to face him again. You see I tried to vamp him on the way home, so that he shouldn't give me away to Daddie. I admit I wasn't in form, in fact I was as feeble as a flounder, but he just went on being polite. Of all the heartless devils,—I couldn't get him to twitch an eyelid."

"My respect for him increases with every word you say," said Miss Hanton dryly. "Vamp him,—you! Diana, you want whipping. You're a nasty little film fan."

"Oh, Auntie, that man's worse than a whipping. He's a nightmare. I've never seen anything so adamantine. Well, now you know about our first merry meeting, I'll get on and tell you about the funeral. Don't expect any expressions of contrition, though. I am too sick with myself to swallow humble pie for anyone else's benefit.

You know that Daddy disapproved of Philip Hayward and his crowd. I saw them quite a lot early in the season. They went everywhere,—Ascot, and Lords, and Grosvenor House, and the Horse Show, and all the rest of it. Then Philip fixed up a moonlight river party and Daddy wouldn't let me go. After that, whenever I saw him, Philip ragged me about my reformed behaviour, and of course I mustn't do this and wasn't allowed to do that. It was all pretty nauseating. I looked such a fool, with a dragon of a parent always at my shoulder. Any old how, I came across Philip last week and he was very touching— the reptile,—and so hurt that he could never see me now. Then he asked if I couldn't play truant one day, and go up the river, or out for a drive,—anywhere where we weren't always dragooned by somebody. I'll just say this in self-defence, Auntie. Philip Hayward's a jolly attractive man. He's a gorgeous dancer, he's witty, and he flirts with just the right mixture of levity and abandon. I enjoyed him. When Daddy said he was going away on Monday afternoon, and would be away the night, I 'phoned to Philip and said, 'What about the river?' It was a corking day, blazing hot, and London was like the Sahara. He jumped at it, and we fixed up for tea at Quarry Woods, and an evening on the river. I wouldn't let him drive me down, I went by train from Paddington. We had tea, we went on the river. Philip had an electric launch,— one of those swift, silent affairs which make the river so seductive. Oh, it was quite idyllic and divinely peaceful. We came off the river about nine,—at least, I believe it was about nine. I had forgotten to wind my watch."

"Idiot," interpolated Miss Madeleine.

"Quite. Don't rub it in. The next suggestion was a drive through the woods to hear the nightingales, and then I was to catch the ten-thirty from High Wycombe up to town. . . . We drove on for some miles with frequent stops. I began to get worried about my train and Philip began to be a nuisance. . . . I'll leave all that out. . . . I got very angry,—and so did he."

Here Diana's cheeks grew crimson and she beat with her fists on the table in front of her.

"Fool, fool, fool that I was! I'd laughed over people having lovers, laughed over conventions and pruderies and fussations, without even giving the thing a real thought, and there was I, alone in the moonlight, with Philip Hayward demanding angrily, 'What had I come for then?' I was so furious that I got out of the car and ran,—not along the road, where he could drive after me, but down a path in the woods. I gave him the slip,—I heard him running after me and calling me. . . . I recovered my wits at last and found my way back to the road. I'd made up my mind to walk into Wycombe. Then I discovered I'd left my purse in the car. Jolly, wasn't it?"

"Poor Diana," said Miss Madeleine, "but you weren't so very far away from here then. Why didn't you come to me?"

"Because I was trying to cover things up. Do you think I wanted to come and tell you what a ghastly little fool I'd been? You, who are the very monument of common sense, and ability, and good behaviour."

"Look here, my dear," expostulated Miss Madeleine, "if you imagine I've arrived at my present age without ever having made a fool of myself, you are supposing I'm worth much less than I am. A grown woman who has never made a fool of herself knows very little about life, or youth, or high spirits. She may be a monument of the virtues, but she's precious little good to other people if she can't understand their point of view."

"Well, I never thought of you as being capable of

anything but one thing,—the best," said Diana, "so I tried
to bluff it out. When I got near Winchstone I met a
country girl whom I didn't know. If you believe me I
stopped and borrowed twopence from her to telephone
with,—and she gave me the twopence like the brick she
was, and I telephoned to Waring from a call box. That's
all. How much of that do I tell the Macdonald man?"

"None of it," said Miss Madeleine promptly. "Your
expedition with Philip Hayward isn't evidence. It's
nothing to do with the case. I can guess what the
Inspector wants to know. Since you were about in the
Winchstone district when this appalling business was
being carried out, did you meet anybody, or see or hear
anybody or anything that could be of use to him? Now
what we'd better do is this. You don't know what time
you started on that wild walk of yours, but you know
what time you met Waring in the car. Since you know the
distance between here and the Haywards' house,—
Woodridings, isn't it called?—you can work out the
times you passed different places. You did come past the
back of Woodridings I suppose?"

"Yes, I did," replied Diana. "I did think of taking a
field path, but was afraid of getting lost in the dark.
Besides, Philip had gone back by the way we came, so I
didn't worry about him any more. I heard him reverse the
car. Well, I got to our corner and met Waring at five past
one. It's over two miles from us to Woodridings, so I
must have passed there about twenty-five past twelve. I
didn't meet anybody on that bit, but I met a man on the
road the other side of Woodridings, about a quarter past
twelve or a little earlier. He seemed to be coming away
from their grounds,—you know the long wall which
encloses the park there. I thought he was Richard
Hayward's chauffeur, but I don't know if I'm right. You

see I was a bit *ennervée,* walking all that way in the moonlight by myself."

"That I can well imagine," said Miss Hanton quietly. In her own mind she was appalled to think of the frightful risk Diana had unwittingly run on that moonlight walk, but the older woman was much too sensible to voice a thought which had apparently not entered Diana's head.

"What about the girl who gave you the twopence?" she enquired.

"Oh that was still earlier,—I'd just passed through Berryhill village. Not a soul stirring of course,—it must have been midnight, just about. The girl's name was Mabel Higgins. She told me she'd been to a dance at the Women's Institute over at Farley, and she'd walked home. I told her my car had broken down, and I couldn't make it move. It was rather funny. She said, 'Ow, you did give me a turn.' I don't expect she's accustomed to London-looking females stopping her and asking for twopence."

"I should imagine not, but I hope you've returned the loan," said Miss Madeleine, and Diana nodded.

"Goodness, yes. I sent her a ten bob note, from 'a grateful pedestrian,' just to encourage her."

"Well, Diana, the best thing you can do is to get a piece of paper and jot down the probable times you passed different places. Then when the Inspector comes, you can try to be a little intelligent to make up for your previous lapses. I shouldn't regard him as a nightmare, if I were you. Personally I liked him. He knows how to behave and he's got more sense in his head than most."

Diana set to work at her aunt's bidding and when Macdonald was announced she was sitting at a writing bureau intent over her papers.

"Good afternoon, Chief Inspector," said Miss

Madeleine tranquilly. "I think you have met my niece."

Macdonald bowed, and Diana rose to her feet.

"I'm Mary Brown," she announced, laughter overcoming her nervousness. "She behaved very badly last time we met, Chief Inspector, but she'd had a very tiring evening. I believe she apologised in the end."

"She did," answered Macdonald gravely, though his eyes were laughing. "As a matter of fact I had a certain amount of sympathy for Mary Brown."

"A very limited amount," retorted Diana, "but if you can manage to forget her, it would be a charitable act."

"She is forgotten already," replied Macdonald. "Now Miss Hanton, I want you to help us if you can. During the course of your walk to Winchstone on Monday night, did you meet anybody, afoot or in a car, or hear any sound of anybody?"

For answer, Diana produced her notes, motioning to Macdonald to sit beside her at the bureau, and Macdonald took a map out of his pocket and began to enter Diana's time schedule in it. When he had completed his task, Diana said:

"I'm afraid this isn't going to help you much."

"It does help,—if only by elimination," Macdonald replied. "Think of it this way. A man,—X, to use a convenient formula,—is at a certain place at a certain time. Half an hour later he is no longer there. Now he can't have vanished into thin air. If he was in a car,— which seems probable,—he had a choice of routes. Now if he had kept to the main road and driven westwards, he would have passed me. He didn't, because I can remember the very few vehicles we passed once we were clear of Oxford. If he had driven east, Londonwards, he'd have passed a night watchman before he reached High Wycombe. He didn't do that either. He might have taken to the by-roads—you can give us evidence about one route at least. It's a very amazing thing, Miss Hanton. You drive along solitary roads at night and think that nobody is likely to see you. It's just then, when traffic is thinnest, that you're most likely to be remarked. It's impossible to remember the traffic passing you in the day time, there's too much of it, but at night you can remember every car you pass because they are so few in number. You can envisage that strip of the Oxford road between twelve-forty-five and one-fifteen as an isolated strip,—my car watching one end of it, a night watchman and police patrol watching the opposite end, and unexpected observers, like yourself, checking the side entries. It's all a matter of a time schedule, and sometimes it's as important to me to know where people were not, as to know where they were."

As he rose to take his leave, Miss Hanton said:

"A cup of tea, Chief Inspector? It will be ready in the drawing-room."

Macdonald shook his head.

"Thank you very much, but I can't stay now,— greatly to my regret." Turning to Diana he added, "Thank you for your help. You were admirably explicit with that time table." Then he added with a twinkle: "You must have been dead tired on Monday night, after all those miles of walking."

"I was," answered Diana. "Dog-tired. If you knew the sort of shoes I walked in, you'd know better how whacked I was."

"I noticed your shoes all right," replied Macdonald. "It occurred to me that they didn't hail from Banbury Road. Pinet's was a more likely place of origin."

"Pinet's they were," returned Diana. "Are you an expert on shoes?"

"Far from it," replied Macdonald, "but I get my living by noticing things, and shoes are an important item. Good-bye, and many thanks."

"Diana, go and make the tea," commanded Miss Madeleine, and when her niece had left the room, the older lady turned to Macdonald.

"I grasp from your conversation with my niece and the general evidence, that Rodmell didn't kill Harrison and Harrison didn't kill Rodmell, but that either of them might have killed anybody else, together or separately."

"Exactly," replied Macdonald. "You have put the matter admirably."

"One other point occurs to me," went on Miss Madeleine calmly. "You pointed out very clearly that a car driven at night, when the roads are clear, is even more likely to be noticed than a car driven in the rush hours. I gather it is not improbable that our Sunbeam was seen, since it was certainly taken out of the garage on Monday evening?"

Macdonald smiled. "You seem to take it for granted that the Sunbeam was not taken out in the afternoon, although Waring was away from the place at two o'clock."

"I know that it was not," retorted Miss Madeleine serenely. "I was in the garden all the afternoon and the gardener was clipping the shrubs in the drive until six o'clock."

"Miss Hanton, you ought to have had my job," laughed Macdonald. "In reward for all the help you have given me I will agree that it is quite probable that the Sunbeam was observed, though that's as far as I'm justified in going at present. Now with your permission I will resume my impersonation of the intelligent mongoose."

"All right, Inspector. Run and find out," said Miss

Madeleine.

.   .   .   .   .

When Macdonald reached home again that evening, he found Vernon once more awaiting him. The Chief Inspector told the journalist just as much as he thought it expedient for him to know, but he made certain reservations concerning his own reading of events. Consequently Vernon learnt all about Harrison's aunt who had come to Macdonald after the inquest.

"Her line of thought was as clear as daylight," volunteered Macdonald. "When she heard the news that Rodmell was dead, she worked herself up into the state of believing that her nephew had killed him. Consequently she lay low and classically said nuffin. When she learnt that the dead man wasn't Rodmell, she reversed her opinion and gave voice, on the probability that Rodmell had killed Harrison."

Continuing, Macdonald told Vernon the gist of his interviews with Diana Hanton and Richard Hayward. Vernon stared at him open-mouthed.

"But Harrison couldn't have been the corpse if he was alive at half-past twelve."

"Time reaction, fifteen seconds," said Macdonald, who had been studying the second hand of his watch. "You're coming on nicely, Peter."

"Confound you. It leapt to the old eye. I thought you were going to tell me you'd copped Hayward for corpsing the chauffeur."

"Nothing so simple," replied Macdonald. "That corpse wasn't a chauffeur's. Hands and feet all wrong. Now listen to me and hear a really exciting bit for to-morrow's copy. At seven-thirty this evening, that bend of the Oxford road where all the trouble occurred seems to have been rather deserted. At seven-thirty-three a van driver had the fright of his life. He came upon a car, capsized in the ditch, burning like blazes. As you know, once a car's afire, it's generally got to burn. This one did, no hope for it,—and I arrived in time to see the smouldering remains. It was an interesting car, Peter. Somebody had removed the number plates for one thing. Also there was no driver."

Peter Vernon sat up with a jerk, his eyes wide and bright.

"Go on!" he growled. "Cut the funny stuff."

"Nothing to cut," replied Macdonald. "It was exactly as I said. There was no sign of a human being aboard and nobody was lying about in the road. The driver was non-existent. The car wasn't a valuable one,—a four cylinder Varron to be exact—but it was noticeable, because it was painted bright grass green. Another funny thing about it is this. Half a mile westwards in the road an A.A. scout was stationed. The car had been coming from the Oxford direction apparently, but it hadn't passed him. Wherefore it must have turned up from a side road. I won't tell you all the possible trials and tribulations of checking the four possible entries by which the Varron could have gained the main road, but we ran it to earth at last, simply by elimination. That car had been standing in the garage of an empty bungalow on the Marlow Road—to the south of the main road that is. Somebody, for purposes of their own, had taken that grass green Varron on to our famous bend, engineered an almighty skid, ditched the thing and capsized it (it was on its side) and got clean away themselves, unseen by anybody. It's an amazing story, but there it is. What do you make of it?"

"George or H.H.?" suggested Vernon promptly.

"Not on your life. They're much too well watched.

Now I'm interested to observe that you, like me, connect that odd accident with other events which have occurred recently in the neighbourhood. You seldom get two lots of abnormal happenings quite unconnected, and the main abnormality about this was the missing number plates."

"The oddest thing of the lot, to my mind, was burning the jolly 'bus bang on the high road," observed Peter. "Why didn't they set light to it in the garage?"

"A Daniel come to judgment, yea, a Daniel," said Macdonald. "That is to say, I quite agree with you. Now I put this reading on it. That car was used by somebody connected with Monday night's affair,—quite possibly it was the dead man's. It was necessary to conceal it, because the colour made it so beastly noticeable. That empty garage was a very good place to hide it in. It might have stayed there unsuspected for weeks, because the bungalow is down a lonely road and no one is looking for an abandoned car. How would it be if some country fellow, noticing something odd about the garage door, poked his nose in and found a perfectly good car, petrol in tank, all in order, and decided to have a joy ride? Accepting that, assume that the driver, none too skilful, makes a hash of it, capsizes the car and gets thrown clear himself? Naturally, he'd make a bolt of it. That seems to me a possible explanation. No skilful or even competent driver would have risked wrecking the car like that. It's against all probability he'd get away unhurt."

Peter rumpled his hair wildly, but waited for a moment before he spoke, and once again Macdonald could have applauded his sagacity.

"Whom does the bungalow belong to?" he enquired at last.

"It's not strictly speaking relevant," answered Macdonald. "Ownership of the bungalow proves nothing, but we had half the natives at the gates when we were investigating that garage. We couldn't prevent them poking round hedges and what nots, and they guessed the rest. At the same time, it's not for publication Peter. Got that?"

"Yes. I have. And I've guessed," said Peter.

"Whose then?"

"The bungalow's Mellon's."

"You're wrong, laddie. The bungalow belongs to Colonel Hanton."

"Great snakes!" exclaimed Vernon, and once again fell silent. "It won't do, Jock. It's silly," he observed after a while, but Macdonald puffed away at his pipe without a word."

"Look here," said Vernon suddenly. "That Hanton girl,—I bet she'd been out with some man or other on Monday night, when we caught her running for home."

"Maybe," answered Macdonald, non-committally.

"Well, confound you, has he disappeared by any chance?"

Macdonald laughed aloud. "You have me there, Peter. To the best of my knowledge and belief, all Miss Hanton's acquaintances are still in evidence. Well, you've had three guesses, the recognised allowance. Your first was Bert Rodmell, your second Mellon, your third Diana Hanton's friend. Far be it for me to say that you're wrong in all of them. By the way, I've got a sad bit of news for you. Your old char at 345, Mrs. Rummidge, was knocked down by a motor-bus on her way home from the egg-tea with which you regaled her."

"Poor old girl! poor old bag of misery," cried Vernon, his voice expressing genuine sorrow. "Don't tell me she was done in."

"I'm afraid she was,—absolutely and completely,"

answered Macdonald. "She tried to run across the Tottenham Court Road and stumbled under a 27 'bus,— the driver couldn't help it. It was just pure accident."

"Accident be blowed!" said Vernon indignantly. "I bet that horse-faced female at 345 poisoned her."

Macdonald shook his head. "I don't think it's very likely, though enquiries will be made on those lines. I expect it's just one of those bits of sheer cussedness which fate indulges in at our expense occasionally. I'd hoped for a lot from Mrs. Rummidge, but as she was dead before I'd even heard of her, I can't blame myself this time. Don't look so mournful, Peter. I expect she died very happy, all bucked up over the excitement of meeting you."

"It was those blasted beans," growled Peter. "Upset her digestion and she got dithery."

"Send her a wreath if it will console you," answered Macdonald. "She'd have considered it a kindly thought. Let me distract your mind from these grave-yard contemplations. We have found Bert Rodmell's motor-bike. . . . I thought that would cheer you up."

"Who found it?" demanded Vernon.

"Sorry. Mere figure of speech. We always try to get a little credit for these occurrences. We advertised and broadcast, and this afternoon the owner of a garage in the Edgware Road came and informed us that he bought that bike from Bert Rodmell himself at three-thirty on Saturday afternoon."

Both men ruminated awhile in silence, and at length Peter said: "What do you make of it?"

"There are so many ways of looking at it," answered Macdonald. "My first idea was that Bert went and bought another one further down the road, so that his own shouldn't be identified if he paid a surprise visit to

Downfield. Then it occurred to me that he might be realising all his available property before he flitted. If that's anywhere near the truth, he could have been out of England by Saturday night."

Vernon smoked away furiously.

"He must have gone straight on to see H.H. at the Potboilers', immediately after he sold his bike," said Vernon. "Then he probably changed his clothes,—say at 345. After which he vanished. I wish you'd say what you really make of it all, Jock. The points I hold on to are these. First, the Rodmell family are all in it, because of their identifying the wrong corpse. Second, H.H. took the trouble to wander round by Warlington instead of going direct. He's going to find it difficult to get away from that."

"It's what a jury considers a nice point," said Macdonald meditatively. "Your game-keeper only thinks he saw him,—he isn't prepared to swear to it. The railway porter at Warlington could easily be confused on the same point when it came to cross-examination. How did you tackle him?"

"Why, I asked him if he'd seen a rather foreign looking bloke,—bit of a waist to his clothes, boots with long toes, and a dark complexion. When he said he had, I showed him the photograph, which he recognised."

Macdonald pondered. "If we had an identification parade with Rodmell in company with half a dozen other dark-haired moustachioed gentry, I wonder if the porter would pick out the right one? Don't think I'm being grudging, Peter, only we've got strong evidence for H.H.'s alibi. It's not going to be a walk over."

Vernon tried the direct method.

"Do you, or do you not, believe that H.H. was on the Liverpool train?"

Macdonald laughed. "In my opinion, for what it's worth, H.H. was not on the Liverpool train. Beyond that I'm not going to answer any questions. I think we've got the necessary data, and it's my business to prove or disprove the theory I've built up. Say if you go home and think it all over. There's more in the business than meets the eye."

With which cryptic announcement Vernon had to be satisfied for the moment.

CHAPTER XI

Thursday found Macdonald at Scotland Yard again, deep in consultation with a tired-eyed man named Castle. The latter was a member of the C.I.D. whose present occupation was investigation of persons suspected of importing and distributing Prohibited Drugs.

"It's a pity I wasn't in England on Monday," Castle was saying. "I've come into contact with your Rodmell friends before, but as it happens I went over to Paris on the tail of some gentry who are well known in the West End of London. I hoped to pick up a few details about them which might be useful next time they came back here. I've been working all day and most of the night for very little purpose, whereas I might have been quite useful to you if I'd been on my usual beat. However, here's the best I can do for you. We have kept an eye on the Rodmells ever since they landed in England a couple of years ago, mainly because they were friendly with some of our most notorious suspects. The Rodmells can be said to hold a privileged position for the purpose of distributing drugs. To begin with, they're British subjects, they can't be sent out of the country as undesirable aliens, but they've lived the best part of their lives in South America, and what they don't know about the cocaine traffic isn't worth knowing. They're slippery customers. Henry Hubert,—your charmer,—is the older. Then there's his brother, Charles Albert, a year younger than he is, and they're as alike as two peas. They give us infinite trouble with their confounded Box and Cox habits. As I've told you, I have never proved a case against either of them, and I haven't even the satisfaction of having collected their finger-prints. If you offer them a card, they always have gloves on. Bless you, I believe it's quite possible that they could exchange parts without anyone being any the wiser. You say you've got Henry Hubert at Downfield,—I am quite willing to believe it's Charles Albert who's there really. I could tell them apart if I saw them both together, but separately they've got me beat. However, one of them was in London on Monday evening. There's a certain party living in Maida Vale,—a drug addict,—and Henry Hubert or Charles Albert called on her at nine-thirty-five p.m. precisely. Hodges saw him go in."

"That's all right from my point of view," answered Macdonald. "What time did Box or Cox leave the Maida Vale house?"

"Ten minutes after he'd gone in. Hodges trailed him to see if he could find out where he was hanging out, but Box-Cox diddled him properly. He walked up St. John's Wood Road and went into that big block of flats in Park Road. There's an automatic lift there. Up goes Box-Cox; Hodges, being too far behind to get into the lift, runs up the stairs. Box-Cox shoots up to the top floor, and runs out along the top landing—(the flats open off balconies) and then takes the other lift down at the further end of the building. Hodges tumbled to the wheeze, but by the time he'd got downstairs again Box-Cox was off in a big car,—too far away for Hodges to read the number,—and that was that."

"Well, all that's quite satisfactory from my point of view," said Macdonald and Castle cut in:

"Glad to hear it. It wasn't from ours."

Macdonald laughed. "No,—but listen to my story. Charles Albert went to Liverpool with Rosario. That accounts for him. Now Henry Hubert had arranged to play some game with his drug-dealing friends, and had squared Charles Albert to do the alibi for him in case of need. Henry Hubert goes down to the Winchstone district and there becomes involved in my story, either as principal or accessory. My own guess is the latter. However, I take it that Henry Hubert had the bright idea of faking the corpse, and my present guess is that he borrowed the Hantons' Sunbeam and probably took the dead man's clothes up to London with him. He'd have had plenty of time to get to Maida Vale by nine-thirty, go back to Charlotte Street and collect Bert's clothes, and then drive back to Winchstone to finish the job with someone else's assistance. So you see we've got them both taped nicely,—Box with Rosario,—Cox in Maida Vale."

"And you can hang either of them with a peaceful mind," put in the weary Castle, "so our good work won't have been wasted."

"Don't anticipate," said Macdonald. "I haven't got a case yet. I don't know who the corpse is. I haven't proved that either Box or Cox had either the motive or opportunity for killing him, and I don't know what Bert is up to, or where he is. If you can keep awake a bit longer, I wish you'd tell me anything you can about the rising generation,—Bert and Vanda and George for instance."

Castle yawned, and stretched his long arms.

"They're all much of a muchness," he said. "George hasn't given us any trouble,—quite the gentleman is George, but Bert is in process of being introduced to his father's friends. About Vanda (that's not her legal name, incidentally, she was christened Emilia, but renamed herself), there's an odd story about her which I learnt from a chap out in Buenos Ayres. When Vanda was only sixteen she ran off with one of her father's friends out there, a chap named d'Alvarez. According to my informant, Vanda and d'Alvarez went through some marriage ceremony in the States, but as d'Alvarez was undoubtedly married at the time, and Vanda probably used an assumed name, it was decided to hush the matter up. That's what I think of Vanda, if you get me."

"Thank you very much," replied Macdonald gratefully. "You believe in keeping the *bonne bouche* to the end, don't you?"

"Glad you're happy and pleased," said the other. "It's bed for me. I'm off."

"Sleep tight," answered Macdonald absent-mindedly, for he was already in a brown study as he cogitated over the news which Castle had given him.

He was still in deep thought when Inspector Jenkins came in, his round cheerful face wreathed in smiles.

"I've been interviewing a dame who thinks she's got a little news for you," he said. "As you were busy with Castle, and she was evidently one of the long-winded sort, I thought I might save you trouble. You can have a go at her later if you think she's worth while. She's staying at the Ritz Hotel,—quite a flyer. Name of Matheson-Villiers,—Mrs. Penelope, to be exact. A widow, she tells me, and I hope it's true for poor Matheson-Villiers's sake, for he must have had a very poor time. The dame arrived in England last Sunday; she's just come from Buenos Ayres in the *Laurentia,* and she's been reading up your advertisements enquiring if anyone's missing from a hotel or boarding house.—By the way that young Vernon's done some very good work for you in that line,—it was reading his articles that got this Matheson dame going. It seems she travelled with a party named Major Harrington, and according to her they were as thick as thieves,—you know the style of thing— 'most intimate friends, Inspector, we knew all one another's thoughts'—and all that. I'll cut the gush and tell you the story. It appears that they came to London together on the boat train and then, when Mrs. Matheson-Villiers said she was going to stay at the Ritz, Harrington said it was the Savoy for him. 'His was one of the most delicate and susceptible personalities, Inspector'."

Jenkins' reproduction of the widow's honeyed accents provoked Macdonald to laughter, and the worthy Inspector continued with much relish.

"Well, she left him alone on Monday, but on Tuesday she 'phoned to the Savoy and he wasn't there,—never had been there. The lady got in a stew and has been spending her time 'phoning half the hotels in London and drawn a blank everywhere. Now she's convinced that Harrington is your find on the Oxford road, and she's providing chapter and verse. Before I go on, would you like to hear my ideas on the subject or not?"

"Fire away," said Macdonald. "Ideas next, by all means."

"Well, I reckon the dame vamped this Harrington man on the boat," said Jenkins. "He probably let himself in, in the first case, and couldn't lose her while they were aboard, but he cut and ran when they reached London. Don't blame him, she's the sort of body to scare a man stiff. She tried the glad eye business on me out of sheer habit. I don't think there's much to it myself, but here's the rest of her twaddle. They discussed all their friends and relations on board, and one of the people Harrington talked about was Colonel Hanton."

Macdonald here groaned audibly, and Jenkins chuckled aloud.

"I thought that'd annoy you. You're banking on the Hantons being all they ought to be. Now this Major Harrington had quite a bit to say about Miss Diana Hanton, and he wasn't above telling a story or two about the young lady which weren't always to her credit. Allowing for the widow lady's exaggerations, Major Harrington said more than he'd any business to say on that subject. Mrs. Matheson-Villiers took it into her head to ring up Colonel Hanton and was told that he did not know Major Harrington, and he was very short about it. Mrs. Villiers reads the papers, and she knew all about the Hantons' car and where the Hantons lived, and she's made a nice little case up on her own account. Now I know you're thinking I'm wasting your time with blether, to use your own expression, but there's something here which may interest you."

Here Jenkins produced a copy of a periodical entitled *The Mayfair Messenger,* which he handed to Macdonald.

"It's a weekly," he said, "one of those foul rags which is always hinting libellous tit-bits, but which hardly ever gets summoned for libel because they know the technicalities of the law. Now this was published this morning, and they must have spent quite a lot on muck-raking to have got all this up yesterday. You'd better read it."

Macdonald took up the paper and glanced through it. It had the usual columns of pseudo-society chatter, full of veiled innuendoes which conveyed nothing to the uninitiated. In the centre pages were two full page portraits:—"Miss Diana Hanton, the season's most captivating debutante." Inset, "Winchstone Manor, Bucks., Miss Hanton's country home." Facing it, on the opposite page, was the heading. "Unusual types of feminine beauty. Miss Vanda Rodmell,—an exquisite and irresistible brunette." Inset, "Miss Rodmell at the fête held in aid of Winchstone Cottage Hospital. Beside her is Colonel Hanton."

"Pretty, isn't it?—but you haven't read their queries column yet. Page 5. The Villiers woman marked the best bits."

Thus instructed, Macdonald read.

"We wonder whether it was by good luck or good management that one of the season's loveliest debutantes was not put into the witness-box to explain just where she was driving in her father's car, and why she was driving it in the early hours of the morning? The police, gallant fellows! are becoming chivalrous this year. (Such a comfort, darling, that our doings are not *always* considered relevant. . . .)

"It is said by people who are in the know that the stern parent is coming into fashion again. Fathers used to be so tiresome in the long-ago, but the jealous father is a *rara avis* these days. Still, it is a bit of a snag if fathers take to sleuthing, darling, isn't it? My own reply is always, 'And where were *you* out last night?' But sometimes even the police remain incurious,—of course it depends on the relevance, doesn't it?"

.   .   .   .   .

"Swine!" ejaculated Macdonald. "I wonder who reads all this trash."

"Bless you, it's meat and drink to half the little idiots who call 'emselves ladies," replied Jenkins. "You and I are too middle class to appreciate it. You've got to be rich and idle or poor and idle to really enjoy it. There's another item you haven't read,—over the page."

Flicking the page disgustedly Macdonald read:

"I am told that Lady Barringer's dinner on Monday night, on the occasion of her silver wedding (held in the famous panelled dining room at Stowe Castle, Hampshire), was a great success, though many who attended the function regretted the unexpected absence of Colonel Hanton, D.S.O., M.C., who was to have been one of the guests. Colonel Hanton was, it may be recalled, best man at Lady Barringer's wedding. . . ."

"They seem to have got a good intelligence department on this rag," commented Macdonald. "One can only suppose that one section of society is always ready to make money by selling the other section, unless the servants do it. I'm a bit intrigued by these references to Diana Hanton and Vanda Rodmell. Somebody's evidently out to make trouble. I shall put Peter Vernon on to this, he'll be able to find out who wrote it up. Of course it was always likely that Diana Hanton would get into the papers over it. Peter wouldn't have given her away, and I don't think Dr. Renford or Hastings would have, but the local bobby knew all about it, and I bet the rest of the station got an inkling. The merest hint does it, and reporters are like starving dogs when there's a hint of a bone in the way of news."

Macdonald glanced down at the *Mayfair Messenger* again.

"It's jolly well organised," he said. "It looks as though someone's building up a case on their own account. I wonder if Miss Rodmell does a bit in the social gossip column. . . ."

"The part that points the moral is that little question, 'Where were *you* out last night?'" said Jenkins. "Our Matheson-Villiers dame will be getting a writ against her if she carries on like she did to me. 'It's obvious that Colonel Hanton has something to conceal, Inspector, and I'm told he'd go to any lengths on his daughter's behalf.'"

"I suppose you didn't suggest that the logical outcome of her line of thought would be for her to be found strangled in Vanda Rodmell's clothes," said Macdonald. "The fact is, Jenkins, you're just yearning to go and ask Colonel Hanton what he was doing on Monday night."

Something in Macdonald's usually placid voice made Jenkins wary in his answer.

"I'm not saying that it wouldn't be satisfactory for you to know," he replied. "Then you could come down on the rag if they go any further."

"Give 'em enough rope," was all Macdonald's answer. "I'm going to make use of your widow-lady's report to the extent of getting in touch with Major Harrington. He interests me."

"I reckon it's all my eye and Betty Martin," answered Jenkins.

"Maybe," answered Macdonald, "but either Harrington is a respectable person who can be found without much difficulty, or he's one of those alias merchants who ought to be traced. You say Mrs. Villiers rang up half the hotels in London. That's an exaggeration, doubtless, but there aren't so many hotels of the Savoy class. How many can you call to mind, Jenkins?"

"Berkeley, Claridges, Grosvenor, Dorchester, Hyde Park, Mayfair, Langham, Piccadilly, Waldorf," said Jenkins promptly.

"Exactly. She'd have tried all those," answered Macdonald. "Allowing that such an individual as Major Harrington exists, he may have gone to earth in one of the smaller hotels,—say the Rubens, or Jermyn, or Queen's Gate,—or he may have left London altogether. If he's a respectable individual he may give us useful tips about his fellow-passengers. I shouldn't be the least surprised if our corpse happened to have travelled on the *Laurentia,* though it'd be a bit marvellous if he turned out to be the lady-killing Harrington. Anyway, we'd better find him, Jenkins, if only as a token of goodwill to the authorities who are getting a bit restless over anonymous corpses. You can get busy on *Who's Who* and reckon up the possibilities, likewise get on to the R.M.L. for passenger lists. To change the angle of the conversation,—you found the clothes were Bert Rodmell's after all?"

"The suit was," said Jenkins readily, taking Macdonald's cue. "I had a bit of luck there, so we can settle Mr. Bert Rodmell's doings for the greater part of Saturday. When I went to Miller's to enquire about the suit, they put me on to the young fellow who'd served him, and when they'd turned up the order book they identified the suit as the one they altered for Mr. Bert Rodmell. This is where my bit of luck came in. Miller's have branches all over London as you know, and the salesman in the West End branch who had served Rodmell knew him quite well by sight. Lewis—their salesman—had been up to their Edgware Road branch on Saturday afternoon, (it's early closing in the West End, but not up Edgware Road) and at five o'clock Bert Rodmell was in the Edgware Road depôt, buying a new outfit. He'd already changed from his tweeds into other clothes, but there he was all right. Lewis says he knew him by sight, but didn't recall his name until he looked up the order. Bert took his new clothes away in a taxi. So that's that."

"Exit Mr. Bert Rodmell," said Macdonald. "Now, Jenkins, just answer this question. Do you think he took his dressy tweeds and made them into a farewell gift to Colonel Hanton? Or does your mind suggest any other method by which the latter gentleman acquired that splendid suit?"

"I'm quite sure he never did acquire it," replied the imperturbable Jenkins, "but you've given no proof that Colonel Hanton wasn't better acquainted with the Rodmell crowd than he cares to admit. That Vanda's a dangerous bit of goods. For all I know Colonel Hanton may be a dark horse. Being a colonel doesn't mean you're above suspicion, but I'm always willing to admit that I may be wrong."

"And I, Jenkins," replied Macdonald, "not to be outdone in diffidence, am perfectly willing to admit that you may be right."

"Well I'm jiggered," said Jenkins,—and he meant it.

Before Jenkins had recovered from his astonishment sufficiently to ask Macdonald what action he intended to take in the matter, the telephone bell rang at the Chief Inspector's elbow. After a brief conversation Macdonald ended up with, "Send him up, then," and replacing the receiver, he turned to Jenkins with a twinkle.

"Information simply rolling in, Jenkins. First, your hyphenated lady, now a worthy member of the unemployed. Idle rich and idle poor, all conspiring to help us."

"Very good of them," said Jenkins genially, "but what I want to know is . . ."

" . . . 'where were *you* out last night?' as our chatty

enquiry column has it," interrupted Macdonald. "Bide a wee, Jenkins, or W. & S. as Peter Vernon would put it,— the slogan of the great Herbert Henry to be applied to the apprehension of our Henry Hubert. . . . Come in."

At Macdonald's bidding a tall, gaunt fellow was shown into the room. His suit was very old and worn, and he wore a muffler round his neck in place of a collar, but his face was clean and his glance alert, and when he spoke his manner was neither obsequious nor aggressive.

"Sit down," said Macdonald. "Your name is John North, and you have come in answer to our advertisement concerning missing hotel visitors?"

"Yes, sir," replied the other promptly. "I may be wasting yer time, but it seemed worth while ter me."

"Go ahead then," answered Macdonald. "I'll soon tell you if it's no go."

"I've been 'ouse-man an' porter in 'otels an' boarding-'ouses," said North, "but I've bin out-er-work fer six months. On Tuesday mornin' the Labour Exchange sent me to an 'otel in Percy Street, orf the Tot'nem Court Road,—name of 'otel Monty Video. They wanted an odd man at thirty bob a week. I jumped at it. I saw the boss— a woman it was, a great fat foreign-looking piece, and she said she'd take me on if I'd start work right away. That was all O.K. Gave me some scrubbing to do in the basement strite orf. In the afternoon the fat madam,—da Soto 'er name is—told me I was to go to Victoria with some baggage. I could take it on a truck and I was to wait with it by the left-luggage office. She said that it belonged to a gent who'd left the 'otel the day previous. I was to tike 'is bill with me, an' 'e was to pay me the money, an' I was ter bring 'er the money an' give the gent 'is luggage. All that quite plain, sir?"

"Perfectly," said Macdonald. "Go on."

"'Well,' I sez, ''ow am I to know 'oo the gent is? Say if I go givin' them bags to the wrong gent?' and she sez, 'Don't be so silly. The gentleman'll be waiting there for you, and 'e'll know 'is own baggage. Also 'e's got to pay you the cash fer the bill before you give 'im the baggage. 'Is name's Mendoza and it's printed right across 'is traps. See?' Well, sir, that was orl right, so orf I went, an' I got ter Victoria at three pip emma as arranged, an' went ter the left-luggage orfice. Strite away a fat dark bloke come up ter me an' sez, 'You from the Monty Video? 'Ere's my card an' you're ter give me my bill,' and he gave me the dibs, three pun-ten it was, an' I give 'im the receipt Madam 'ad given me ter give 'im, after I'd got the cash. Also 'e signed a receipt 'imself fer the luggage an' give me 'arf a crown, so I reckoned I was in luck."

Here North took a deep breath, as though the effort of narration was telling on him, and Macdonald encouraged him.

"Well, that's all very interesting. Anything else?"

"Yes, sir, plenty more. I took the money back an' giv' it to Madam, all in order, and the receipt the gent 'ad signed fer is dunnage. It was four o'clock by then an' she told me to go an' 'ave some tea. After tea I was doin' an odd job repairin' a lock on one 'er the bedroom doors— I'm good at odd jobs—it was the room that that Mendoza 'ad 'ad, an' I 'appened to pass the time 'er day with the chamber-maid on that floor an' we got chattin'. Now she was complinin' she'd got a wart on 'er 'and, and I remembered that that Mendoza 'ad a wart on 'is 'and. I noticed it when I was standin' beside 'im, an' I said to 'er, 'That gent w'at was in 'ere in No. 23 'ad a great big wart on 'is 'and.' 'Oh git along,' she sez, ''e 'adn't. I know 'e 'adn't, cause 'e got a bit fresh, see, and tried skylarking round. I told 'im orf fer it, but I know 'e's got no wart on 'is 'and, 'cause I noticed w'at nice 'ands he'd got, all done up like a lidy's.' Now just then Madam came along the corridor an' she didn't 'arf give me an ugly look. 'I won't 'ave this noise in my corridors,' she sez, 'if you can't work quietly, you can git. This is a first-class 'otel this is, an' I won't 'ave none of yer row.' Real nasty, she sounded. Well, it weren't more than 'arf an hour after that I was goin' along to the service lift, an' one of the waiters ran inter me with a tray loaded with tea things. 'E fairly banged into me, I tell you, an' there wasn't 'arf a proper bust up. There was bits of that china fer yards, an' tea an' cream cakes all over the carpet,— oh, a real old mess up it was, an' then while the waiter was cussing me in foreign languages, Madam comes up, all in a great rage. 'What's this?' she sez. 'It's disgraceful, that's wot it is,' an' the waiter, 'e swore I'd run 'im down. Well, arter that, it was all up. Madam tol' me I could go to the orfice an' draw a week's wages an' git,—she'd no use fer me in a decent 'ouse, an' I tell yer I got ten years' reference from the 'otel Petersburg before they closed down. A put up job, that's wot it was."

"Bad luck," said Macdonald. "Still you got your week's wages and your half-crown, so it wasn't so bad. Now can you describe this Mendoza for me?"

North scratched his head.

"'E was a tallish chap, bit shorter than me, say five-nine or five-ten. 'E was a bit fat an' dark, an' 'e 'ad a little dark moustache. 'E was smart, good clothes an' all that, but 'e looked a foreigner,—greasy, if yer know wot I mean, like that Madam-da-Soto. 'E'd got coloured glasses on, an' a wide 'at. And 'e'd got a big wart on 'is right 'and, I saw it when 'e signed me receipt for the luggage."

"That's quite a useful description," answered

Macdonald. "Now say if you tell me what you can remember about his baggage. Had he a trunk?"

"Yes, sir, big cabin-trunk with 'is name right across it,—J. S. Mendoza. 'Ere you are," and North pulled a much thumbed card out of his pocket on which was engraved the name he had given. Macdonald and Jenkins looked at the card and then looked at one another, each shaking a disappointed head. From that card, it was clear, no finger-prints would be obtainable save those of the house-man, John North.

"E 'ad a trunk an' two big suit-cases, sir, all 'eavy things, an' covered with labels all over 'em,—'Cabin' an' 'not wanted on the voyage.' I'm used to them labels 'avin' been in 'otel jobs."

"You didn't notice what ship he'd come home on, I suppose?" enquired Macdonald.

"That I did," replied North promptly. "I had them labels under me eye all the way from Percy Street to Victoria. The *Laurentia,* 'is ship was, an' 'e'd come from South America."

Macdonald sat silent for a moment and North said:

"Any 'ope of a reward, sir? The pipers mentioned that a reward was to be given. I saw your notices outside in Cannon Row."

"Quite a good hope," answered Macdonald, "only we shall have to verify what you say first."

"Then I'll 'ave wasted me trouble," answered the man sadly. "It's like this. You've only got my word for it, but I'll bet any money that that bloke at Victoria wasn't the same bloke who stayed at the Monty Video in No. 23. Strikes me that Madam took me on that morning 'cause she didn't want the regular porter to go, seeing he knew this Mendoza and I didn't, and then when I'd served her turn, she fired me."

"That sounds quite possible to me, too," answered Macdonald, "but Madame da Soto has to have her visitors registered, so we ought to be able to place him somehow."

Watching the man, Macdonald saw his face brighten, and it was evident that he feared nothing from investigation.

"That's good," he said, "for I'll lay my bottom dollar old Madam wouldn't tell you a word if she could help it. That 'otel's all for foreigners. Funny lot they are."

After spending a few moments interrogating North as to where he lived and the Labour Exchange which had given him news of the job, Macdonald pulled some photographs out of a drawer in his desk and asked North if he recognised any of them. The man turned them over dubiously and at length selected one of them.

"I think I've seen this chap," he said, and fell into a brown study.

"Well, this is a funny go, this is," he went on, and Macdonald said sharply:

"If you've got anything to say, say it. Hurry up, because I'm busy."

"Sorry, sir," replied North. "Now this 'ere photo puts me in mind of a chap who's got rooms in Charlotte Street. I've seen 'im several times. I told you I got a room in 'Owland Street and Charlotte Street is just at the corner. And when I said it was a funny go, I meant that this same photo might be the chap with the wart on 'is 'and. I don't say it is, I only say it might be."

"I see," answered Macdonald; "now only one more question. What did Mendoza do with the luggage when you left him at Victoria Station?"

"Put it in the baggage orfice," returned North promptly. "I dumped it on the counter for him."

"Very good," replied Macdonald. "Now you can call here again the day after to-morrow and we'll let you know about that reward. Here's half a crown on account, just so that you shan't feel that you've wasted your time. Good morning and thanks very much."

"What do you make of that?" enquired Macdonald of Jenkins, when the door shut behind North.

Jenkins grinned.

"Sounds like a cert to me," he answered. "Though I don't quite see Major Harrington or Colonel Hanton fitting into that galley."

"Sorry you're disappointed," answered Macdonald, and then the telephone rang again.

After he had hung up the receiver, Macdonald heaved a large sigh.

"That was Hastings, Jenkins. He's rung up to tell me that Colonel Hanton's gardener has dug up a pair of boots in the rose border at Winchstone Manor. Miss Madeleine Hanton 'phoned the news to Hastings who went there and collected the boots. They fit the corpse perfectly, Jenkins."

Jenkins followed Macdonald's example and sighed heavily.

"Somebody's being funny," he said, and Macdonald replied:

"They are that. In the meanwhile we've got jobs to keep us busy for twenty-four hours on end."

CHAPTER XII

The Hotel Montevideo, though it might not have come up to Madame da Soto's description of it as a first-class hotel, was a pleasant, prosperous-looking place in an unpretentious way. Its stucco front was freshly painted in cream, its windows and doors were the brightest shade of emerald green, and the clipped bay trees which stood in tubs on either side of the front door were healthy and flourishing.

On Thursday evening a plump, dark man drove up to the Montevideo in a taxi, and after a prolonged scrutiny of the hotel entrance made his way to the office inside the lobby. The porter studied the newcomer shrewdly as the latter stood by the counter at the office, and put the visitor down as a Spaniard. His clothes were of distinctly foreign cut, his shoes long-toed and too brightly tan in colour for an Englishman. His hat was new and looked as though it might have been bought close at hand in the Tottenham Court Road, but the tilt at which it was worn was distinctly foreign. Moreover the gentleman was smoking a Brazilian cigarette,—the porter sniffed the aroma appreciatively. He liked it, but very few Englishmen did, as he knew quite well. The porter hovered in the background while the new arrival negotiated for a room.

The clerk in the office was a slim dark girl; she had fine dark eyes and was exquisitely neat, and in response to the visitor's request she handed him a printed tariff. The porter watched with experienced eyes while the gentleman produced a pencil and made some notes on an envelope he had taken from his pocket. The porter knew all about that,—it isn't everybody who can translate British currency into francs, or lire, or marks in their heads. Apparently the sum was a success; the gentleman turned back to the clerk, this time raising his hat with a fine twirl and displaying a luxuriant crop of black hair.

"I guess that'll be what I'm wanting, Miss," he said. "One single room, at the back of the house and the quieter the better. I'll reserve it for three nights. My traps are outside,—guess that guy of yours had better bring them right in."

As he spoke, another woman came and surveyed him over the counter of the office. She was enormously fat, and she smiled pleasantly at the visitor, but her eyes examined him with a shrewdness which missed nothing. She noted the dark skin and red lips, and the little bristling black moustache cut so as to clear the upper lip. A dandy, that was obvious, with a suggestion of make up on his face, and a diamond pin in his tie. He wore heavily rimmed glasses, slightly tinted like those many people wore in the tropics, and his black eyebrows nearly met across his nose.

"It is customary, señor, to pay a deposit for a room which has not been booked in advance."

Thus spoke the stout woman, apparently indifferent as to whether the visitor liked her statement or not.

"That so? It's all the same to me, ma'am," he retorted, "but I'm no señor. I'm a British subject."

Here he pulled out a roll of notes from his pocket and the stout woman watched him while he counted them carefully and selected two, shoving the others back into his pocket, but not before the observant black eyes watching him had seen that the notes were not all British currency.

She smiled and pushed forward a book.

"Perhaps you would register your name, sir?"

The man took a fountain pen from his pocket and wrote: "John Robinson. Liverpool." Pushing the book back again he observed:

"Guess I shall be just fixed right here. I've been recommended to come here by several friends."

Here, as though on an afterthought, he pulled the

Registration book towards him and began to glance through the pages.

"Your number is 23," announced the fat lady. "Here is your key and your things shall be sent up immediately. Have you dined, sir?"

"What's that? Oh yes, I dined on the train. I'll have a black coffee and a liqueur brandy. Send 'em upstairs. There's a guy here named Rosario. Sounds sort of familiar. I got some relatives living in a place called Rosario,—near Buenos Ayres,—yes?"

"Yes, sir," replied the fat woman. "I, too, have lived in Rosario."

"Say, that's fine. Reckon we ought to have a chat some time. 23, you said? I'll go right up."

"Espero que hallara todo a su satisfaccion, Señor."

John Robinson stared at her with raised eyebrows.

"No bon, ma'am, I don't speak Spanish. I told you straight, I'm a British subject, see? English, just plain English."

"I beg your pardon, sir. The Mr. Rosario whose name is entered in the register left some days ago."

Mr. Robinson shrugged his shoulders as though to indicate that the fact didn't interest him, replaced his hat with a careful glance in the mirror, and swaggered across to the lift. As he was borne upwards, the slim clerk indulged in a wide smile and turned to the older woman.

"He's a good comic turn, Auntie. About as much like an Englishman as I'm like an Esquimaux."

"No matter, child. His money's none the worse, and I have seen stranger fish than that one," and with that the proprietress returned to her accounts which she was checking when her new patron had arrived. It was not long, however, before she was interrupted again. This time the porter decided that the solidly built gentleman

with the healthy rubicund face was definitely English,—
nothing continental about him. Indeed Inspector Jenkins
looked as uncompromisingly British as any man could
look, and he was proud of the fact. Advancing to the
office, he raised his hat politely and enquired for
Madame da Soto, the proprietress.

"Yes, sir?" enquired the stout lady calmly, and the
Inspector laid his card on the counter.

"I want to see a Mr. Mendoza, madam. I understand he
arrived here last Sunday."

"Yes," replied Madame da Soto. "That is so, and he
left on Monday."

"Can I have a word with you in private?" enquired
Jenkins, and the stout lady rose and opened the office
door, beckoning Jenkins to follow her to a small room
which led out of the office.

"What do you wish to know?" she demanded
tranquilly.

"I want to know where Mr. Mendoza went to when he
left here," replied Jenkins, and was met by the same
placid stare from Madame's unwinking black eyes.

"I regret. I do not know," she said. "He left no
address."

Jenkins scratched his head and looked foolish.

"Hm," he said, "that's awkward. I want to get into
touch with him. It's important. Now you have a lot of
foreigners here, ma'am, and sometimes we have to keep
our eyes on them. Now we've nothing against you,—this
hotel has a name for being well managed,—all very nice
and proper, and it's not your fault if some of the folk who
stay here aren't all they should be. The fact is, this Mr.
Mendoza has been giving us a lot of trouble. I take it that
you are willing to assist the police, ma'am?"

"But yes, the question answers itself," replied

Madame. "It is desirable to be on good terms with the police, and for me I have nothing to conceal."

"Exactly," replied Jenkins cheerfully. "Now did this Mr. Mendoza take his luggage and go to a railway station do you know? Perhaps your porter would know?"

"No, but I think I know," replied the imperturbable Madame. "It was like this. Mr. Mendoza arrived on Sunday night and booked a room for three nights. Although I did not know him, I had a recommendation of him from a gentleman whom I know well. When Mr. Mendoza came to me on Monday morning and said that he was going to see a friend in the country and might be away for the night, I did not disturb myself. Besides, he left his luggage here,—a big trunk and two suit-cases,— and the waiter had observed that his things were good things," she added with a charming simplicity which Jenkins applauded with:

"Quite so, quite so."

"On Tuesday morning," continued Madame, "Mr. Mendoza telephoned to me saying that he was going over to France, and as he was much occupied he asked that his luggage might be sent to Victoria, saying that he would be waiting at the luggage office at three o'clock. He said that he would give to my messenger the money he owed for the three nights he had booked his room here, and also, of course, pay for the porter's time. Naturally I agreed. His luggage was sent,—I might add that his cases were all strapped up ready. All went as arranged. He paid his bill and signed a receipt for his luggage, and there the affair ended."

"Quite so, ma'am," replied Jenkins. "Now could you tell me who recommended Mr. Mendoza to you?"

"But certainly," replied Madame, not to be outdone in amiability. "A Mr. Juan Rosario."

"And his address?" demanded Jenkins, note-book in hand.

"25 Avenue Las Rosas, Buenos Ayres," replied Madame. "Mr. Rosario sailed in the *Melitic* on Tuesday morning. His home is in Buenos Ayres."

Jenkins looked non-plussed.

"That makes it a bit difficult for me," he said. "Now your porter might remember if Mr. Mendoza took his luggage straight on to the train at Victoria."

"But no, he did not," was the answer. "The luggage was put into the cloak room. There is no boat train leaving Victoria in the middle of the afternoon."

"Ah, I ought to have thought of that myself," said Jenkins, "but I'll have a talk to the porter all the same."

"That is impossible, for he is no longer here," replied Madame, "and if he were, he could tell you no more than I have told you. I was a little curious,—I enquired, but I learnt no more than I have told you."

"Seems a blind alley whichever way you look at it," replied Jenkins. "Perhaps you could show me his registration and the receipt he signed for you."

"Willingly," replied the lady complaisantly. "If you would be so kind as to step into the office?"

Jenkins gallantly opened the door for her, and as he did so became aware of a slight commotion in the office. Apparently Mr. John Robinson had come downstairs again for his chat with Madame, and he seemed to be making the best of her absence by conversing with the dark-eyed girl; he was leaning negligently against the jamb of the door, gesticulating with his cigarette which was fitted into a long scarlet holder. Apparently the sight of Jenkins did not please Mr. Robinson, for after a quick glance at the Inspector's face, the dark man swung round on his heel with astonishing celerity, and walked away across the lounge to the main door.

"Now who might that gentleman be?" enquired Jenkins promptly.

For answer Madame da Soto stretched out her hand and reached for the hotel register. Opening it, she showed Jenkins the last name written therein. "Mr. John Robinson. Liverpool."

"Well I'm jiggered," replied Jenkins. "All I can say is that he doesn't look the part to me. I've seen him before and he's seen me, too, or I'm a Chinaman. . . . Now about this Mendoza. Hm . . . here's his signature, I suppose? He signed himself, I take it?"

"But yes," answered Madame da Soto patiently, bending down to unlock a drawer in the desk beside her, "and here is the receipt for the luggage."

Jenkins studied the document carefully, comparing the scribbled signature on the receipt. At a first glance the writing on each was very similar,—a flowing foreign hand which Jenkins would have found it very difficult to imitate, but despite his air of transparent foolishness, the Inspector was something of an expert at handwriting and the difference in the two signatures rapidly became apparent to him. At length he turned to the proprietress.

"With your permission, ma'am, I will keep this document. I will of course give you a receipt for it and when it has been examined it will be returned to you."

"It's important that I keep that paper," she said. "If Mr. Mendoza has any complaints to make or any enquiries . . . it is a receipt, you understand."

"Ah, so you're not quite happy about it yourself then?" enquired Jenkins. "You thought there might be something fishy about it, too?"

"I thought nothing of the kind," retorted Madame da Soto, "but a receipt is a receipt. I am a business woman. I keep my receipts."

"Quite right," applauded Jenkins, "and you're thinking it's not entirely beyond the bounds of possibility that you've been had, ma'am? Now if the man at Victoria who took over delivery of Mendoza's baggage wasn't Mendoza, you'd be in a bit of a difficulty, wouldn't you?"

The stout lady studied the Inspector thoughtfully, but gave no sign of perturbation.

"He paid my bill," she observed succinctly, as though that disposed of the matter.

"Well, if you ask me, I call that a cheap way of getting hold of another chap's belongings, if you happen to fancy them," answered Jenkins. "Now what about the porter who took the luggage to Victoria. He knew Mr. Mendoza by sight I suppose?"

"I do not know," replied the other, "but what is more important to me, Mr. Inspector, I knew Mr. Mendoza's voice. I talked to him myself and received his instructions about the baggage. I am satisfied. You can have the receipt, provided, as you say, you give me an official acknowledgement of it."

"Very good," said Jenkins. "Then you'll be willing to swear, if need be, that you spoke to Mendoza on Tuesday morning?"

"But certainly," replied the lady placidly.

"And I shall want the name and address of the porter who took the luggage," continued Jenkins and Madame da Soto promptly wrote out a name and address. (The name, Jenkins observed, was correct. The address was not.)

"Still in your employ, ma'am?" he persisted, and Madame shook her head.

"No. I am sorry to say he had to go. A good worker but

mannerless. We cannot afford to employ clumsy ones here. He was like a bull in a china shop, that one."

Jenkins looked her very straight in the face:

"Then you can tell me nothing more, ma'am? I warn you, this is an important matter. You may have to give sworn evidence later."

"I have told you all that I know," replied Madame steadily. "I know nothing of the gentleman you mention. He came, as I say, with a recommendation. He paid. He has gone. That is all."

"Very well, ma'am. I won't trouble you any further just now, but I warn you that you had better be very careful of that Register of yours. We may want to examine it later."

Here Jenkins took a sheet of paper from his note-book and wrote out a receipt for the paper he was taking, carefully copying the form of words on it and finally signing the whole.

"That quite satisfactory?" he enquired cheerfully.

"Then I'll bid you good night. Thank you, ma'am, good evening."

Madame da Soto replied with a placid "good night, sir," and when Jenkins had disappeared into the street, she turned to her assistant, who had been sitting in silence, listening attentively to the words of the other two.

"You may go now, Sanzia. I shall not want you again to-night," said the older woman, and Sanzia knew her employer too well to make any comments on what she had heard.

"Good night, madame, and thank you," was all that she said before she walked gracefully away—a very composed and discreet young woman.

A few minutes later Mr. John Robinson, of Liverpool,

reappeared at the office.

"Say, ma'am, have you got such a thing as a map of London. I don't know my way about as well as I should like to."

Madame descended from her stool and motioned to the young man to follow her into her private room.

"I think I can find you what you want," she said. "London is difficult for a stranger. One needs to be careful lest one loses the way."

"Difficult. I should damn well say that's so," replied the other. "To look for a man in London is like looking for a needle in a haystack."

Madame looked at him with her non-committal gaze.

"Men are not marked on maps," she observed, and the other laughed.

"Nope, they're marked in people's minds. You, for instance, haven't forgotten a man named d'Alvarez. Pedro, he called himself. Now I'm wanting to find d'Alvarez. We have interests in common, if you get me."

Madame smiled. "I am afraid a map of London will not help you, sir. You want a map of the world."

"That so? I reckon you're wrong, ma'am. D'Alvarez came to England to raise money, and he came here because he liked to be considered one of the family. Perhaps he made a mistake, but I'll lay any money someone else made a mistake, too. Now I'm not wanting to poke my nose in where it isn't wanted, but I happened to be in Las Palmas four or five years ago, and I saw a bit of d'Alvarez there. When I heard he'd come to London, I came too. I wasn't far wrong in my reckoning when I came here, was I?"

For answer Madame opened her hotel Register. "If you think that your friend has been staying here, you are mistaken," she said softly. "You can look for yourself."

"I've looked already," replied the other, "and seen what I wanted to see. The guy who was in here just now had a look too, but he's not so well up in family affairs as you and me."

"Yet he seemed to know your face," retorted Madame quietly.

"He's welcome," replied John Robinson. "He's got nothing on me, but I could tell him a whole lot he'd find interesting. He knows Bertie and Charles, for instance, and he's gotten a mighty good idea where you fit in. He's looking for trouble and you know best where he's likely to find it. D'Alvarez was a flat to come butting in. You ought to have told him so. Vanda's done very well for herself, and she didn't want d'Alvarez over here."

"You talk in riddles, sir," replied Madame da Soto coldly. "I have told you that I do not know your friend."

"No, and you don't know Quixado or de Vries or William Lambert either," answered Robinson. "Now see here. I want to find d'Alvarez. You can guess my business without me shouting it. When d'Alvarez came over here he was playing two hands. One was the usual thing, and one was Vanda. He can have his Jane but I want a straight deal for the other. If you tell me d'Alvarez has gone to France, or Jericho, or Salt Lake City for that matter, I won't contradict you, but he hasn't taken his traps with him. Now I took an almighty risk when I came here. I didn't reckon to meet Scotland Yard on the mat. When I made tracks just now, it saved you a lot of bother. Yep?"

Madame sat with folded arms and studied John Robinson thoughtfully. "If I send for the police and tell them I have an impostor in the hotel——" she began slowly.

"That's so," interrupted Robinson. "A guy with a wig,

and a complexion which is his own because he paid for it, who signed your registration with a bum name, and who knows more about Prohibited Drugs than's good for him. Yes, ma'am, they'll come running. But do you want 'em to? They'll be just tickled to death when I say my piece about d'Alvarez."

"What do you want?" demanded Madame suddenly.

"Now you're talking!" replied the other. "I want to know where d'Alvarez's traps are located. You can tell me that, though you can't tell me where I can find d'Alvarez himself. Old man Peter's the guy for that job. You've said it."

"I have said nothing at all," replied Madame scornfully, "except to tell you that you are mistaken, and that I say again. I repeat that I cannot help you. You must find Charles."

"Santissima! Tell me something I don't know. Charles went to Liverpool with Rosario; he came back and picked up the traps at Victoria, and then he walked off the face of the earth. If you put me wise where Charles is hanging out I'll be satisfied, but if you try any funny business with me, I'll turn King's Evidence, and you know what that means."

In reply Madame da Soto pulled a sheet of paper towards her, and wrote down an address: '60H North Mansions, N.W.8.' and she pushed the paper across for Mr. Robinson to read.

That gentleman read the address and then tore the paper on which it was written into fragments.

"Keep a thing in your head, but never leave it about on paper," he said sagely. "A lot of trouble might be saved if everybody remembered that rule, ma'am."

Here he produced another of his exotic looking cigarettes, and lighted it thoughtfully.

"I guess you've worried yourself blue over this bum business," he said sympathetically. "Fact is, Bertie ought to have kept clear of the doings. You can't pull off a frame-up in this God-darned country. It was a good idea, but it just side-slipped on an off chance. He's asked for trouble and I guess he's going to get it. I'm sorry for Bertie, ma'am, but he's got his fingers burnt good and true this time. He should of let the other guy face the music."

Madame da Soto heaved a large sigh. "You talk in riddles, sir. To please you I do the same. Bertie never knew d'Alvarez was in England."

"That so? He must have had some facer when he saw him, then. Did some quick thinking did Bertie, and over-reached himself for once. It's a funny thing to think you're at the bottom of it, ma'am. Here are we, two honest citizens,—that's us, and if the police guys could do a spot of mental telepathy they'd be in clover. Sure. You've told me one thing I didn't know, ma'am, and I can guess the rest right away."

Madame made no answer. She just watched the strange young fellow with her melancholy eyes.

"Got you guessing there? You've said it. If Bertie didn't know d'Alvarez was in England, who told d'Alvarez that Vanda was fixed? You meant well, ma'am, but you started the trouble when you put him wise there. 'Something in this for me,' says d'Alvarez, 'I'm on the dollars.'. . . . That's what we call a psychic bid, ma'am. . . . I'll bid you good night. See here. Don't you go calling up Charles when I quit. You've got to leave things to sort themselves straight."

"Good night, sir," replied Madame, her large body monumentally still, though her eyes looked wicked. "You have forgotten to take your map of London."

"Oh that," returned the other. "I'd say it's too small, that map. What I'm wanting is a map of the Oxford Road."

And with that Mr. John Robinson made his way once more to the street door.

CHAPTER XIII

It was very late on Thursday evening that Mr. Charles Rodmell returned to his modest flat in North Mansions, St. John's Wood, but just as he was approaching his front door a figure detached itself from the shadows, and Mr. Rodmell perceived that a tall man was standing in the little recess in which the door was situated.

"Mr. Charles Rodmell?" enquired an even voice.

"What's that got to do with you, and what the devil are you wanting at this hour?" demanded Charles in retort.

"I am the officer in charge of the enquiry concerning the murder of a man on the Oxford Road, and I wish to ask you certain questions. My business is urgent and cannot be delayed," replied the other.

"That's all very fine and large," answered Charles. "How am I to know who you are? No confidence tricks on me, now. You call again in daylight, and I'll have a look at you."

"Your attitude is quite reasonable," replied the first speaker patiently, "but there is a constable further along the balcony who will vouch for it that I am not an impostor. Wilson!"

In answer to the call, another figure approached, and turned the beam of an electric torch on to the two men. In the reflected light Charles could make out the policeman's uniform.

"My name is Macdonald, Chief Inspector, C.I.D.," said the original speaker. "You vouch for my identity, Wilson?"

"Yes, sir. All correct," replied the man in uniform, and Mr. Rodmell's voice was pitched on a different note as he replied:

"Very good, Inspector, very good. I won't apologise for my caution, there are some funny characters about to-day and I don't want to entertain any wrong 'uns. Come right in, Inspector. Very glad to see you."

So saying Mr. Rodmell put his key in the lock and pushed open the small front door.

"Pardon me going first," he said affably. "Not too much room in these entrances. Would the constable like to come inside?"

"Since you're so kind as to suggest it, and it's a nasty night, thank you very much," said Macdonald.

When the three men stood inside in the tiny hall they seemed to fill the place, and the owner of the flat pushed open a door opposite to the front door, and ushered Macdonald into a cosy small room. There were two large arm chairs and a small chesterfield, and a syphon and whisky bottle were standing on a table.

Mr. Rodmell rubbed his hands cheerfully.

"Nice convenient little place, this," he observed genially. "Just a quick one, officer, to open proceedings?"

Macdonald had closed the door of the room behind him, leaving Wilson in the entrance-hall beyond.

"Not for me, thanks," he replied. "I assume that you are cognisant of the events in this case, Mr. Rodmell?"

"Pretty well, pretty well, and a fine old muddle it is," replied the other, mixing himself a stiff drink. "As a matter of fact, I have been in Paris since Tuesday, but a letter from my brother, giving me the facts,—as they appear,—brought me back home in a hurry. You're all at sea, if you don't mind my speaking frankly. All at sea. I shall be able to correct a few misapprehensions for you. A very difficult case, I might remark, most obscure."

"Quite," replied Macdonald, "but we have a lot of routine work to do before we can make any headway. Since this case has involved your whole family, so to speak, you will appreciate that it is necessary for us, as a preliminary, to rule out any possibility that any of you could have been implicated in the actual murder."

"Just so, just so," replied Charles, smacking his lips appreciatively over the drink he had just disposed of. "Now you want to know just what I was doing on Monday night? Quite an interesting little narrative there, Inspector. Sit down, won't you, and make yourself at home now. A cigar now?—that's a brand I can strongly recommend."

"Thank you, not for me," replied Macdonald, taking the seat indicated, but refusing the cigar. "On Monday evening, Mr. Rodmell, I think that you travelled to Liverpool in company with Mr. Rosario."

"All wrong, my boy, all wrong," answered Charles. "That was my brother, Hubert. The fact is, you've been getting confused and I can't blame you, because it's a very puzzling little story. Well, on Monday evening I went by train to a little place called Warlington. Ha! ha! my boy. You weren't expecting that now, were you!"

"I can't say I was," replied Macdonald pleasantly, "but I'm always willing to learn. Having told me so much, Mr. Rodmell, say if you carry on and tell me the rest."

"Just what I am wanting to do," replied the other.

"Why am I here, Inspector? I'm here to give you facts. Hard facts, my boy. Now I shall have to go back a little bit. It came to my knowledge some months ago that there was a little affair between the lady in the case and a certain South American gentleman who was received in London society. The lady being very young, her father did not approve of the business at all. I don't want to mention more names than I can help, Inspector, I hate to make trouble. You get me?"

"I think so," replied Macdonald. "You refer, of course, to your niece, Vanda?"

"Not on your life, sir! don't you believe it," returned Charles indignantly. "Nothing of the kind. If you want names, then you'll have to have them. I refer to the lady in the case,—the lady you found at the outset. Miss Diana Hanton."

Macdonald sitting with his legs crossed, swung one foot to and fro, but his voice was bland as he said, "I'm afraid that I don't follow then. You'll have to enlighten me," and Charles responded.

"Just as I said! just as I said! Enlightenment is the very word I should have used myself. Now it came to my knowledge that this South American gentleman whom I mentioned,—you shall have his name later if you find it necessary to cross-examine me in the witness-box,—was returning to England. Now, I've told you I'm a peaceful man, hate trouble, especially for the young folk. We were all young once, my boy,—you still are, ha! ha! Well, I thought I'd say a word in season to the lady's father. A delicate business, if you take me, Inspector. One that needed careful handling. Well, the upshot of it was all this. The gallant Colonel made an appointment with me for Monday evening. We were to have our little talk in a bungalow he owns on the Marlow road. The place was his choice, not mine. Now you'll have to forgive me if I seem to diverge a bit and get off the point, but there are certain details which ought not to be overlooked."

Here Charles mixed himself another drink and smiled at Macdonald in the pleasantest way in the world.

"Don't hesitate to stop me if I fail to make myself clear," he said. "I'm not accustomed to giving evidence, not in my line really, but I'll do my best. Now you know all about my nephew, Bert. He's a good boy, Inspector, one of the best, and if I had been informed about all this bother before I left England on Tuesday, his parents would have been saved a lot of unnecessary anguish. Bert left England on Sunday morning, Inspector. I know it. I saw him off. If it hadn't been for that coincidence about the old bullet wound in the leg, his people would never have identified him with such assurance. A most harrowing experience for them, Inspector, most harrowing, upon my soul it was. But that's neither here nor there. I saw Bert on Saturday and he told me that he was determined to leave England. I needn't go into all that,—another of these little *affaires-du-cœur*,—but I do know that he left England on Sunday morning. Now before he left me on Saturday night he asked me if I'd be willing to take a suit-case back home for him. Just a few things he didn't want on the voyage. I knew I should be seeing Hubert shortly,—my brother, that is,—I wanted to have a talk with him about the boy, so I was quite willing to take charge of the case,—meaning the suit-case, ha! ha! Now that's point number two, Inspector, and a very important point, too."

"Very," agreed Macdonald, who, it must be admitted was listening to the narrative with unfeigned interest. He was wondering how on earth Charles was going to vindicate his own innocence concerning Monday night.

"Now you'll appreciate from what I'm telling you that I must be very certain of my own position in the matter, Inspector," went on Charles. "I can assure you that the last thing I want to risk is a capital charge; nevertheless, I'm going to tell the truth. It always pays in the long run and no one has ever suffered for it yet. Well, when I made this appointment with our friend on the Marlow road, it occurred to me that it was a good opportunity to take Bert's suit-case back home for him."

"Quite," said Macdonald, who was beginning to see the way the wind was blowing, and Charles continued,

"I went to Warlington by train, arriving there at six-eleven. The station is not a great distance from the bungalow and I walked there, reaching the place at six twenty-five."

"Taking the suit-case with you?" put in Macdonald.

"Exactly. That's very important. Taking the suit-case with me, just as you say. When I arrived I found the whole place locked up. I put the suit-case down in the porch and sat down in the garden at the back of the house. If you'll believe me, I waited there for an hour, Inspector. 'Pon my soul, I've never been more put about in my life. I had an appointment in London at nine o'clock,—a most important appointment, too, and there was I, cooling my heels and wasting valuable time, all out of sheer good nature. I waited for an hour, as I told you, and then I decided to quit. The fact was I was seriously annoyed. I don't often lose my wool,—I'm an easy going chap taking me all round, but I hate being made a fool of. I waited by the garden gate a bit longer and then I decided I'd walk back to Wycombe and catch a train up from there. Now you can see how annoyed I was when I tell you this: I'd left Bert's suit-case in the porch, and I forgot all about it,—went clean out of my head, and I didn't give it another thought. If you'll believe me, I didn't remember that suit-case again until yesterday. Careless, of course,—but there you are. . . .

Now what was the word you used?—enlightening,—that was it. Able to see daylight a bit now, Inspector?"

Macdonald laughed. "Lime-light expresses it better, Mr. Rodmell,—a spot light, focused on you, so to speak. You've only omitted one thing, and that is to tell me by what train you travelled back from Wycombe."

"Ah, yes,—always dot your i's—quite right, my boy. But I didn't travel back to London by train at all. I had a spot of luck at the last. Just when I'd got on to the main road a car overtook me and then pulled up. The driver of that car was young Tony d'Allessandri. He picked me up and drove me back to town. We got to Marble Arch at eight-thirty to the tick."

Macdonald nodded. "A very convenient coincidence, Mr. Rodmell. Of course you've realised that your whole story will have to be investigated in detail? Do you think that Colonel Hanton, for instance, is likely to substantiate it?"

Charles broke out into a shout of laughter. "Very good one that! very good indeed. No, my boy, I don't. Colonel Hanton's the very last person who is likely to admit the truth. But come now, play the game! I've been very open with you. Have you asked Colonel Hanton just what *he* was doing last Monday night? I don't lay claim to any powerful intellect, Inspector, but I'm not quite the simpleton you're thinking. I haven't produced a cock and bull story for you to play skittles with. You look into it, that's my advice to you. There's more in it than meets the eye."

"I'm quite sure there is," responded Macdonald. "I don't think you a simpleton by any manner of means, Mr. Rodmell. I have a lot of respect for your ability and I'm like you in this respect,—I don't like being made a fool of either. The situation's a difficult one, as you've said.

Say if we discuss it without prejudice. You have been very frank in admitting that you were in the danger zone, so to speak, between six-thirty and seven-thirty. What proof can you offer me that you weren't implicated in the actual murder? You'll see the reasonableness of that question I'm sure."

"Quite so, quite so! I saw it coming all along, Inspector. That's the risk I took when I decided to be open with you. You suggest that deceased joined me during that hour at the bungalow and that I knocked him over the head with a spanner, and—er—left him there?"

"It might be suggested," replied Macdonald. "For instance deceased might have arrived by car. . . ."

"In the green Varron for instance? I read that little bit of evidence, Inspector. Well, assuming for argument's sake that I committed the murder,—and as good as told you so in plain words, since I've told you I was at the bungalow,—how did deceased move himself to the spot where you found him? I can't prove what I did during that hour, but I can prove that I was in London at eight-thirty, and that I stayed the rest of the evening in London. Say if we put down the case for the prosecution: "There is not a particle of evidence against the accused save that which he has provided voluntarily, out of his own mouth. He was so unwise as to tell Chief Inspector Macdonald that he—accused—was in the—er—danger zone around zero hour. He had no motive for the murder, and not a fragment of evidence can be produced to show that the deceased met his death at the hands of the accused. This charge is brought solely on the strength of his own voluntary statement. Medical evidence indicates that deceased met his death at least seven and a half hours before his body was found, say about five-thirty p.m. Accused was not at the bungalow until an hour later. It is suggested that accused put body of deceased on the main road in broad daylight—say about seven-thirty, but the body was not observed until six hours later. That, sir, is the case for the prosecution."

Here Charles mixed himself another drink and raised his glass to Macdonald.

"Here's how! my boy. Feel that the facts fit the case?"

"Only to some extent," replied Macdonald. "I don't think that the charge is likely to be a capital charge, you know. Of course I'm speaking in a hypothetical manner as far as you are concerned; at present no case is formulated. On the whole I think you'd do well to reconsider your attitude. One thing that has struck me very forcibly is that your family is a very united one; you all understand the essence of the old adage that unity is strength, and you have been very successful in backing one another up. But a murder case is a very different matter from other cases, it is subject to a more detailed analysis. Bearing this in mind, perhaps you will listen to my own ideas on the subject,—all hypothetical, of course, but the exposition may help you to elucidate certain points, and if you care to modify your evidence hereafter, you may find it to the good of the family to do so. Later, of course, you will be on oath. At present you are kindly assisting me by a voluntary statement."

"Exceedingly well put," applauded Charles. "If I may say so, I envy you your power of speech. You should have been an advocate, Inspector. You have the knack, so to speak."

"Thank you," said Macdonald gravely. "Say if we examine your suggestions quite dispassionately. One is led to assume that your altruistic intentions towards Colonel Hanton in the matter of the South American gentleman were anticipated by that gentleman on confronting Colonel Hanton in person. You are of the opinion that the latter was so deeply incensed by the imputations made to him that he gave way to violence. Such a thing is not beyond the bounds of credibility of course. Blackmail has been at the root of similar events before now,—but let us continue the reconstruction. Perhaps, you might suggest, Colonel Hanton remembered his appointment with you at the bungalow. He arrived there to find that you had already left, but that a suit-case was standing in the porch. He examined the contents of the case and had a sudden brain wave. Is that it?"

"That's it, Inspector. Fits all the facts. Very circumstantial of course. You'll never be able to prove it."

"Probably not; it looks as though a confession is essential to determine those facts, though I'm not optimistic about that. Well, the rest of the business can be assumed, but there are just one or two points you could help me with. When we examined your nephew's bedroom at Downfield we found in that room a small pocket mirror which gave excellent finger-prints coinciding with those of the corpse. Can you tell me how Colonel Hanton introduced the mirror to that room? . . . It's a very nice point, Mr. Rodmell. You have explained to me that you saw your nephew off on Saturday, and the victim of the murder did not arrive in this country until Sunday,—we are agreed on that point, I think? I am assured that there were no visitors at Downfield on either Sunday or Monday. It's a difficult point. . . . Then there is that little matter of the luggage which you collected at Victoria Station from the porter of the Montevideo. Am I to assume that Colonel Hanton enlisted your aid in that matter, Mr. Rodmell? It really looks like it. Otherwise I can see no point in your taking the luggage over to Paris by the evening train. You have said that you had no motive to get rid of your South American friend, but you seem to have had a motive in moving his luggage. Quite frankly, Mr. Rodmell, you seem to have allowed your enthusiasm for Colonel Hanton to get the better of your judgment. You'd have been much more safely placed had you travelled to Liverpool with Mr. Rosario."

Charles had a good poker face. He never turned a hair during Macdonald's last speech, and his face showed only the expression of innocent surprise which the occasion demanded.

"That bit about the luggage at Victoria is all Latin and Greek to me," he said. "I've told you I'm no scholar, Inspector. I don't know anything about any luggage, and I crossed to Paris by the morning boat—ten-five boat-train from Charing X. I can show you my reservation. As for your suggestion of collusion between Colonel Hanton and myself, it's not worthy of your consideration. I'm willing to do a man a good turn by giving him advice, but that's all there is to it. The other suggestion won't wash."

"I thought it wouldn't myself," replied Macdonald placidly, "but you never know how counsel will interpret things. As I told you, I have been very much struck by the strong sense of unity in your family. You are all anxious to help one another. Now in the interest of your family can you make any suggestion which will show how the finger-prints of deceased were found in your nephew's bedroom? You have demonstrated that you yourself could not have been there, and neither your nephew nor your brother. There must be an explanation somewhere."

"Now let's think this thing out," said Charles gravely. "Deceased met his death round about five-thirty or six o'clock and his body was found after midnight. That gives plenty of time for cooking evidence. A desperate man seeks desperate remedies you know, and entering a house is a small matter in comparison with murder."

"Not very convincing I'm afraid, Mr. Rodmell, but not, as you say, utterly impossible. If one accepts your reading of the facts, one is led inevitably to the conclusion that the murderer had an accomplice, and that his accomplice had access to your brother's house at Downfield. That would fit all the facts. Just one other point. It appears that you are pretty well acquainted with Colonel Hanton. I am sure that you would not be so anxious for me to investigate his actions if you were not convinced that I should find something interesting about them."

"Exactly, dear boy, exactly," said Charles warmly. "Really it's a pleasure to talk to you, Inspector, you go straight to the point."

"I only wish I did, Mr. Rodmell," said Macdonald, "then I shouldn't have to go on wasting your time asking you questions when you want to go to bed. Now it appears to me that this case resolves itself into three separate parts and I have got to find the connection between them before I can reach a conclusion. The first part concerns the disappearance of your nephew, Bert. The second part concerns the transactions,—if any,— between your family and Colonel Hanton. The third part concerns the transactions between the deceased and the murderer. I am sure that you could supply the information linking up these parts, and I feel very strongly that you would be well advised to supply it. In spite of your optimistic anticipation of the case for the prosecution, I don't think you're out of the wood yet."

"Damn it, my boy, you're right!" said Charles enthusiastically. "I quite realised the difficulties I shouldered when I set out on this policy of frankness. Believe me, if I hadn't seen my way clear, I doubt if I'd have risked it. Public spirit is all very well but number one is bound to be considered. Now about your little problem in three parts—A. B. and C. A. refers to Bert. You can wash him right out, my boy, he's a wash out, ha! ha! His decision to clear out had nothing to do with the case, it's as irrelevant as the flowers that bloom in the spring, tra-la-la. I make you a present of that,— absolutely. Now about B. The transactions between my family and Colonel Hanton are only relevant so far as they gave us an opportunity of knowing that he was in the danger zone on Monday night, once again they're not concerned with the origin of events, they're accidental. There's an amazing amount of accident in this case, Inspector. As for C.—transactions between deceased and murderer, it's a case of, the lady in the case, my boy."

"I think you're probably right there," said Macdonald, in the tone of one who has decided on a great truth.

"And now, Inspector, I hate to be inhospitable, but it's very late and I need a good sleep. I've given you the data—it's up to you to cross the T's you know."

"Exactly," replied Macdonald, rising promptly to his feet. "I'll leave you in peace, Mr. Rodmell. By the way, I see you've had an accident to your hand."

Charles waved a bandaged hand airily.

"Just a trifling burn," he said cheerfully. "Funny what silly things one can do. I let a cigar roll off the ash tray and found it by putting my hand on the live end. Quite a nasty little blister it made."

"It would," returned Macdonald sympathetically. "Good night, Mr. Rodmell, thank you for all your information."

"Glad to help you, dear boy. Good night,— and you

just take my tip and think it all out."

"I'll do my best," returned Macdonald gravely.

CHAPTER XIV

"Morning, Macdonald. I don't want to rub it in, but I can't help a sneaking feeling of satisfaction that this infernal Box-Cox combination had diddled somebody else besides me. If you knew the number of times I've been put back to the starting point looking a fool, when you've been solving your cases without a hitch, you'd understand how well I can sympathise with you now."

It was Inspector Castle who spoke and Macdonald turned to him with an exasperated countenance.

"It's the devil and all, Castle. I thought I'd got the beggars taped, but they've fairly got the laugh of us. There's going to be a fine old rumpus over this,—it looks like the worst sort of incompetence."

"Whoever mentions the word incompetence in connection with those qualified eels ought to be put on to shadow them himself," replied Castle. "Whatever the moral qualities of the precious pair may be, and there's not much villainy they're not capable of, they're genuine artists in the disappearing line. They ought to have made their fortunes in the Maskelyne and Devant line. How did it happen? I'm to be given the jolly task of picking 'em up again."

"Right,—you know more about them than I do, and you'll do it in half the time anyone else could," answered Macdonald. "I'd got H.H. safely at home at Downfield,— Reeves was watching the house, and he's a good man. I spent yesterday evening making a fool of myself at Madame da Soto's place and got her guessing all right.

She thought I was part of the family and took me into her confidence and gave me Charles's address. You'll be interested to know that he's got a nice snug little lair in North Mansions, where he diddled Hodges with the automatic lifts. He's known there as Mr. William Watson, a bagman in the fancy gadgets line, beads and anklets and chokers and all that tripe. I had a real heart to heart talk with Charles, and he was as clever as they make 'em. Took all the onus of the Warlington business on his own capable shoulders and put H.H. right out of it. When I left I had a man watching each of the exits,—it was obviously essential to keep in with Charles.

"After I'd left he came out of his flat and went downstairs, chatting to Wilson on his way to the lift. Said his telephone was out of order and he'd got to go to the phone box at the street corner. Well, he put his call through and went back to his flat. This morning he re-appeared at his front door and Wilson noticed something unfamiliar about him. . . ."

"Hell! don't I know the game!" interrupted Castle. "He'd changed in the night and turned into H.H."

"Exactly," answered Macdonald. "Do you know that all the time I was talking to Charles last night, H.H. must have been in the next room . . . then after I'd gone, H.H. put on Charles' hat and coat, went out and telephoned in the role of Charles,—thereby absorbing the attention of my men while Charles himself slipped through the barrage and disappeared. H.H. went back to the flat and stayed the night there, and when Wilson investigated this morning the only occupant of the flat was H.H.

"They played a very similar game on Reeves at Downfield. George came running down the drive with a story of burglars and they all began chasing shadows along the road. In the meantime H.H. slips quietly up to

London to consult with Charles,—and there you are."

"Quite," replied Castle. "I know the little game,—and now I'm to comb out all the likely spots where Box and Cox foregather."

"At any rate you've got a warrant this time," replied Macdonald. "That ought to help. It's not so easy for a man to vanish when there's a warrant for murder out against him. People don't mind being involved in Prohibited Drugs, but some of them are bound to squeal when it's a murder charge."

"Ummm . . . nothing like being an optimist," answered Castle. "Charles will have got his hidey hole all prepared against an eventuality like this one. I bet he's snugly settled in a prearranged niche, name and occupation all complete. Chameleons are nowhere in it with this pair. They're polyglot for one thing and they know every capital in Europe. Charles will be doing the virtuous bourgeois somewhere in Belgium to-day, probably with a wife to swear she's never let him out of her sight. Incidentally, if I get him, do you think you'll be able to prove your charge?"

"Losh, no!" said Macdonald. "For one thing I don't believe he did it and I expect he can prove he didn't, but he's an accessory all right. Once we get him, we can give him a bonny run for his money."

"Right. I'll do my best," answered Castle. "It's a comfort to have a definite charge for a change. As a rule I'm merely trying to prove that he's a suspicious character. No one's ever succeeded in proving it yet. What are you up to this morning?"

"I'm the scapegoat. Going to be hauled on the carpet to explain our negligence. It looks a bit obvious, I grant you."

"Bad luck!" said Castle. "Well, you don't get much of

that sort of thing. Your luck's been too good lately. Cheerioh,—I hope we cop the brute."

Ten minutes later Macdonald was with the Assistant Commissioner, outlining his case.

"We have got over the initial difficulty, sir," he said to Colonel Wragley. "We can take deceased's identity as proven. He is a South American, known as d'Alvarez or Mendoza. The Argentine Police have had him in prison over there and cabled us an exceedingly detailed description of him on the Bertillon lines. Deceased is known to have had dealings with the Rodmells in America, so that connection is clearly established."

"Very good, Macdonald," replied Colonel Wragley. "It seems to be necessary to decide which of the Rodmells could have been involved in the murder."

"Exactly," assented Macdonald, a flicker of amusement lighting his grey eyes. "I should like to make this part of the problem clear to you, sir. It wasn't the son, George, he is clearly out of it. So far as Bert is concerned, we haven't an atom of evidence to show that he was in the neighbourhood at the time, or that he had any motive for the murder. H. H. Rodmell supplied an alibi which we haven't been able to disprove. I couldn't have arrested him on suspicion, because all the evidence went to prove that he was miles away. That leaves us with Charles. Having with difficulty learnt the latter's address, I interviewed him last night and his evidence establishes his brother's innocence completely. Charles Rodmell admitted without hesitation that he himself was in the Winchstone neighbourhood on Monday night. In fact he went out of his way to impress on me that he, alone of the family, was the suspect, and he told me that the reason which took him to the district was an interview with Colonel Hanton. Now I am convinced that he had very good reasons for all his assertions, however mendacious they may be. If I had arrested Charles Rodmell then and there I felt pretty certain that circumstances would have forced me to charge Colonel Hanton also. I did not arrest Rodmell,—I thought that he was efficiently watched,—and I intended to interrogate Colonel Hanton before I took any further steps. In the meantime, Charles Rodmell has given us the slip,—he and his brother have simply fooled us for the moment."

Here Macdonald gave Colonel Wragley an outline of the same facts which Castle had heard a few minutes earlier.

"The responsibility was mine," said Macdonald. "I decided to wait before I made an arrest, because I wanted to cut the ground from under Rodmell's feet. In the meantime, this is where we stand. Charles has got away after having given evidence which clears his brother, and the greater part of the evidence which I have collected can be interpreted in Charles' favour. Mendoza undoubtedly stayed at the Hotel Montevideo; on Monday he hired a car from a firm in Portland Street,—this car was the green Varron which was burnt out on the Oxford road. (Incidentally we have proved that that was the work of two country lads who took the car out of the bungalow garage and capsized it, the boys themselves escaping almost unhurt.) To return to Mendoza. It appears that he left London in the Varron on Monday afternoon and drove by the Thames Valley road through Maidenhead and Marlow. He stopped at the latter place for tea, shortly after four o'clock, and he was seen on the Marlow road about three miles from Downfield and Winchstone, about five-thirty.

"There is an element of assumption in all this, of course. I am assuming that the man who hired the Varron and drove it through Marlow really was Mendoza and not an impersonator of him. We can be satisfied with the evidence that the corpse is Mendoza's and that he met his death approximately between five and six o'clock, so I think I am justified in assuming that it was he who was actually driving the Varron when it was seen near Winchstone at five-thirty. Now the road which the Varron took after leaving Marlow is the road in which the bungalow is situated. The Varron passed the bungalow at five-forty. A local market-gardener, named Higgins, who was driving into Wycombe had a breakdown just beyond the bungalow—on the side nearest to the main road, and he saw the Varron pass.

"He had sent his boy on to a garage in Wycombe to get a car sent out to tow him in, and he sat in the car from shortly after five until nearly seven o'clock. Now we have established that Higgins saw the Varron pass him just after five-forty. He is prepared to swear that neither the Varron nor its driver returned down that road while he was there, and that no one of Charles Rodmell's appearance passed him either. Our evidence as it stands at present is to this effect—the Varron and its driver were on one side of the market gardener, and Charles Rodmell, according to his own statement, was on the other. Now when Charles proffered his evidence last night I am convinced that he was cognisant of these facts. In other words, sir, I think that the Rodmells have done a lot of very competent intelligence work. They are an exceedingly intelligent family and we are going to have our work cut out to bowl them out."

"Exactly, Macdonald," replied Colonel Wragley with some asperity, "and it's an exceedingly unfortunate thing that you did not detain Charles Rodmell on suspicion. I should be interested to learn if you think that there is any doubt that he is the murderer."

"I can answer that question very easily, sir," replied Macdonald. "I am convinced in my own mind that Charles is not the murderer. It is far more probable that he was in the Liverpool train. He was never at Warlington at all on Monday evening, but Henry Hubert was, only I have got to get clearer evidence to prove the point. This is a case where the facts can only be interpreted with the aid of a little imagination."

Colonel Wragley gave a sound indicative of exasperation. "I have no use for psychic methods, Macdonald. You're up against a subtle and elusive pair of scoundrels, and you're likely to let them give you the slip if you don't close with them. I consider you have ample evidence to charge Henry Hubert Rodmell."

"I must admit, sir, that it would be a comfort to have him in a lock-up," said Macdonald, "but I hate making charges which I can't substantiate. My case against Henry Hubert is something to this effect. On Monday evening he went to the Winchstone district via Warlington, where he arrived at 6.11. The green Varron was seen at the bungalow at 5.40. After that we can gather no further information about it. Since it was not seen passing through either Winchstone or Downfield, and was not seen on the main Oxford road either, it looks probable that Rodmell and d'Alvarez met at some point north of the bungalow but south of the Oxford road. However if we attempt to establish that the Varron was driven to the Rodmells' house at Downfield we shall certainly be defeated,—I can't find an atom of evidence to support the point, but plenty of evidence against it. Assume, however, that the Varron was concealed at some point not yet located—and that H.H. Rodmell joins Mendoza there and kills him. Having done this he conceals the body, goes and gets the Hantons' car out of their garage, drives up to London in it and secures Bert's clothes. He also executes his commission in Maida Vale; then drives back to Winchstone, dresses the corpse in Bert's clothes and stages the affair on the Oxford road with the assistance of Mellon's lorry. It's interesting to work out how he spent the rest of the night and how he got back to London. Personally I imagine he remained concealed in the Winchstone district till morning and then caught an early train up from some station where he was not known,—say Princes Risborough. Assuming that this reconstruction is anywhere near the truth, I'm certain of one thing—he had to have assistance. The man's physique isn't good enough for him to have done the job single handed. It's the assistant whom I'm so interested in."

"Why, his precious son, Bert," retorted Colonel Wragley.

"Well, in that case Bert is still in England," replied Macdonald. "I got on to the case early enough to have all the ports watched on Tuesday morning and Bert couldn't have sailed before Tuesday if he were busy on the Oxford road at midnight. However, all these hypotheses aren't going to help our case much until we have solved what Castle calls the Box and Cox problem. The Rodmells believe in backing one another up, and the whole case turns on the family and its ramifications. I'm sure, sir, you'll agree with me that you don't see Colonel Hanton in that galère, yet I'm certain that Charles Rodmell has something damaging up his sleeves in that quarter."

"The suggestion's preposterous," said Colonel Wragley.

Macdonald had an impulse,—to which he did not yield,—to ask his superior if he had ever seen a play called *Loyalties*. Instead he replied, "I am going to interrogate Colonel Hanton as to his movements on Monday night before I put a warrant against H. H. Rodmell into effect. I take it that that course will have your approval, sir?"

"Certainly," replied Wragley stiffly, and then spoke in a rather different tone. "I appreciate the fact that you have shown the Hantons every consideration, Macdonald. While I am convinced that Colonel Hanton's actions are impeccable in every respect. I realise that it might have been very unpleasant for him to have had to repudiate slanderous statements in court. It's the old story about mud being sticky material."

"Thank you, sir," replied Macdonald, "in that case I will get on with the good work."

"And don't give rein to your imagination sufficiently to allow H. H. Rodmell to join his brother in obscurity," said Colonel Wragley. "What you've got to do is to lay hands on the pair of them, and Bert Rodmell into the bargain. It's not like you to be caught napping, Macdonald."

"And if I told him of the particular bee I've got in my bonnet, he'd denounce me as an impractical theorist, having no contact with reality," said Macdonald to himself as he went downstairs, "yet reality is making me obey the preposterous injunction of the *Mayfair Messenger* and ask Miss Hanton's father, Where were *you* out last night? One person will be pleased over it, at any rate, and that's Jenkins."

When Macdonald arrived at Eaton Place, Colonel Hanton seemed to welcome his appearance wholeheartedly.

"I'm exceedingly glad to see you, Inspector. As a matter of fact I had thought of calling on you myself. I have been very much troubled in my mind, but I didn't like to bother you over my own affairs when you were so fully occupied with your case."

"Well, sir, it looks as though the things which have been troubling you may not be so remote from the case after all," replied Macdonald. "It seems that someone has been interesting themselves by casting aspersions on you, and it is obviously desirable to prove that such remarks are baseless. To put it quite simply, I want a statement of your movements on Monday evening. A witness has stated that you were in the Winchstone district that evening. I take it that this witness erred?"

"The witness,—whoever he may be,—was perfectly correct," replied Colonel Hanton quietly. "I realise that this belated admission will undermine your confidence in me, Inspector. You will argue, quite correctly, that it was my duty to have informed you of this fact at the outset, instead of using my own judgment in deciding if the facts were relevant. I withheld the statement for personal reasons, believing that no actions of mine could have any relevance to this case. If you care to listen to a statement of the reasons which led up to my presence near Winchstone last Monday evening, I will do my best to enlighten you."

"Thank you, sir," replied Macdonald quietly, "I think that complete frankness is essential. Although I have made no investigations of your actions myself, it is evident that someone else has done so."

"I shall have to go back some months," began Hanton. "You have met my daughter and you will probably understand me when I say that her welfare is more important to me than my own. Early this year I began to receive small press-cuttings, commenting in a veiled and ambiguous manner on the doings of my daughter and of other young people with whom she was associated. Now none of these excerpts was in any way libellous; I disliked their tone, and I disliked the thought that Diana's actions should be commented upon, anonymously or otherwise, in the less reputable section of the Press. I had no idea who my informant was,— for all I know it might have been some individual of a friendly disposition who was endeavouring,—very ill-advisedly,—to enlighten me as to the difficulties which beset a young girl of unconventional mind. I did not tell Diana anything of all this, but I did endeavour, unsuccessfully I fear, to limit her social activities, and to prevent her coming into contact with undesirable acquaintances. A few weeks ago my unknown informant changed his methods; instead of press-cuttings he sent me brief descriptions, in type-script,—of the manner in which Diana spent her time. It was all very exasperating; there was nothing objectionable in these communications beyond the fact that some Paul Pry was making my daughter the focus of his activities. One thing was very clear,—he was well informed, the facts which he occasionally chose to send were always correct. After some consideration I consulted my solicitor in the matter. He was disposed to put the whole matter down to some obscure press-agency,— people who hoped that their talents might be employed in the direction of press publicity. Although it is to my mind an odious business, I do know that certain people are not above employing such methods to keep their names before the public. As my solicitor pointed out, even though I traced the origin of these letters, I could do nothing. I had no legal ground of complaint as I had received nothing of an objectionable nature. . . . I hope I have made all this clear."

"Perfectly clear," answered Macdonald, and Colonel

Hanton continued,

"On Monday evening I had an engagement to dine with Lady Barringer. I was at my club for lunch, and just before I left in the afternoon I was given a letter,— delivered by hand,—which proved to be another of these anonymous communications. This time it was quite a different sort of statement. You can read it for yourself if you care to."

Here Colonel Hanton handed Macdonald a sheet of paper on which the following message was typed:

"Colonel Hanton has recently received certain communications concerning his daughter's actions. These letters were a guarantee of good faith, to establish the fact that the writer has accurate knowledge of facts, as their recipient will doubtless have found.

"If Colonel Hanton is interested in his daughter's welfare, it would be desirable for him to go this evening to the bungalow he owns on the Marlow road. Miss Hanton has an appointment there during the course of the evening."

"To say that I was horrified is an inadequate manner of expressing what I felt," went on the Colonel. "I had realised some time since that Diana was capable of actions which could be interpreted most unpleasantly by an inimical or base-minded observer, and I knew also,— to my great distress,—that she frequently avoided telling me what she had been doing. My first action on the receipt of this letter was to try to get into touch with her. She was not at home, and I could get no news of her from any of our friends I spent several hours in useless attempts to find her, and eventually made up my mind that the only thing I could do was to go to the bungalow and satisfy myself that the insinuation in this letter was baseless. I drove there in my own two-seater Austin, going by the Thames Valley route, as I did not wish to be seen in Wycombe. I arrived at the bungalow shortly after six-thirty and I stayed there till nearly midnight. I can hardly tell you the distress in my mind during that interminable vigil. The result was completely nil,—I saw nobody and heard nobody, and when I came away I felt that I had been ignobly fooled. When I reached home,— just before one o'clock,—I found a telephone message awaiting me from Diana saying she was at Lady Bredon's dance. I telephoned to that house immediately and was told that she was not there. The rest you know."

Macdonald had listened very gravely to the older man's statement and he answered after a brief pause.

"For your own sake, sir, it is very regrettable that you did not trust me with these facts at the outset. It is inevitable that somebody will make capital at your expense from this story. In the event of a charge against the Rodmells, their counsel will stress the point, and examine you as to your reasons for having withheld such evidence."

Colonel Hanton's voice showed that he appreciated the point of Macdonald's speech when he replied, "Heaven knows that I realise all that,—yet, taking everything into consideration, I could have acted in no other manner. This letter,"—pointing to the type-written sheet,— "indicated that Diana might have been in the Winchstone neighbourhood on Monday evening. My one desire was to keep her clear of any contact with the case, to keep her name out of the papers. I told you frankly just what she had done and where she had been. If I had also told you that I had been to the bungalow because I had reason to expect that I might find her there, you would have been bound, in all reason, to connect her with those other very deplorable events which occurred during that night. Had you asked me for a statement of my own doings on Monday night, I should have had two courses open to me,—I could have refused to tell you, or I should have given you the facts without explanation. You made no enquiries; consequently I hoped that this statement need not be made"

For a while Macdonald said nothing; his mind was busy over the facts which Colonel Hanton had just given him, and at length he said,

"The simplest thing for you to do is to answer the questions I am going to ask you, sir. Have you any idea at all of the origin of these letters, and have you made any enquiries into their origin?"

"In reply to both questions, no," answered Hanton. "I have told you that I consulted my solicitor over the earlier letters. With reference to the last one I have been unable to arrive at any decision. Whatever action I contemplated seemed only to make matters worse, not better."

"What time did you leave London on Monday and what was your exact route?" continued Macdonald.

"I left the garage in Eaton Mews at five o'clock," was the reply, "and I drove through Hounslow, Slough, Maidenhead and thence by Marlow, arriving at the bungalow at six-thirty. I ran my car round to the back of the house, and sat in the porch until after dark. Then I walked up and down the garden."

"Whom did you see while you were at the bungalow?" was the next question, and Colonel Hanton replied instantly,

"I saw nobody at all. I myself was concealed from anyone approaching from the road, and I did not seek to see anything further than the garden. One or two cars passed, and a few pedestrians, but I neither saw anyone nor spoke with anyone."

"Did you enter the bungalow?" persisted Macdonald, and the other shook his head.

"No. It was all locked up and the keys safely put away in my desk at Winchstone. Short of breaking into the place, I could not have got inside, and a brief observation enabled me to see that no one else had forced an entrance."

Macdonald felt that he was able to understand why Colonel Hanton had found it difficult to manage his daughter. It seemed to the Chief Inspector that the man he was interrogating had the mind of a child,—unless this simplicity was assumed for his own purposes. Sticking to his interrogation without comment, Macdonald went on,

"What time was it when you left the bungalow?"

"Shortly after eleven-thirty," replied Hanton.

"And by what route did you return?"

"By the same route which I took on the journey down," was the answer.

"Did you stop anywhere on the road for petrol?" went on Macdonald, and the Colonel shook his head.

"No, I filled the tank at the garage before I left London," answered Hanton.

Macdonald paused a moment before his next question.

"Have you ever at any time been blackmailed, or threatened with blackmail, on any subject whatever?"

"Never," was the laconic reply.

Macdonald rose to his feet.

"That is the extent of my questions for the moment, sir," he said. "In the event of my having to interrogate you further, shall I find you here, in town?"

"Certainly," replied Hanton quietly. "If you wish me to give you an undertaking that I will not leave this house, I am quite willing to do so."

"Thank you, sir, I don't think that is necessary at present provided that you are easily available," replied Macdonald.

Hanton looked at the younger man with troubled eyes. "I owe you an apology, Inspector. I feel I have ill repaid the consideration which you have showed to my daughter and myself. Had I realised that I was putting difficulties in your way, I should have behaved otherwise."

"My difficulties don't matter so very much," replied Macdonald. "I generally manage to surmount them in the long run,—I'm hoping to do so this time. Good morning, sir."

"Good morning, Inspector," replied Colonel Hanton.

CHAPTER XV

Macdonald felt in an irritated frame of mind when he left Colonel Hanton,—because he was aware that his own judgment had let him down. The Chief Inspector was wounded in his *amour propre* to think that a man whose integrity he had accepted so unquestionably should have played him so scurvy a trick.

"Motto, never trust anybody, and above all never trust a man who is interested in a woman, be she daughter or wife or mere acquaintance," reiterated Macdonald to himself. "I'm told that Hanton was highly respected in the army, and yet we won this war. Reflects badly on the ex-enemy, that's all."

But when he reached Scotland Yard, Macdonald soon forgot all about his annoyance with Hanton and became absorbed in the possible development of a fresh clue. On entering his office, the Inspector found a message awaiting him from Detective Rogerson,—a young man who had recently been promoted from the constabulary to the C.I.D. Rogerson wanted to see Macdonald as soon as possible as he had news which might conceivably have a bearing on the "Oxford road case." When summoned to the Chief Inspector's presence, Rogerson came to the point with admirable promptitude.

"A pawnbroker named Cohen in the Whitechapel Road sent us information to the effect that he was being offered for sale goods which had most probably been stolen," began Rogerson. "I was sent to investigate the matter, and Cohen told me that a man had come into his shop yesterday in order to sell a beaten silver goblet, a gold cigarette case and a man's wristlet watch. The two latter articles were commonplace enough, but the silver goblet was a different matter. It appears that Cohen is a bit of an expert over old English silver, and he says this thing was a masterpiece,—hand-beaten silver of the Stuart period. Cohen took the goblet to a friend of his who is an expert at Christie's and the latter recognised it at once. He says it was bought early this year by Mr. Vincent Hayward, the owner of the Forward Car Company. I thought that any incidents from that neighbourhood were worth reporting to you, sir."

"Excellent," said Macdonald. "Anything else?"

"The man,—who gave his name as Martin—is to go to Cohen this afternoon. Cohen did not want to arouse Martin's suspicions; he said he couldn't assess the value of the goblet off-hand but could probably offer a decent price for it if the vendor wasn't in too much hurry. He also added that its value as old silver would not amount to much, and Martin readily agreed to leaving it with Cohen in the hope of getting a good price. . . . I've been studying your case a bit, sir," went on Rogerson diffidently, "and I read your 'all-stations' notice giving a description of the Haywards' chauffeur Harrison. This man Martin fits the description pretty well."

"Well done, Rogerson," applauded Macdonald. "If everyone used the wits the good Lord gave them as profitably as you seem to have done, we shouldn't have to waste so much time unravelling muddles. When is this fellow Martin to go and claim the loot?"

"Two o'clock this afternoon, sir," replied Rogerson. "The address is 549B Whitechapel Road. I told Cohen to let us know if Martin appeared earlier, and a constable on point duty has instructions to keep within sight of 549B."

"Very good," answered Macdonald. "We'll go there this afternoon, Rogerson, and hope for the best. Just ring up Cohen and tell him to arrange so that we can observe the interview. We'll get there at one-thirty. Report in this room at twelve-forty-five."

"Very good, sir," replied the younger man, with a grin which showed how much satisfaction this arrangement caused him.

"There's a man named Vernon waiting downstairs to see you, sir. Shall I ask him to come up?"

"Vernon?—oh yes, send him right up," said Macdonald, and leaned back in his chair feeling that affairs showed a distinct turn for the better since he had returned from his last visit.

"Hullo, Jock,—case progressing favourably and both doing well?" was Vernon's characteristic greeting.

"So so, Peter. Everybody's handing everyone else the baby to hold," replied Macdonald, "and the seemingly impeccable are looking such fools that they can't be true, and the obviously unvirtuous are behaving so altruistically that they can't be true either. Any news?"

"Bags of it," responded Vernon. "I have been sleuthing

in the sewers of journalism, and what I don't know about society chit-chat isn't worth knowing. I have talked to a hard bitten toper of seventy who writes under the pseudonym of a 'Modern Mother'; I have consulted with a male athlete of twenty who writes such articles as 'Why I married late in life' by an 'Elderly Bride,' and I have met the world's ugliest male, who makes a good thing out of writing 'beauty culture hints' under the name of 'Orange Blossom.' It was 'Orange Blossom' who lent me the helping hand with the *Mayfair Messenger*. He took me to a binge in modern high-life,—held in a Mayfair Mews of course. I suggested that the latter was a spicy alternative to the more banal title of 'Messenger' and it was considered a good suggestion.

"Incidentally, among the distinguished guests were Miss Vanda Rodmell and Mr. Philip Hayward, the latter a bit screwed, the former remarkably sober. She can put down cocktails by the score and keep as sober as a judge,—never met such a head in my life. We were right in our guess, Jock.—Vanda's responsible for the newsy bits in the Mayfair Muckheap, and Philip Hayward lends an occasional finger in the pie."

"Who told you that?—not Vanda?" enquired Macdonald.

"Not much! I kept well out of the lady's way," replied Vernon. "She's a dangerous bit of goods, Jock. If there's any blackmailing on hand, Vanda's just the type to carry it through. She sees to it that other folk lose their heads while she keeps hers. No, I thought I'd keep out of Vanda's way, and cultivate her dearest friend in a corner, —safer and more productive. I learnt quite a lot through the simple expedient of pretending that I knew everything. Vanda has been trying to get herself accepted in the county—just as Miss Madeleine Hanton told you,—and the Hantons have handed her the frozen mitt. I'm no believer in popular sayings as a rule, but the one about 'Hell holds no fury . . .' is true enough. Anyway Vanda's been trying to get her knife into Diana for a long time and I should say she'd cultivated Philip Hayward assiduously with that end in view. I think it's time someone spiked her guns,—she's getting nasty."

"Maybe," answered Macdonald, "but these feline amenities aren't in my line. Any signs of Richard Hayward anywhere in this galère?"

"Not a ghost of him," replied Vernon. "He's quite a different bag of tricks, Jock. Nothing of the muck merchant about him. I'll bet he doesn't know one word of Vanda's little journalistic flights. He'd never stand in with a low down game like that one. Philip Hayward's quite a different customer, he wants strangling."

"Quite," said Macdonald, "only so far as I can see, strangling's not coming his way, not officially, anyhow. I think the story's beginning to take shape, Peter. Did you get any enlightenment on the 'Where were you out last night, father?' touch?"

"If you'll accept a bit of guess work, I believe I can see the workings of their tortuous minds," replied Vernon, "though it doesn't appear to have any connection with your case at all. Although Vanda is certainly out to get Richard Hayward for better, for worse, and all that, she's not above ogling Philip when Richard isn't there, as I saw last night. As I read the case, she twitted Philip over his fancy for Diana Hanton, and twitted him a good deal more when Colonel Hanton nipped the acquaintance in the bud so to speak. Now on Sunday morning, as you've probably ascertained, Philip and Vanda both went out riding. They met either by appointment or chance and rode over Winchstone Common together. Now if Vanda ragged Philip over his frustrated romance, what would be more natural than for Philip—who is a born cad—to boast to her about his assignation with Diana for Monday night. Vanda, thinking she's got the chance of her life to play Diana a dirty trick, passes the news on anonymously to Colonel Hanton. . . . I bet it was something like that, Jock."

"And I'll not be saying you're wrong," murmured Macdonald cautiously, "altho' the timing won't fit as you've worked it. See here, Peter. Someone handed in a letter at Colonel Hanton's club on Monday after lunch, telling him that Diana Hanton had an assignation at the bungalow on Monday evening. Now Philip couldn't have told Vanda about his appointment with Diana on Sunday, because Diana says she didn't make that appointment until Monday."

"Humm . . ." was all that Vernon replied, and Macdonald laughed.

"Meaning you wouldn't put much reliance on the Sphinx-cum-Minx? Well, it doesn't matter for the moment. It's quite as likely that Philip thought he'd turn the tables on Vanda by telling her a non-existent assignation, thinking that if curiosity took her to the bungalow to score over her hated rival, he would cope with the situation in his own pleasant way. Only as it happened Diana did ring him up, and full of hopefulness Master Philip engaged a suite at the Quarry Hotel, say,— seeing he undoubtedly returned there on Monday night."

"Well, I'm everlastingly and eternally damned," said Peter fervently.

"And you'll deserve to be if you utter words like that here," said Macdonald. "There's another factor you haven't reckoned with, Peter, and that's friend Charles,— Bertie's loving brother. Charles knew all about the

Bungalow story. Ergo, it's Charles and Vanda who have been making Colonel Hanton's life one long worry."

"How the deuce did you get so matey with Charles?" demanded Peter. "I thought he was the mystery man of the story."

Macdonald began to laugh, and having started laughing, he seemed to find it difficult to stop. At last he opened one of his drawers and produced a photograph.

"You deserve to be given the benefit of the joke, Peter. Who is this merchant?—whose curly locks are so dressy and yet so chaste, as the advertisements say."

Vernon shook his head. "Don't know," he replied, "if it's meant to be a Rodmell, I don't know him."

"It is not," replied Macdonald. "It is I. Me. Meaning myself. I got Reeves to snap me before I went out. Losh, laddie, I had the evening of my life, tricked up as a Latin."

"You!" cried Vernon in disgust. "I wouldn't have believed it of you. I thought you didn't approve of monkey tricks."

"I don't either," replied Macdonald. "I've never yet seen a man in a wig at close quarters without his wig proclaiming its origin. The whole point was that for the job I was doing that night, the fishier I looked the better. No C.I.D. man would have been seen dead in the outrageous make up I appeared in that evening. The whole object of the funny business was to make me look a suspicious character. If I could only get the proprietress of the Montevideo to regard me as a fishy fellow of alien origin, my work was half done. So I chose a wig which was intensively wiglike, rouged my cheeks and padded 'em out a bit, did some good work with an eyebrow pencil and lip-stick, and off I sailed to interview Madame da Soto, proprietress of said hotel. That lady's maiden name was Rodmell, and she's one of the family in the most literal sense of the word,—always ready to lend a hand to assist the others. I tell you, Peter, the Rodmells have got the Girl Guides and Boy Scouts beat in their own mottoes. Their telegraphic address is 'Helpful,' to use your own way of putting it."

"And you mean to say that Madame da—whatnot fell for you in those. . . ."

"Don't be vulgar, Peter," remonstrated Macdonald. "Madame da Soto took me for one of the family. She gave me Charles' address—thereby materially, if unintentionally, assisting the course of justice. I was lucky in catching Charles at home, and he welcomed me with open arms, and told me a really ingenious story whose main theme concerned Colonel Hanton and his doings on Monday night. Charles is a very well informed man, Peter, and all is fish that comes to his net, be it Prohibited Drugs, profitable scandal or spotting the lady. . . . Well, I'm very grateful for all you've done, Peter. I'm sorry you can't stop now, but I've got to ring up a lady friend of mine,—who, who, who? and so *ad infinitum*."

"You like to leave me guessing, don't you," growled Peter, "anyway I don't envy your lady friends; they're optimists if they hope for anything out of you."

"Don't get terse, Peter. Go home and think it out, as Charles said to me. Tie a wet towel round your head, and go and search the records at Somerset House, particularly those of last December. Good-bye."

"Births, marriages and deaths, likewise wills and testaments," murmured Peter. "I say, you've heard that old Hayward died last night?"

"Ay,—I heard," replied Macdonald. "Push off, Peter. You'll be no end pleased with yourself if you think it out all on your own account."

"Weeping and tearful I bid thee farewell," proclaimed Vernon, "but if the title of this drama is *The Missing Heir,* I shall be a bitterly disappointed journalist. Missing heirs are no-go. The public's sceptical about them."

"To the best of my knowledge the heir isn't missing," replied Macdonald. "It's all very well to be flippant, Peter, but it's a miserable business really. Buzz off, and do some guessing on your own account."

Vernon surveyed his friend quizzically for a few seconds before he took his departure.

"Right oh, Jock," he answered, "only people like you and me can't afford bowels of compassion. They're a luxury for folk with independent incomes," and with that he left Macdonald to himself.

The man who had given his name as Martin turned up at Messrs. Cohen's establishment in good time for his appointment at two-thirty, and strolled casually up to the counter. He was a well-built, neatly-dressed fellow, cool and self-contained in manner, and his voice expressed no anxiety as he put a question to the assistant behind the counter.

"I left some stuff here to be valued yesterday. Your boss is expecting me. Name of Martin."

"That's right, sir," replied the assistant, a shrewd young Jew. "Just step right through into the office. Mr. Cohen's quite ready to make you an offer, and he always gives good prices. Pity it wasn't all gold though, gold's got a good market just now."

Bowing politely, the assistant ushered Martin into the office at the back of the shop, and closed the door behind him. Martin gave a quick glance round and saw two men seated at a table,—one of them was Mr. Cohen, the other a stranger. Glancing quickly behind him, Martin observed that a third man was standing by the door through which he had just entered, but before he had had time to take in the situation, Mr. Cohen had risen.

"Good afternoon sir," he said, "you have come about the sale of these goods,"—indicating a beautiful silver loving cup which stood on his desk. "The silver cup is, as I supposed, of some value as an antique. Before I can make you an offer for it, however, I should like to know something of its history. Perhaps you could tell me where you acquired it?"

"Old family heir-loom," answered Martin promptly. "Been in the family since the year dot. We've come down in the world a bit,—most of the old stuff's gone the way of this, you know,—up the spout as the saying is."

"Quite so," replied Mr. Cohen amiably, "and the watch and cigarette case are yours, I take it?"

"Yep. They're my own," replied the other easily, "and damned sorry I am to part with them."

"Possibly, Mr. Harrison, and I think you'll eventually be sorrier still that you ever came by them," said a quiet voice,—that of the man who was seated beside Mr. Cohen. Martin gave a perceptible start and wheeled round on the last speaker, his face flushed and truculent.

"Who do you think you're talking to?" he demanded.

"To you," replied the other, "Charles Harrison, till recently chauffeur to Mr. Richard Hayward. It's not worth while arguing about your identity, is it?

"We'll see about that," retorted Martin. "Who d'you think you are, Mr. Know-all?"

"Macdonald, Chief Inspector, C.I.D.," was the laconic reply. "It's no use trying a rough house, Harrison. There's a constable outside, in addition to ourselves. I want to know how you came by this stuff?" pointing to the valuables on the table which Martin had come to realise.

"I've told you," answered the other curtly, but Macdonald replied,

"It won't wash. That watch and cigarette case have been identified as the property of a man who was murdered on the Oxford road on Monday night. If you'd taken the trouble to open the back of the watch you'd have found his name engraved on it. Now I have evidence that you were seen in the Winchstone district on Monday night. You'd better be careful or you'll find yourself facing a capital charge."

The self-styled Martin looked at Macdonald with a very different expression on his face His jaw dropped and his cheeks assumed a livid hue, he looked round the room as though seeking an escape.

"Wake up, Harrison," said Macdonald sharply. "I want to know where you got that watch and cigarette case. Did you rob a corpse?"

"My God, no! I never seen him. I don't know anything about it," he cried.

"Then answer my question," said Macdonald, "and tell me in addition where you got that silver cup from."

The man gave no answer and Mr. Cohen suddenly joined in the conversation; picking up the silver cup, he studied it quietly.

"It looks so safe," he said, apparently in soliloquy, "just plain silver, no name on it, no inscription. Who could place a cup like that? I tell you, my friend, the hallmark and year mark on a piece of hand-beaten silver can tell me a lot. This piece was designed in one of the most famous silversmith shops in England in the year when London was burnt. It belonged until lately to Lord Alastair. He sold it at Christie's last January. There's a catalogue of theirs on the table with a photograph of the cup in it. You were unfortunate, young man. You brought that cup to the one pawnbroker in London who could recognise it. It's no use talking about family heirlooms when you offer a thing like that for sale."

"Well, Harrison, I'm waiting for an answer," said Macdonald, when Cohen's voice ceased.

"And you can go on waiting," said Harrison unexpectedly. "That's stuff's mine because it was given to me,—planted on me,—I see that now. If you know so much about it, you and your friend there, go and ask the owner of that cup if he didn't give it to me as a parting present, token of good-will, and all that. . . . You're asking me a damn' lot of questions, just answer this one for a change. Has the owner of that cup reported its loss to the police? Has he come to you and said that he wants you to recover it because it's stolen property? Put that in your pipe and smoke it, Mr. Clever C.I.D."

"That sort of stuff won't help you, Harrison," answered Macdonald. "You have offered for sale goods which belonged to a man who was murdered, you are known to have been in the vicinity on the evening of the murder."

"Very well. Then charge me with the murder," snapped Harrison, "and if you don't know the rules of the game, I do. You can't ask me questions, you've got to warn me. I won't tell you a thing beyond what I've told you already, and be damned to you."

"Very well," replied Macdonald, "then you'll be detained on suspicion, pending further enquiries. You seem well up in the rules of criminal procedure, you've evidently had experience of police methods before."

"Clever, aren't you?" sneered Harrison, "but you can't get anything out of me. Go and ask the other party. He'll tell you, I don't think!"

Macdonald nodded his head to Rogerson, and the latter

opened the door of the office, beyond which stood a constable in uniform.

"Take him away, Rogerson, and don't lose him," said Macdonald. "He's going to be useful for once."

The young C.I.D. man and the constable each took Harrison firmly by the arm, one on either side, and led him outside to a car which was awaiting them, and then Mr. Cohen turned to Macdonald.

"If it hadn't been for me reporting the matter of that cup to you, you wouldn't have got him," he said, "yet how many of you give the Jews credit for anything but avarice?"

"I do, for one," answered Macdonald, "and I've met a good many of your race during the pursuit of my job. I think you've a lot of common sense, Cohen. Would it really have been profitable to you to display that cup for sale? You wouldn't like to have offered it at Christie's, would you?—and it wasn't worth very much as old silver, as you said. It was much more worth while to earn the good-will of Scotland Yard than to traffic with stolen goods, and you know it. I have already thanked you for the help you have given us, and we shan't forget it."

The Jew shrugged his shoulders.

"The owners might be willing to give a reward for its recovery," he said.

"You can always try," replied Macdonald, "but in the present instance I think you must wait awhile. Mr. Vincent Hayward died last night. I must take those articles away with me now, Mr. Cohen. I'll sign you a receipt for them and then I must hurry off."

"Do you think this man Harrison was the murderer?" enquired the Jew, as he took his receipt and neatly wrapped up the cup, cigarette case, and watch, but the only reply he received was:

"Quite honestly, Mr. Cohen, I don't know. Good-bye, and many thanks."

CHAPTER XVI

About three hours after he left the pawnbroker's shop in Whitechapel, Macdonald was shown into Richard Hayward's presence in the big house at Woodridings. This time it was not to the study that the Chief Inspector was taken, but to a large room in the upper part of the house, which Hayward evidently used as a workshop. There was a carpenter's bench beneath the window, and another table, rather like a laboratory bench, made of teak wood, stood beneath a skylight in the middle of the room. It was at this table that Richard Hayward was seated, apparently absorbed in work over some intricate piece of mechanism. He looked up quickly as Macdonald was shown into the room, and greeted him pleasantly enough.

"Come in, Inspector. I was rather expecting to see you. As a matter of fact, I might have asked you to come earlier, only I had other things to think about concerning my father's death."

"If I may, I should like to express my sympathy with you over his loss," said Macdonald quietly. "It is none the less sincere that it is offered while I am on duty."

Hayward studied the other man thoughtfully.

"That's very decent of you," he said. "To put it quite honestly, the dear old man's death was a relief, inasmuch as recovery of his health was impossible, and life could have meant only perpetual suffering for him. . . . And now for your present business?"

"Last time I saw you," said Macdonald, "I asked you for an account of your actions on Monday evening. In view of evidence which has recently come to hand, I want to know if you would like to review the statement you made to me."

"Thanks,—that's very thoughtfully put," answered Hayward, a little smile lighting up his pale face and tired eyes. "Life is often a damnably complicated business, isn't it? I would much rather have made my statement on the last occasion I met you, but I didn't want to involve some one else in needless suffering, so I temporised. Now, however, I feel more detached. I have decided that everybody has to bear the brunt of their own performances. . . . If other people had behaved decently, I might have been more disposed to stand by them, but there has been such a lot of dirty work that I'm more than content to wash my hands of it."

"One moment, Mr. Hayward," said Macdonald. "Let's get things a bit clearer. When I asked you if you wished to modify your previous statement I ought to have added that you are under no compulsion to do so. You have a perfect right to adhere to what you said previously. . . ."

"In other words, you are repeating the good old slogan that anything I say will be used as evidence against me," interrupted Hayward. "I know the rules of the game that far, but if I wish to make a statement to you I have the right to do so, haven't I? and if you find it desirable to formulate a charge based on my evidence afterwards, then you can do so. Is that all in order?"

"Certainly," replied Macdonald, "but under the circumstances, it might be desirable to have another witness besides myself,—to save us both from possible misunderstanding later."

"That is to say I can have my lawyer at hand if I wish?" enquired Hayward. "Well, I don't wish it. Judging from the way you have conducted your case so far, I am quite willing to trust you with what I am going to tell you,—but if you want a witness on your own account, call one in by all means. You have a man downstairs, I believe. Perhaps, as you say, it might be mutually advantageous to have him in."

Here the speaker rose and crossed over the room to press the bell-push by the mantelpiece, and then returned to his seat at the table, facing Macdonald who sat with his back to the window watching intently.

"There's been an infernal lot of gossip in this place lately," went on Hayward, turning sideways in his chair, one arm resting on the table, the other lying on the arm of his chair. "I'm afraid the Hantons have suffered from it quite unfairly. It's a case of wheels within wheels, and the mud-slinging's been pretty general. It's high time somebody spiked the guns of the slanderers. Don't you agree with me?"

Before Macdonald had time to answer, the door was opened by the butler and Hayward said, "Send up the other inspector, please."

The servant stood aside with a worried movement of his hands, as though to indicate that he could not cope with the present trend of events, and Jenkins entered the room at his heels.

"Come and sit down," said Macdonald to the latter, and the butler was dismissed by a gesture from Hayward. As the door closed Macdonald said:

"Mr. Hayward wishes to make a statement and I want you as a witness, Jenkins."

Then turning again to Hayward, he said:

"You understand clearly that you are under no compulsion to say anything at this juncture?"

Once again Richard Hayward smiled.

"You have made that abundantly clear, but I'm quite

capable of deciding this issue for myself. It's improbable that anything I have to say will be news to you, but I may help to clear up a few odd points. The dead man whom you found last Monday night was named Juan Mendoza. He was a South American gaol bird of distinguished appearance and considerable address. In 1926 he underwent a form of marriage in the States with Miss Vanda Rodmell, and he came to England to blackmail the man whom Vanda Rodmell had subsequently married in this country. It was with that purpose that Mendoza came to this locality last Monday, but having found his quarry, he overstepped the bounds of prudence, and enraged the man he came to exploit to such an extent that Mendoza was worsted in a rough and tumble, and his skull was crushed in by a violent fall on to the corner of an iron-bound box. You'll find the box in the small pavilion down in the garden here, or more correctly speaking you have found it already. . . . You can realise the position easily enough. Mendoza was dead on the floor of the pavilion, and the man who had killed him was a bit bewildered by the sudden turn of affairs. It wasn't a promising situation. Here was a dead man and the car in which he had driven himself was standing in the avenue which leads from the garden entrance on the Marlow road. In an instant of time a law-abiding man had become a murderer, and a very little consideration decided the murderer to make an effort to avoid the consequences of his act. . . ."

Here Macdonald intervened.

"If death occurred accidentally in a struggle, it wasn't murder, it was accident."

Hayward shook his head.

"I'm not going into intricacies of that kind. When Mendoza was killed, his opponent meant to kill him. He deserved to be killed, no one need be ashamed of having caused his death. Circumstances alter cases, as I told you to begin with. Here was the husband with a wife whom he adored, wanting to protect her, wanting also to protect other people from the results of his actions. You may well wonder why I'm telling you all this,—it's because there's no longer any purpose in protecting anyone. Don't interrupt, Inspector! You undertook to hear my statement and it's only fair play that you should hear it to the end. You can argue out the ethics of this case at your leisure, but I'm going to tell you the circumstances. You want to know why I'm throwing up the sponge? It's not only because I'm beaten,—because all the beastliness of the past has been to no purpose,—it's because I'm disillusioned. I was willing to put up a fight for it to save my wife from being branded as the wife of a murderer, and to save my father from knowing that he'd been deceived and let down by his son, but now my father is dead,—and my wife— But we can leave her out of it. Suffice to say that this last week has shown me that the family into which I married consists of drug traffickers and blackmailers. In the first case, when I thought that Mendoza's death could be passed off as an accident, I jumped at the chance of a way out, but since I have discovered that my wife's family are trying to fasten the crime on to a decent man like Hanton, and stirring up mud round a girl who has done them no harm, I'm through with it. . . . It's a little bit late in the day for me to adopt the moral tone perhaps. I know that I've got to face the issue because I have recently become the subject of blackmail myself. You remember my chauffeur, Harrison? It appears that he chose Monday evening to do a little housebreaking here, to revenge himself for his summary dismissal. How much he saw I don't know, but he managed to break open the drawer of my desk and remove Mendoza's watch and cigarette case which I had locked up until I had a chance of disposing of them. When I got back to the house and found the things had been stolen, I knew that my goose was cooked. After that I only played for time. I got the grace I needed, for the old man died in peace. That is my statement, Inspector. Mendoza came here to blackmail me, and I killed him. After that I did my best to fake evidence to give the impression that another man had been killed by accident. I alone was responsible for the whole thing, but I am not responsible for foisting the blame on another man. So far as Bert Rodmell was concerned, I knew that he was already out of England, and if you ever caught him it was plain that he couldn't have been the culprit, because he was in mid-Atlantic when the murder occurred. I think that's all,—if you want to dot the I's and cross the T's, you might just glance through this statement."

Leaning forward in his chair, Hayward passed a folded sheet of paper to Macdonald, and then sunk back in his chair, his right hand stretched out across his desk. Jenkins, who was watching intently, sprang up as he saw Hayward's hand close over something on the desk. As Jenkins sprang to his feet, a shudder seemed to run through Hayward's limbs and he suddenly fell forward, his head sinking over on to the table and Macdonald's voice cried out,

"Don't touch him, Jenkins, don't touch him!"

Jenkins became aware that Macdonald was gripping him by the arm, pulling him away from Hayward's crouching figure, and he turned to the Chief Inspector in bewilderment. "He's had a heart attack,—collapsed under the strain," he said, but Macdonald shook his head, and held out the piece of paper which he had just unfolded. In amazement Jenkins read the words typed on it.

"Don't touch me until you have switched off the electric power. The control switch is by the door. Richard Hayward."

.   .   .   .   .

Late that same evening when Macdonald returned to his flat, he found Vernon awaiting him. In his hand the journalist held a copy of the evening paper, across which ran huge head lines,

"Richard Hayward commits suicide after confessing to the murder of the man on the Oxford road."

"Is it true, Jock?" he asked.

"Perfectly true," answered Macdonald. "He killed himself under my eyes. He had connected up the electric current to a metal rod on the bench in his workroom, and he electrocuted himself. I'm glad he didn't wait for us to hang him, Peter. He was a decent chap really. . . ."

"Tell me," said Vernon, "you'd guessed he did it? I knew what you meant when I found the certificate of his marriage with Vanda."

"Guessing's the word for it," replied Macdonald. "I guessed my way all through, but the only definite pieces of evidence I got were the fact of his marriage, and the fact that his study had been robbed on Monday evening. . . . Let's start at the beginning. It was the Hantons' evidence that set me guessing in the first place. Old Hanton said he couldn't understand why people like the Rodmells had come to live at Winchstone. Miss Madeleine said that Vanda Rodmell was out to catch Richard Hayward, and that old Hayward intended

Richard to marry into the county. Now Vincent Hayward was a millionaire and Richard was his heir. If there was any chance of the Rodmells bringing off that match they'd stick at nothing to do it. Hence I argued that the Rodmells had staged the murder for some reason connected with Richard and Vanda. Sheer guess work. When Mellon did not report about his lorry, I didn't immediately leap to the conclusion that Mellon had committed the murder, but that he was shielding someone he cared about. Now Mellon loved Richard Hayward dearly. I was right in that guess, because Mellon has admitted it since. On Tuesday morning he found one of Richard's gloves in his lorry. Later, when he was questioned, he suppressed that fact. Then a pencil was found at the spot where we found the body. It had originally been Mellon's pencil, but Hayward had picked it up off his desk. That pencil was a link. The Rodmells couldn't have had it—unless Bert had, but Bert never set pencil to paper. He was the true mechanic, and a HH Koh-i-Noor pencil wouldn't have interested him at all. . . . Now I led off with the certainty that two people had been concerned in the crime of whom Rodmell *père* was one; Richard Hayward I bore in mind as a possible second. When I went to see him, I came away convinced that he knew something about it. He was generally an acute enough fellow, observant, with regard to his fellow beings and thoroughly logical over them. Yet he jumped at the very foolish suggestion I offered him that the dead man was his chauffeur, Harrison. Harrison, I have since learned, had a maimed finger by which he could have been identified, and Hayward knew it. Yet knowing that the dead man couldn't have been Harrison, he didn't say so. It's odd how one can arrive at conclusions with practically no data. When I left Hayward that evening I was convinced in my own mind that he knew the truth of the whole matter, and I was certain, too, that he had guessed the trend of my thoughts, but I had no evidence worth calling evidence.

"I liked Richard Hayward, Peter. He was easily the best of the whole bunch in this case. There's Colonel Hanton,—he's a decent sort, doubtless, but he's more than a bit of a fool. If he had behaved sensibly at the outset, we could have got Vanda and Charles into the picture with very little trouble. As for Charles Albert and Henry Hubert, they're the most transparent pair of rogues I ever set eyes on,—the one thing that I'm grateful to them for is the comic relief they provided. They're genuinely funny if you look at them the right way."

"Have you copped them, by the way, or does a case no longer lie?" enquired Vernon.

"A case! Hell's bells! There's enough evidence for twenty cases," exclaimed Macdonald. "Yes, we've got them both, though in the case of Charles, it was more by good luck than good judgment. Wragley was a bit terse over that business of losing Charles; however the blighter jumped out of the frying pan into the fire. He went to Paris by this morning's boat and joined some of his drug dealing friends over there at the very moment when the French police were making a comprehensive haul of those very gentry, so Charles and Bertie will be able to stand shoulder to shoulder in the dock. It's no use their prevaricating any more, because H.H. lost his nerve and told the whole story. The usual bluff worked,—he was told that Hayward had confessed everything and he supplied the missing links when we questioned him."

"Just one question before you put me wise over the whole show," interrupted Vernon. "About this confession of Hayward's, how did the Press get hold of it so soon?

Did you notify them?"

"No, we didn't. Hayward did himself," answered Macdonald. "It's one of the most remarkable points in the whole case. Hayward must have written out a statement, taking the entire guilt on to his own shoulders. He left this document under cover at his lawyer's, with instructions that it was to be delivered as and when he instructed them. He telephoned to the lawyers a few minutes before I was shown into his room, and told them to send the letter by hand to the *Evening Post.* Relvin— the editor—knew Hayward personally, and recognised his writing. He must have had a shock when he read that letter, but news is news."

"And journalists are ravening wolves," said Vernon, "but do you believe that Hayward was responsible for the whole thing?"

"Heavens, no!" answered Macdonald. "Here's the story, Peter, and keep your ears skinned, because I'm not answering any more questions to-night.

"Mendoza drove to Woodridings, via Marlow, intending to turn to account the information which Madame da Soto had unhappily presented him with,—the fact that Vanda was secretly married to a rich man. He must have mistaken the entrance to the house and driven in by the garden avenue at the back and he came on Hayward when the latter was just going into the tennis pavilion. Hayward killed him there, after a long conversation. I can imagine the provocation easily enough. Mendoza was one of the worst sorts of swine, and he got Hayward on the raw on two points, his wife and his father. I expect that the thought of Mendoza going to old Vincent Hayward, and telling him about that secret marriage, was as appalling to Richard as the things Mendoza had told him about Vanda. Be that as it may,

Richard Hayward killed him; he probably went for him blind with rage and brought him down on the angle of a metal bound chest, so that Mendoza's skull was smashed in by the impetus of their falling bodies. It was at this juncture that Rodmell *père* put in an appearance, and realised what had happened; the very encounter which he had been scheming to avoid. It was to prevent Mendoza meeting Richard Hayward that Rodmell went to Warlington that afternoon, when he ought to have been lying doggo in London, according to plan, to carry out his private trafficking. I can imagine Henry Hubert taking in the situation at a glance and saying in that accommodating manner of his: 'Don't worry over a little thing like this, dear boy. I'll fix it,' and he very nearly pulled it off, too. They stripped Mendoza, and made a bundle of his clothes and locked up the body in the Pavilion. Rodmell took the actual clothes,—the things he could dispose of without much risk. Hayward took the cigarette case and watch and probably any papers which they found. He then returned to the house and locked up the metal things in a drawer of his desk, from which they were purloined by Harrison later that evening when Hayward was helping with the lorry business. H.H. then set out on his return journey to London. He is really one of the most ingenious rogues I have ever met, and he took the wildest risks, assessing them with a true gambler's coolness. A car was necessary,—very well, he would borrow a car. He knew Waring was away and I think that the thought of the Hantons' car awoke in Henry Hubert's fertile mind the thought of laying the blame at Hanton's door if the scheme miscarried,—but it didn't miscarry. It went through according to plan and he returned the car after his business in London was done,—all very successfully, save for that inexplicable carelessness about dropping his cigarette case in the Sunbeam. . . . Once he was back in Winchstone the rest was easy. We have worked out just how it was done, including the business of Mellon's lorry. The only remaining jobs were to dispose of the Varron, which H.H. planted at the bungalow garage; and to clear up any finger-prints in Bert's bedroom. I bet H.H. attended to that detail himself. It was jolly well done. The one point which neither could have foreseen was that Harrison would go into Hayward's study by the garden door and purloin those damning pieces of evidence. When Hayward got back after all that hideous business with the lorry, he found that his room had been burgled. He couldn't do anything about it,—he just lay low and said nothing. Of course the servants noticed that the silver cup was missing. It had been standing on Hayward's study mantelpiece at ten o'clock that evening. Next morning it had gone, and Richard told the butler that he had put it away himself. . . . Luck was continually against him. There are only two other points. . . . George Rodmell was instructed by telephone to go and identify the body as Bert's in the morning. H.H. must have got Madame da Soto to do the telephoning for him, because he certainly did not do it himself; that's just another example of the way this remarkable family aided and abetted one another. They all helped and they'll all be in the dock together. Charles it was, of course, who collected Mendoza's baggage at Victoria. . . . I was sorry for Hayward, Peter, but he's well out of it. When he married Vanda Rodmell he signed away all hopes of a peaceful and prosperous future. He just did for himself. And that's that."

Silence fell on the two men until Peter Vernon asked:

"And what about the Highlands, Jock?"

Macdonald's face lighted up at the question.

"Man, that's a grand thought," he said, "let's sleep on it. . . . I shall be clear of the whole show next week, Peter, and then over the Border for both of us. . . ."

"Shake on it," replied Vernon, thrusting out his hand.

And they shook.

THE END